I was a small time PI, so what did the FBI want with me?

Special Agent Foster reached over and shook hands. "I understand your concern. This might be a first for the Bureau, signing up a PI firm, but it's legit. Not only do we *not* want to shut you down, we're hoping your help will speed along our investigation."

I wondered how that would happen as long as this remained a one-way operation in terms of sharing, so I decided to ask. "I'm interested to hear how you plan to assist us in assisting you, since a few minutes ago, I believe I heard you say you couldn't share information with us?" I turned my statement into a question so they had to answer and not just acknowledge.

"Oh, it's not that we can't share *some* information," Peters said. "Just not information on the Dockweiler Beach investigation. There are plenty of other ways we can help, and when we have something concrete, we'll get back to you. I hope you'll do the same for us?"

"We will," I promised.

"Then we'll be in touch," Foster replied, as the two agents wriggled their butts off the couch and moved in tandem to the front door.

"I appreciate your confidence in Berger Investigations," I said to their retreating backs.

Special Agent Peters turned and handed me her card as Bunny hurried past her to hold the door.

"Email is the best and fastest way to reach me if you have any questions," she said. "Or, you can text me. That's fine, too."

Bunny closed the door behind them and turned to me. Or rather, turned *on* me. "What the blankety-blank is the matter with you?"

"What do you mean?"

"Letting in two armed strangers when I'm out of the office. How do you even know they are who they say they are? I mean, did you contact the Bureau for verification, or call Johnny?"

I admitted I hadn't. "I checked over their creds and you agreed they looked legit—had all the proper markers: solid gold badge, Federal Bureau of Investigation spelled out across the top—"

Bunny sat down, put his elbows on the desk, and cradled his head in his hands. "Wait'll Johnny hears this one."

I wondered if that was a threat or a warning.

A dead body, identified as Lenny Spinoli, washes up on Dockweiler Beach in Southern California. Spinoli was last seen on Santa Catalina Island, leaving on a fishing trip with his friend, Ricky Martin. When Ricky goes missing, his realtor wife hires Hollywood PI Polly Berger to find him. Meanwhile, Polly's firm has been hired to tail the wife of a big-time Hollywood director of zombie movies, who claims his wife is cheating on him. Within days, the director's wife dies of a purported suicide. Polly suspects the director of murdering his wife, but how can she prove it? And as she digs for clues to the whereabouts of Ricky Martin, the FBI horns in, demanding that she help with their investigation. But will they return the favor, or are they just using her as bait?

KUDOS for *The Case of the Missing Mobster*

In *The Case of the Missing Mobster* by Harol Marshall, a body of a man shows up on the beach in Southern California. The dead man is identified as Lenny Spinoli, who was heading out for a fishing trip with his friend Ricky Martin, who is missing. Did Ricky kill Lenny, or is he dead too? And if he is not dead, where is he? This is the question Ricky's wife wants PI Polly Bergin to answer. But no sooner does she start investigating than the FBI shows up asking for her help on the same case. She doesn't trust them—after all, she is just a small-time PI, so why would they want her help?—but what can she do? Fast paced, intense, and intriguing, this is a story that will grab you by the throat from the very first page and hold on tight all the way through. ~ *Taylor Jones, The Review Team of Taylor Jones & Regan Murphy*

The Case of the Missing Mobster by Harol Marshall is the story of an LA private investigator, Polly Bergin. As the story opens, a man in New York, named Lenny Spinoli, gets a call from his brother who delivers a message to Lenny from a mobster. Some time later, Lenny's body washes up on the beach in California. Lenny was last seen with his friend, big-time LA realtor, Ricky Martin, who is now missing. Martin's wife, Sally, hires Polly to find her husband and prove he did not kill Lenny. As Polly begins to investigate, she calls her cop ex-husband, Johnny, who tells her that the feds have taken over the case and he has been told to stay out of it. He tells Polly to stay out of it too. Then she gets a visit from the FBI, who to her surprise, don't want her to stay out of it, but to help them solve the case. Knowing they don't really need her help, she doesn't trust them, but how can she refuse? Marshall has crafted an intriguing and enthralling tale, combing mystery, suspense, and superb character development to make *The Case of the Missing Mobster* one you won't be able to put down.~ *Regan Murphy, The Review Team of Taylor Jones & Regan Murphy*

ACKNOWLEDGEMENTS

I want to thank those who've been especially helpful to me in writing this novel, including my husband, Jerry Meisner, daughter, Sharol Gauthier, and brother, Brett Armstrong. Plus, my friend, Dixie Land Jakubsen, and the Writer's Group of the Triad: Agnes Alexander, Betty DiMeo, and Nancy Gotter Gates. Thank you all for your encouragement and support.

THE CASE OF THE
MISSING MOBSTER

A PI POLLY BERGER NOVEL

HAROL MARSHALL

A Black Opal Books Publication

GENRE: MYSTERY-DETECTIVE/WOMEN SLEUTHS/SUSPENSE

THE CASE OF THE MISSING MOBSTER ~ A PI Polly Berger Novel
Copyright © 2019 by Harol Marshall
Cover Design by Rob Furr
All cover art copyright © 2019
All Rights Reserved
Print ISBN: 9781644370773

First Publication: JANUARY 2019

Published by Black Opal Books **http://www.blackopalbooks.com**

DEDICATION

To my brother Brett with thanks for all his great stories.

PROLOGUE

Coxsackie, New York:

L enny Spinoli was a dead man, thanks to unfinished business from his sordid past. Two questions danced in his head—not the why, but the how and when. If he could eliminate one of those two uncertainties, maybe he could beat the rap. After all, he was smarter and better educated than the mobster who put a price on his head. And he had a heart. Otherwise, he wouldn't be in this bind, a predicament he'd thought about a hundred times, wondering how he'd feel, how he'd handle himself when the devil came calling. Now he knew.

He'd have quit on his own if quitting had been an option, but that was not how things worked. You didn't quit the Mob. The Mob quit you. Like it or not, signing up amounted to a life sentence, a message drilled home to him when his brother Mickey phoned.

Lenny failed to put two and two together in the beginning. Figured the call was another effort to keep Mickey in their clutches. Mickey, who'd been walking the straight and narrow for twenty-five years. Hadn't thought about the life, hadn't missed it. Married a nice lady, had two kids, opened his own bakery in downtown

Coxsackie. Lived well. Mickey was happy and Lenny was happy for him.

Lenny turned off the burner under his pasta when his cell phone chirped. Caller ID read Anita Spinoli. His sister-in-law. She never called him. Had something happened to Mickey?

"Nita. Somethin' wrong?"

"It's me, Mickey," his brother said.

Must have forgotten to charge his phone. Not like him.

"What's up, Bro?"

"Jeez, Lenny, I got a real scare today."

Mickey's voice shook, like he might be standing on one of those phony weight loss machines with the vibrating belt that jiggled your middle. Lenny wondered how anyone lost weight on those things. Maybe the shaking action liquefied your stomach contents so the food ran right through you instead of absorbing into your intestines. Only way he could see the thing might work, not that he ever used one. Losing weight wasn't a problem for Lenny. He worried the pounds off.

"What happened? You in trouble?"

"Not now, Len. It's over, but I tell ya, I thought I'd seen the last of this world today. All for doin' a friend a favor."

Lenny sighed, drained the pasta, and dumped it into his red clam sauce. His mouth watered at the sight, but he turned his attention back to his brother. He had a pretty good idea what this was about. "Who's the friend and what was the favor?"

"See, Father Moretti was in the bakery picking up his weekly order of cannoli. He likes the ones with pistachios in the cream, which is my favorite too."

"Father Moretti's the friend?"

"No. He happened to be in the bakery when Eddie Dagostino comes in. Tells Father the cannoli are gonna make him fat. But Father says these are Holy Cannoli. Once he blesses them, they're no longer sinful. So, we all have a laugh about that. Then after Father leaves, Eddie tells me he has a problem."

I knew it, Lenny thought, stirring the pasta and stifling a sigh. "What kinda problem?"

"With his kid. Kid's got no brains. Doesn't know his butt from his elbow, but he got lucky."

"If he's so lucky what's the problem?"

"Kid's lucky his father called on *me*, that's what. Problem is, his father called on me."

"What'd the kid do?"

"I don't ask. I'm guessin' he screwed up a drug deal. Bottom line, some jerk downstate stiffed the kid. Owed him a lot of money and wouldn't pay up."

"So, what's this got to do with you?"

"Eddie didn't want his kid handling the problem alone. Asked if I'd accompany him when the kid went to collect the money."

"Why you? Eddie's got plenty of friends in the business. Collecting is what they do."

"That's the point. The deadbeat's connected. Eddie didn't wanna start a war or nothin' so he needed somebody clean. Like me."

"Let me guess. You were smart enough to turn him down, then he sent somebody to your place today to convince you otherwise, especially since you know he knows where your kids live."

"No. I told him I'd do it."

Lenny exhaled slowly, unsure what his brother expected him to say. Unsure what to say himself. A quarter of a century his brother had kept his nose clean. Started his own business. Worked hard, put two kids through college. Son earned an MBA and worked as an accountant, his daughter taught school. Mickey had a lot to lose saying yes to Eddie. More to lose saying no. That's the business for you. Always squeezing their own.

"Guess you didn't have a choice."

"Exactly."

"So, what happened?"

"Me and the kid, we drive down to Brooklyn yesterday morning."

"You packin'?"

"You kiddin' me?"

"Keep going."

"The SOB talks tough. Says if we don't get out of his territory, meaning the City, we're dead meat. You know the routine."

Lenny nodded like they were on video chat. "Then what?"

"I put a gun to the creep's head, and he saw the light. Handed over the money and we split. Kid's happy, Eddie's happy, I'm happy."

"Until?"

"Until today. I close up the bakery and head out to my car with the last of the cannoli. Black SUV's parked next to mine. Inside are three guys I never seen before. One of 'em gets out and tells me to get in. I say, 'hold on a sec, gotta run back in the bakery and take a leak,' but the guy opens the back door and tells me, 'you ain't goin' nowhere except with us. Get in.'" Mickey paused. Lenny could sense his distress. "Guess he knew if I went back in the bakery I'd come out carryin' heat. Anyway, right then, I think to myself this is it, my last day on the face of this good earth. Honest Lenny, tears came to my eyes when I thought of Nita and the kids. I couldn't move, stood there like a freakin' statue. I'm tellin' ya, if I was captured by ISIS, I couldn't o' been more scared."

"Where'd they take you?"

"Coxsackie Mall. Back of the parking lot I see this black limo. Thing looked like a hearse, which didn't make me feel too good. Alls I can think is, how they gonna do this? Shoot me? Slit my throat and dump my body in the river?"

"Stop draggin' out the suspense."

"Just paintin' a picture so's you know why I'm so upset. I puked my guts out when I got home. Couldn't settle down enough to call you. Told Nita I had a stomach bug."

"Okay. Calm down, and tell me what happened."

"We pull up beside the limo and stop. The back door opens up. I wait for somebody to get out, but instead, the goon in the seat in front of me turns around and tells me to get out and climb in the limo."

Lenny was running out of patience. Mickey was the worst storyteller ever. Had to include every detail, no matter how insignificant. Drove his kids crazy. Every time he started another story, they'd wave their hands in circles telling him to speed it up. Lenny glanced down at his right hand drawing the same circles. He wondered how long this story would go on, and if in the end it was even worth listening to, but when it's flesh and blood you do what you gotta do.

He sighed audibly, a hint for his brother to get on with it. "Since you're on the phone talkin' to me about this, I take it nobody bumped you off, so what's got you so agitated? They threaten you, have another job for you? And who was in the limo, anyway?"

"One question at a time. I'm still shook up. Remember, this just happened to me. I ain't recovered yet."

"You tell Nita about it?"

"Of course not. I've never told her nothin' about the life. You know that. She'd leave me in a heartbeat.

Couldn't deal with it. The kids neither. You're the only person I can talk to, Lenny, and sometimes I just have to vent, you know?"

"I know. Go ahead and finish your story, but I haven't got all day. I got things to do."

"So, my knees are quaking, I almost break my neck climbin' outta the SUV, but I make it without fallin' on my face. When I slide into the backseat of the limo, I see Eddie sittin' up front. He turns around, introduces me to the guy next to me, and sez, 'sorry about this,' and I think to myself, *you little punk. I do you a favor and now you're gonna have me wacked?* But it wasn't like that." Mickey hesitated. Lenny could hear him catching his breath again. "Guess who he introduces me to? I'll give you a hint. The limo had Connecticut plates."

Lenny didn't need a hint. He'd once worked with the Connecticut mob. They ran Coxsackie, so he guessed they sent a mid-level capo to town, maybe to put the fear of God into Mickey, or maybe sign him on for more work since he'd done such a good job, suck him back into the business now they had something to hold over his head.

"Sounds like your New York deadbeat was not just connected," Lenny said, "but *well*-connected. I don't suppose you looked into his background before you took the job, try to find out if maybe he was the son of somebody high up in the organization, a little higher up than Eddie, say?"

"Didn't have time. What's your guess? Who was in the limo?"

"Look, I don't have time for games, but I'll play because you're my brother. Easy. Some bone-breaker with a vowel at the end of his name."

"Wrong on both counts. The Big Boss himself."

"Pauly Budin?"

"Yup."

"Jeez, Marie. What did he say?"

"Asked me about 'that thing.' I said, 'what thing?'"

"Not the smartest answer."

"I know. He says, 'that thing this weekend in the City.' I shrug and tell him I was doin' a friend a favor, like I'd do for any of my friends if one of their kids was in trouble."

"That it?"

"Hell no. He asks me a coupla more questions, then he says, 'You dig up your gun?'"

"He asked that," Lenny said, "'cause it's an important question."

"I know and I tell him the truth. I tell Pauly, 'No. I been straight for twenty-five years. This is the first time somethin' came up. It had nothin' to do with the business.' I say, 'Eddie's kid got in some kind of trouble that I don't know nothin' about, other than the kid was getting stiffed by some sleazebag in the City. Eddie was afraid to let his kid confront the guy alone, and I don't blame him. Clearly the guy was connected, but he made a big mistake. Thought he could abuse his connections in order to make a little money off o' one of our own. But we all know that ain't the way things work.' I mean, I said, 'if your kid was in trouble, Pauley, and you asked me for help, I'd o' helped you out, too. Don't mean I'm back in the business because I ain't.'"

"Then what?"

"Pauley tells me I done good. I was so relieved, I handed him the box of cannoli sitting in my lap, told him they were Holy Cannoli blessed by a priest, and he could eat all he wanted without gainin' a pound."

"Pauly's not known for his sense of humor," Lenny said, "so that might not have been the wisest answer. More like a wise-ass one."

"On the contrary. He opened the box of cannoli,

stuck his finger in the cream, and licked it off. Said it was the best cannolo cream he ever ate. I told him I was glad he liked it. Then he looks me in the eye and says, 'Now I'm gonna do you a favor. Tell your brother that Angel Bianchi found the two cannoli your brother was supposed to polish off, and Angel ain't happy about it.'"

A chill ran through Lenny, like someone sealed him in a meat locker, one of those places where they slaughter animals and hang 'em in long racks. Lenny's heart raced, but he controlled the tenor of his voice. "What else did Pauley say?"

"I ask him, 'What's that supposed to mean?' But he shakes his head, tells me to pass along the message. Says you'll know what it means, then he tells me, 'get outta the limo, go home, and keep your nose clean,' which is all I was hopin' to do. I thanked him, said I was pleased to meet him, and split. The three goons drove me back to my car. Nobody, including me, said a word on the trip over or on the trip back."

"Always best to keep your mouth shut when you don't know what's going down."

"I know. I probably should keep my mouth shut now, but my curiosity is gettin' the better of me. What's this about you refusing to eat the cannoli Angel gave you?"

"Nothin' to worry about," Lenny said, knowing the message was about a contract on his life. He wondered about the price tag, but not about who placed the order and why.

ↄ◦ↄↄ◦ↄ

One week after Lenny Spinoli received Pauly Budin's bad news, two things happened: the first pertained to an apparently unrelated celebration of good news taking place inside the second-floor office of Berger

Investigative Services, a small PI firm in Hollywood, California. The second occurred in Coxsackie when Mickey Spinoli received a visit from the FBI informing him of the drowning death of his brother Lenny, whose body washed up on a beach in Southern California.

CHAPTER 1

Hollywood, CA, Day 1:

L anded our first Hollywood bigwigs, boss. We've finally hit the big time." My secretary and associate investigator, Bunny Contreras, crowed happily about our newest client as I came through the door a little later than usual. "One elite client leads to another, Polly. You'll see. We're gonna be rollin' in *dough* now that we've finally penetrated the upper crust. Pun intended."

"Upper crust is stretching it," I snorted. "Clive Hooper specializes in zombie films for Pete's sake."

"They're big money-makers right now, which you'd know if you read *Variety* on a regular basis. He's considered the premiere director of horror films in this town, not to mention the fact that his wife ranks number ten on the top fifty sexiest horror film actresses."

"I'll agree Melody Knight's sexy," I said, "which no doubt is the reason her husband thinks she's stepping out on him, and clearly the reason you're stoked about tailing her…"

My wisecrack slowed Bunny down for a beat or two. He sent me a look of genuine hurt and outrage, enough to make me feel bad. "Hey, ever since Franny came into my life," he said, referring to my identical twin sister, the current love of his life, "I don't even look at other women. As for Melody Knight, if she isn't having an affair, I'm a donkey's backside. You ever see her husband?"

"Not in person. Wasn't he nominated for some award last year?"

"Yeah, a Fright Meter. Anyway, he looks like a zombie, and I think he might be one, which is why he likes making movies about them."

"Seriously? You think zombies are real?"

"Could be. Just because you've never met one doesn't mean they don't exist. You ever meet a wombat? No, but they're real."

Our conversation had reached a new height of absurdity, and for the sake of maintaining some semblance of office professionalism, I decided to change the subject.

I'm a private investigator, Polly Isabel Berger, a PI in name as well as occupation. My agency, Berger Investigative Services, Inc. is located in beautiful downtown Hollywood, California, on the wrong side of the tracks but the right side of the law. Private investigators in general have a dicey reputation, so I work hard to maintain high professional standards, which isn't easy when you live and work in the land of false promises and broken dreams.

As for our current workload, Bunny and I had more business than usual when the Clive Hooper case landed in our laps two days ago, and I was beginning to worry about how to handle the case load while still catching some much needed R&R.

"All I hope," I told Bunny, "is that Clive Hooper's bank account is large enough to cover the costs of hiring extra help because we're swamped right now."

Bunny raised an eyebrow. "Swamped. You channeling *Swamp Bludgie?*

"What are you talking about?" I knew I shouldn't ask, but sometimes I can't help myself.

Bunny shook his head in mock despair. "You've never seen a Clive Hooper movie, have you?"

I wrinkled my nose. "I don't do zombie movies. Wouldn't recognize one if I fell over it."

"Hooper's films all have two-word titles. It's his signature. Latest is *Flesh Mob.*"

"So, he's into puns?" I was having trouble keeping snide thoughts to myself, despite our latest client's cash cow potential.

Bunny sniffed. "You are a snob, you know that? A movie snob."

I ignored his accusatory tone. "I might not go to zombie movies," I told him, "but I keep abreast of the Hollywood scene."

"Ever heard of *All You Can Eat?*"

"I thought you said Hooper's movies had two-word titles."

Bunny sniggered. "Just seeing if you were paying attention."

"Okay, I'll play along. Who directed *All You Can Eat?*"

Bunny grinned. "Nobody. I made up the title to see if you'd pretend you heard of it."

"Having a little fun at my expense, are we?"

"You passed with flying colors, boss, so don't get your knits in a snit. How about *Death Horde?* Heard of that one?"

"No. Let's get back to business, shall we?"

"Another Clive Hooper movie. His biggest flop."

"No wonder," I said, "with a title like that. Maybe he should think about moving up to four-word titles. I mean, *Dawn of the Dead* may be the greatest zombie movie ever made. They filmed it outside of Pittsburgh, near my hometown.

That was ten years or more before I was born, but a friend of my parents was an extra."

Bunny made a honking sound like a quiz show buzzer. "Wrong. You're thinking of *Night of the Living Dead*. Nineteen sixty-eight. Also one of the greatest zombie movies of all time, written and directed by George Romero. Only cost one hundred fourteen thousand dollars to make and grossed millions. A cult classic."

"Okay, enough about zombie movies. What I'd like to hear is your latest progress report on the Hooper case, beginning with last night's surveillance of Hollywood's leading zombie bait, Melody Knight."

"Borrrring," Bunny said. "She never left the house and nobody stopped by for a visit. I had a tough time staying awake. Left at midnight when the house finally went dark. If she's seeing somebody, I'm guessing daytime flings are her thing, like when Clive-baby is away on set directing the next terrifying attack planned for his wife."

"Wouldn't she be on set then, too?"

"Not necessarily. Even when she's the leading lady, she never appears in more than half the movie. Melody's there to be seen not heard, unless the scene calls for a lot of screaming. I'm not even sure that's her you hear. Probably some opera singer dubbing her shrieks."

I took a deep breath. "So much for the lives and times of the Hollywood *upper crust*. I think you just proved my point," I murmured, heading back to my office, before adding, "I hear paperwork calling, I'll talk to you later."

Bunny stopped me. "Hey, Polly."

I drew in my breath waiting for the bad news that usually accompanied those two words. "Yes?"

"I just wanna thank you for turning this case over to me. I promise I won't let you down."

I tried to hide my surprise, chiding myself for always thinking the worst when it came to Bunny. "I know you won't disappoint me, Bun. I have confidence in you. Just don't up and leave me when you finally get your PI license."

"Not planning to, boss. Besides, Franny would kill me."

"A good thought to keep in mind," I told him.

CHAPTER 2

I hadn't mentioned this to Bunny yet, but I'd been thinking of offering him a partnership in the business. He started working toward his PI certification about the same time he began dating my sister and should have his license in the next couple of months. I don't want to lose him. I depend on him a lot, even though he only works for me part-time. Well, more like full-time lately, and overtime last week.

On weekends he moonlights as a stand-up comic. Bunny considers comedy his profession, and claims he only works for me for beer money, which if that's the case, he drinks enough to keep the local pubs in business for a year or more. I'm hoping he'll change his ideas about his profession when he has that PI license in his hand.

Today, for the first time in recent memory, Bunny arrived at the office ahead of me. I called in to leave a message on the answering machine saying I'd be late, but instead of the machine, Bunny answered.

"Hi, Bun. I have some errands to run this morning so I'll be in a little later than usual."

"No problem. I couldn't sleep, so I came in early to catch up on the filing. Earning real money sure brings on a load of paperwork. Who knew?"

I knew but held my tongue. I appreciated having him tending the office while I took care of a few personal chores, one of which involved a new pair of shoes. Our office earned a fat ten grand the previous week for solving the case of the Reverend Harvey Kow's missing wife. Pretty nice pay for six days' work, except for the fact I nearly lost my life in the process, which is why I decided to reward myself with a new pair of Jimmy Choo's.

Leaving my house, I headed straight for Nordstrom's, hoping they had a pair I might like for under five hundred dollars, but no such luck. So, I settled for option two, treating myself to Michael Kors "Logo Bow Thong," a style I'd been eyeing for a month or more. Even those weren't cheap, but I'd promised myself not to feel guilty. I know I spend too much money on shoes, but it's my only real vice, if you don't count men, and I don't.

Anyway, the main reason I agreed to let Bunny handle the Hooper case was because I needed a rest. Fortunately, we had another ten big ones coming our way in the next week, our share of the Harvey Kow reward fund. In all, this was more money than we'd seen in the past three months combined. With that kind of financial security I could afford to relax for a bit. A cool twenty grand in two weeks meant that if Bunny screwed up the Hooper case, we still had sufficient funds in the bank to cover our bills.

With my morning shopping wrapped up, I'd jumped on the 101 back to the office, parking my RAV4 two spaces away from the dumpster in the lot next to my building. My PI headquarters occupies the second floor of a two-story walkup. On the way in I hollered a "good morning" to my friend and former client, Rosa the tarot card reader whose shop is on the first floor, making her rent double that of mine. She felt the price was worth it because a lot of her clients were elderly and couldn't handle the stairs.

"Worrying about how soon they'll meet the grim reaper?" I'd asked her once.

"Oh, no. More concerned about their status in the afterlife. I get a lot of movie people in here, and, you know, with the lives they've led, especially in their youth, they want some reassurances about wiping the slate clean."

"So, they come to you instead of going to a priest?"

"Actually, most of them, the ones who worry the most, do both." She couldn't keep from smiling. "I do what I can for them."

"That's the story of this whole town," I'd told her. "Everybody's into cover your butt, even when it comes to the afterlife."

"Afternoon, Polly," Rosa called out to me as I passed by her door, correcting my "good morning" slip as my foot hit the bottom rung of the stairs to my office. "You're running kinda late today. Have a busy night?" I caught the sly wink in her voice even if I couldn't see her face.

"Running errands this morning. We've had a busy week. On client overload at the moment, but Bunny's holding down the fort while I take care of business."

"Same here," she said. "I barely have time for lunch these days."

I never cease to be amazed at the number of people who file through Rosa's front door paying hard-earned cash for a few words of false hope.

But she's good at her craft. Always predicts rosy futures, knowing it's the reason behind her clients' visits. Telling people what they want to hear is Rosa's idea of therapy, as well as good customer service. I wasn't about to find fault with her business model.

I climbed the stairs and breezed into my office suite, feeling smug and happy. Bunny was at his computer and barely looked up when I arrived.

"Mornin', Bun," I said, sauntering over, briefcase in one hand and a cup of Starbucks in the other.

"Afternoon, boss. Guess you had a rough night, huh?"

I ignored his question since what I do at night is no longer any business of his.

"Any bulletins for me?" I asked.

"Nothing new. You could take the whole day off if you want, which I'd say you pretty much did."

That was the point where I changed the subject to zombie movies and our latest client.

ↄჂↄჂ

After shutting my door hard, and loud enough to keep Bunny from even thinking about disturbing me, I sat down at my desk still in no mood to work, even though I had two case files in front of me. Both required substantial internet research, but neither were time critical. I could put them off until the end of the week or into the following week with no serious downside.

I glanced around my desk for an amusing distraction and found just the one. I must be a high achiever, I thought, because according to some social science researcher somewhere, high achievers work best under pressure and that certainly described me.

I retrieved my briefcase and pulled out a copy of Agnes Alexander's latest western romance. What could be better in the middle of a lazy afternoon than a Smoked

Butterscotch Latte from Starbucks and the taste of love in the air?

I'd barely finished reading chapter sex, er six, when the intercom buzzed.

So much for love in the afternoon, I thought, pressing the *Talk* button and wondering what now?

CHAPTER 3

B unny's voice came in loud and clear. "Headin' for your office."

"Thanks for the warning," I said, which wasn't as snippy as it sounded. It's not that I was annoyed with Bunny, only disappointed at the interruption. There goes the rest of my day, I thought, shoving *Edwina's Husband* under my butt as I grabbed the nearest manila folder and slid it to the front of my desk, answering Bunny's knock with, "Okay. Come on in."

He strolled through the door and glanced at my desk. "What are you readin'?"

I tapped the bright orange folder in front of me. "Just some tax stuff. Now that we've earned real money we're required to donate a share of it to the US Government."

He reached his foot back to close the door and handed me a business card. "Really?" he said with a questioning look. "I saw *Edwina's Husband* on your desk and thought you were probably in here feasting on another bodice ripper, dreamin' of…uh, making it with cowboys."

I hid my annoyance only because Bunny was doing a good job lately of abiding by my office rules when it came to tempering his language. Rule number three in my company's official guidelines contained a prohibition against profanity, which wasn't easy for Bunny, considering his weekend vocation.

"First of all," I said, "Agnes doesn't write bodice rippers and second, who appointed you book police?"

He shrugged and nodded at the business card. "I'd like to read it when you're done. This is our latest client's business card. She goes by the name of Sally Martin. She called early this morning for an appointment. I didn't know when you'd be in, so I scheduled her for the afternoon."

I picked up the card, a fancy design I guessed hadn't come from Office Depot. "Sally, not Sarah?"

"Why Sarah?"

"Because Sally's a nickname for Sarah, so most Sallys are really Sarahs."

"Oh, she's not a Sarah," Bunny said, giving me his best impression of a seductive look—one eyebrow raised over an eye half-closed.

Bunny had the most flexible eyebrows of anybody I'd ever seen, and he made good use of the trait in his comedy routines, mostly to signal the audience when to laugh.

My turn to lift an eyebrow, even though I could only raise my left one a quarter of an inch, one of the many things Bunny did better than me. Quick comebacks was another. "What does that mean?"

"You'll see."

I took a deep breath. "Invite her in."

As Bunny turned to leave, I removed *Edwina's Husband* from under my derriere and dumped it in my bottom drawer. He caught me, sending an over-the-shoulder gotcha look on his way out, one of his more annoying habits.

I removed a yellow pad from my middle drawer, set

it squarely on top of the orange folder, and wrote: *Sally Martin* across the top of the first page.

The click-click of high heels announced the presence of my prospective client. The sweet sound of her shoes reminded me of the snakeskin Jimmy Choo's I'd passed up earlier that morning. So here I was, already lusting for a second expensive pair of shoes, thinking I'm dangerous with real money in my checking account, but what the heck, that snakeskin number was calling my name and maybe one of these days, I'd be able to afford it without suffering a boatload of guilt.

Sally Martin appeared at my door, drawing me back to reality. Bunny introduced us, and I could see him hiding a smile. I knew the reason as soon as I laid eyes on Sally's angular, well-endowed figure. She reminded me of someone I'd seen in the news, but I couldn't remember who.

"We were recommended to Ms. Martin by one of our former clients," Bunny said, clearly trying to keep a straight face. "Cinda Mae Bradbury."

One look at Sally Martin and I should have figured that out for myself. Former stripper turned restaurateur Cinda Mae Bradbury was one of my agency's first clients. She'd hired us to find her husband's killer, and we'd obliged. I wondered if Sally Martin faced a similar problem.

My new client was taller than Cinda Mae, about five-ten, and attractive, though I'd say handsome more than pretty. Her long blonde hair, size thirty-eight chest, and unconventional outfit harked back to the first time I'd set eyes on my former client. I seemed to be the strippers' PI of choice these days.

I reached across the desk and shook her hand. "Hi. I'm Pauline Berger, but I go by Polly. Welcome to Berger Investigations."

"Thanks for meeting with me." Her voice had the gravelly quality of a long-time smoker, with an accent straight out of Brooklyn.

I pointed her to the chair across from my desk. "Have a seat and tell me how we can help you."

I gestured Bunny to the second vacant chair knowing his curiosity was killing him and if I sent him back to his desk he'd only stand outside with his ear glued to the door.

From the sedate way Sally Martin seated herself I guessed she was in the midst of a career change similar to Cinda Mae's recent decision to turn her deceased husband's strip club into a Mexican restaurant.

"You may have seen the article in the *Times* yesterday?" A slight lift in tone turned her statement into a question.

I'd barely had enough time to eat last week let alone read the *Sunday Times*, which I wasn't prepared to admit to a new client. "About?"

"About the body that washed up on Dockweiler State Beach?"

"Sorry. I guess I missed that one." Which was the truth. I'd neither read about the discovery nor caught it on the news, but then a dead body in La La Land wasn't exactly news. I shrugged an apology. "I had a busy day yesterday. Was this person a relative of yours?"

"No. A friend of my husband's." The hesitation in her throaty response suggested grief or maybe uncertainty. I wasn't sure which.

"Male or female?"

She answered with a slight tip of her head as if she'd taken offense at my question. "Male, of course."

I waited for her to continue, wondering what she wanted me to do about a dead body washing up on a beach south of Santa Monica. She hesitated, and I urged her along. "The dead guy's name is?"

"Leonardo Da Vinci Spinoli."

"Like the artist."

She nodded. "He went by Lenny."

"But Leonardo Da Vinci was his real name?"

She shrugged. "It's the name he gave my husband."

I had a bad feeling about the answer to my next question. "And your husband is?"

"Missing," she said. "My husband is missing."

CHAPTER 4

Hearing Mrs. Martin's response reminded me of another former client—my friend, Cinda Mae Bradbury, who wouldn't know the meaning of the term *figure of speech* if you drew a diagram and pasted it on her forehead. On the other hand, thanks to Cinda Mae, I had plenty of practice handling the type seated in front of me, so I charged ahead.

"Let's start at the beginning. When was the last time you saw your husband?"

"The night he and Lenny Spinoli went fishing together. They never came home. I called the Coast Guard the next morning. Told them my husband went fishing with Lenny Spinoli and never came back. They took down all the information and said they'd get back to me." She hesitated, daubing at her eyes with a tissue from the box on my desk. "I got a call the next day saying the police had found their boat adrift off Santa Catalina Island with nobody on board. That was like, three days before Lenny's body washed up on Dockweiler Beach."

I scribbled a few notes before repeating the question I thought I'd asked earlier. "And your husband's name is?"

"Ricky."

"Ricky Martin," I said. "Like the singer." I dropped my voice at the end of the sentence, but she got the message anyway, which suggested she was another pretend dumb blonde like Cinda Mae. Since I'm a dishwater blonde myself, I'm always happy to run across smart blondes. If I counted my sister Franny along with Cinda Mae, then the addition of Sally Martin made four of us. I figured a quartet of high I.Q. blondes was enough to start a Twitter fad of smart blonde jokes. Once I thought of one I'd try to get the craze started.

Sally pulled a face at the mention of her spouse's famous namesake. "Except my husband's first name is Richard, not Enrique, but everyone calls him Ricky. He says it's been his nickname since childhood, and that was way before Ricky Martin's time." She hesitated again, clearly unhappy with the comparison I'd drawn. "And despite his age," she continued, "my husband is better looking than—than his more famous doppelgänger."

"He must be a looker, then," I said, which I probably shouldn't have because she cast her eyes down as if she'd lost a contact.

As she sat across from me, head down, saying nothing, just wiping her eyes, I couldn't help but feel sorry for her. If I were my twin sister, tears would be streaming down my face right now, but I'm not the sentimental side of us. Hollywood has turned me into a hard-boiled broad, much as I hate to admit it, but this town will do that to you.

I surveyed my new client, wondering how many years stretched between her and her missing spouse. I guessed Sally Martin to have a good ten years on me, years she was good at disguising, which meant she might be pushing fifty-five.

An unwelcome thought flitted through my head, that maybe she had something to do with her husband's disappearance. I brushed aside my suspicions, deciding to give her the benefit of the doubt.

"How uh, old—*is* your husband?" I asked, almost using the past tense, which would give away my best estimate as to the current disposition of her spouse. I wondered if she was familiar with the *Schrödinger's cat* physics paradox in which a cat may be both dead and alive at the same time—the identical state in which Ricky Martin currently existed in my mind, and which would exist until somebody found him alive, or recovered his dead body. In the case of the latter, I didn't want to be the one resolving the paradox.

"Fifty-three," she whispered. More tears formed in the corner of her cocoa-brown eyes, which were nearly hidden by an expensive set of black lashes. "He's in the prime of his life." She reached for another tissue and wiped her nose. "Or at least, he *was*."

I appreciated her use of the past tense, saving me the embarrassment of using it first. I watched my client's eyes glaze over as the enormity of her husband's disappearance hit her, perhaps for the first time, and decided to focus her thoughts elsewhere. "When did the Coast Guard begin searching the waters around Catalina Island for your husband?"

The question seemed to snap Sally Martin out of her stupor. "Five days ago, but it seems like an eternity."

"Is the search still on?"

"No. The mission coordinator called me yesterday to say they were suspending operations as of today."

I drummed a number two pencil on my desk in another effort to distract her from her grief. "That doesn't mean they've given up," I said, attempting to offer a modicum of hope in what seemed to me a pretty hopeless situation. "Only that they've halted search activities pending further developments. Don't worry, it's still on their radar."

She sniffed up her tears. "I know. That's what they told me."

I had no idea what she wanted my firm to do when it came to finding her missing husband, but I knew one thing: Bunny and I were not about to hire a boat and troll the waters around Santa Catalina in hopes of locating a body, since I was pretty sure Sally's husband hadn't survived bobbing alone in the sea for nearly a week. Besides, I don't do small boats. I'm afraid of the water, and I don't trust Bunny out there on his own, even if he does like to surf.

"I'm a little confused here," I said. "What is it you think I can do for you?"

She took a deep breath. "I think somebody murdered my husband *and* Lenny Spinoli, and I want you to catch the SOB."

CHAPTER 5

My client's accusation came out of the blue, and I took a minute to compose my response, but Bunny piped up before I could spit out my first word.

"We can do that," he said, without missing a beat, "for a price."

I couldn't believe how mercenary Bunny had become and wondered if it had anything to do with his recent marriage proposals to my sister Franny, who fortunately, has had the good sense to turn him down. So far, anyway.

"What Mr. Contreras means," I offered, trying to soften the message, "is that we need to negotiate a financial arrangement before we can agree to take on your case—"

She interrupted me, clearly not offended by Bunny's bluntness. "Whatever it takes. Money's no object, and Cinda Mae says you guys are the best. I only go with the best."

I appreciated Cinda Mae's recommendation, especially when I took another look at my client's shoes and realized she must be loaded.

"In that case," I said, responding to Sally's "going with the best" comment, "you and I can continue our discussion while Bernardo brings in a contract for you to review. The contract requires a snapshot of both you and your missing husband. If you don't have one of yourself, Bunny can snap a pic."

She shrugged one shoulder as if she wasn't happy about the photo idea, but she'd go along with it.

Bunny stood up, waiting for a clue on how much to charge. "Same as last week," I said.

Bugsy Bernstein, our favorite shyster lawyer paid us one-fifty per hour plus expenses the previous week to help find Holy Kow's missing wife. I saw no reason why we should take less to track down a killer. In fact, if I'd had more time to consider it, I might have raised the rate to two hundred, but I can always reserve the option of add-ons. Extra expenses have a way of accumulating on their own when a client has deep pockets, especially since a full day's work at Bugsy's rates still might not allow me to buy that pair of snakeskin Jimmy Choo's. Not that Michael Kors are cheap, but when it comes to shoes I can be obsessive. Not as obsessive as Mariah Carey, who owns over a thousand pairs. Even if I could afford it, I wouldn't go that far.

"Right, boss." Bunny practically saluted before leaving the office. I knew he was happy to be working for Bugsy's rates, which I hoped to make our standard fee structure.

My avaricious assistant investigator left without shutting the door, but I made no effort to close it behind him because I knew an open door would save me the bother of repeating to him the rest of my conversation with Sally Martin.

I turned back to my client. "Have you known Cinda Mae for long?"

She squirmed in her seat, and I had a good idea why.

"Years ago—" She hesitated. "—in my former life…"

Here it comes, I thought, the 'I was a stripper' admission.

"Uh, my company and the CatWalk shared a hairdresser."

"The CatWalk, where Cinda Mae used to work," I said, assuming my new client worked at a different strip joint. "And your company is?"

"Was. I skated with a local roller derby team. Maybe you heard of us, The Jammer Slammers?

"Sounds familiar," I said, covering my faulty assumption and trying to hide my surprise.

"Cinda Mae and I both worked nights, so we often had afternoon hair appointments together. That's how we became friends. She's one of the nicest people I've ever met. I'm glad she finally got away from that creep of a husband." She shot me a questioning look. "You helped find the perp who murdered him, didn't you?"

I nodded. "That's when we met. Cinda Mae hired me to track down her husband's killer."

"Right, I remember. Cinda also told me you had a lot to do with helping her get a fresh start, and she's doing a great job with her new restaurant. Ricky and I were hoping she'd go for Italian, but we're regulars, even though we don't care much for Mexican food." She paused. "*Were* regulars, I should say. I know I shouldn't give up hope of finding my husband alive, but I'm a realist. The chances are slim to none that he'll turn up alive and I can deal with that. What I can't deal with is knowing some freakin' loser is getting away with the murder of a good man."

"I understand," I said, noticing she hadn't said *two* good men, "and I'll do my best to see that the killer or killers are found and brought to justice."

"I appreciate it. Whatever it costs, I'm good with it. Cinda Mae said if anybody could find the SOB, you could."

Sally's accent was getting to me, making me homesick for the east coast, Pittsburgh, in particular.

"I appreciate Cinda's confidence in me," I said, getting down to business. "Now I have a few questions for you, the first of which is the obvious one. Why do you believe your husband and his friend were murdered?"

She reached in her purse and pulled out an envelope, opened it, and handed me the document inside. "My husband gave this to me and told me to open it *only* if something happened to him. At the time, I was shocked by his request. 'What do you mean,' I asked, 'if something happens to you? Are you in some kind of trouble? If so, we should contact the police.'"

"What did he say?"

"He laughed like it was no big deal. 'The real estate business can be dangerous these days,' he said, 'even for an honest person like me.' I work with him in the business, but I don't know all the ins and outs because he handles the money. I just show houses and answer the phone."

An honest real estate developer, I thought, trying to hide my skepticism. LA real estate development was a favorite front for laundering drug money, as well as a host of other shady financial dealings. I made another note to myself: *Loan shark becomes shark bait?*

I unfolded the paper and looked it over before scanning the contents into my computer. The text appeared to be nothing more than a short summary of the couple's financial statement and an overview of their business accounts. The name and address of a local CPA showed up on the bottom of the last page.

"This looks like an account of your husband's finances. Is that correct?"

She nodded. "Correct as far as I know. Ricky handled our personal finances, too. Said he didn't want me to worry my pretty little head about anything as mundane as money."

"I see." I took in this information with a grain of salt since Sally Martin was a far stretch from the helpless little woman.

She leaned over my desk, which should have squashed her boobs down to nothing, but they remained intact, telling me they were mostly fake, and flipped to the last page. "This is the name of the accountant I'm supposed to contact, but I haven't called him yet."

"Why not?"

"How do I know I can trust him? How do I know I can trust anybody in Ricky's life now that he's disappeared under mysterious circumstances?"

"That's a good point," I said, because it was. "I can hook you up with a trustworthy accountant if you'd like." I hesitated before adding, "*and* a good lawyer." I had no plans to recommend my pal Bugsy Bernstein. Much as I owed him a favor, he wasn't the kind of attorney I'd go out on a limb for, but I did know someone I'd be willing to refer. "I'll get to that in a minute," I said. "First, I have a few questions about the body on the beach. Just out of curiosity, you said Lenny Spinoli's body washed up on Dockweiler Beach. Any idea who discovered it?"

"A local TV crew."

"TV crew?"

"Yeah. They were shooting a commercial for a local Dr. Sellout."

"Dr. Sellout?" Given the name game so far, Dr. Zhivago or Dr. Watson wouldn't have surprised me.

A semblance of a grin crossed my client's lips. "It's like, uh, slang, for a plastic surgeon. You never heard the term before?"

I had, but I shook my head. "Guess I travel in the wrong circles. What's the doctor's name?"

She looked thoughtful. "I should remember because it was all over the news. His slogan is, *Stop Aging Forever.*"

"Ironic," I said.

"Ironic?"

"That he'd be the one to turn up a corpse." I glanced over to see if she made the connection.

She pursed her lips. "Maybe it was, uh…like a message?"

CHAPTER 6

I thought about Lenny Spinoli's body washing up on Dockweiler Beach, which, when compared to other beaches around LA, is not a particularly popular spot. Probably the reason the ad company chose to film there. Maybe it was the killer's choice, too. If I wanted to dispose of a dead body in a way that suggested it washed ashore, I'd choose a deserted beach where the body had time to putrefy a bit before being found.

I tented my fingers as I mulled things over in my mind, debating about whether or not to take on her case. Something about it smelled worse than a decomposing corpse on the sands of Dockweiler Beach. Besides, for the first time since I started Berger Investigations, Inc., I wasn't desperate for money. I could even afford to take some time off, maybe take a trip with my sister Franny and escape the grind.

Problem is, Franny would want to take Bunny along. And if that weren't bad enough, my ex, once he learned I had time on my hands, would push for a renewal of our marriage vows followed by a Hawaiian honeymoon. Neither idea appealed to me, so I gave up on the travel idea. For now, anyway. My ex, Hollywood Police Department Detective third grade Johnny Birdwhistle, keeps pressuring me for another go at marriage. I love the guy and I've already promised to re-marry him some day. I'm just not certain how soon I want that day to arrive.

After a few minutes of vacillating, I made an executive decision to handle Mrs. Martin's case, even though finding a murderer appealed to me less right now than finding myself married, for a third time, Johnny being my second husband. As for the present, he and I had a good thing going, and I couldn't see any reason for ruining it. Unfortunately, Johnny refused to buy into my logic and periodically bugged me to set a date. I could buy myself some time by taking on the case of the missing Ricky Martin and the dead Lenny Spinoli.

I wrote a few notes on my yellow pad while thinking about what to ask next. Before committing one hundred percent to this case, I needed a bucket load of additional information. I began with, "What can you tell me about Mr. Spinoli?"

Sally Martin blinked a few times before offering her next gem. "Not much. Like, I didn't really know him."

"You said he was a friend of your husband's?"

"More like an acquaintance. A business acquaintance."

"For how long?"

"Not long, which is why I never got to know him."

"You must know something about him."

She shook her head.

Her answers frustrated the heck out of me. Not exactly a cooperative witness, I thought, especially for someone who wanted answers to some pretty difficult questions. "Anything at all will help me get started." I was thirsting for a productive clue. "Where is your husband from, anyway?

"Poughkeepsie."

"Poughkeepsie, New York?"

"You ever hear of another Poughkeepsie?"

"I guess not, otherwise, I'd remember."

"It's an Indian word. Means house by the water or somethin', but Ricky did tell me where Lenny lived," she offered.

I began to feel hopeful. "That's a start. Where?"

"Coxsackie. But I don't know if he still lives there since he called Ricky to look at properties out here. Could be he splits his time between the two places."

I noticed her use of the present tense in referring to Lenny, which was odd given she'd referred to her missing husband in the past tense. I wondered if the coroner had made a definite ID on Spinoli's body yet, but I'd save that question for later. I had a feeling Sally Martin knew more than she was saying so I decided to switch tactics. "Okay, then, tell me about your husband."

"What do you want to know?"

"Anything that might help me figure out what's happened to him."

"We met three years ago. I was auditioning for a part in the movie *The Place Beyond the Pines*, and so was Ricky. Did you see it?"

"Missed that one."

"It takes place in Schenectady, so they were looking for actors from Upstate New York."

Since Sally apparently answered the call, I assumed maybe she grew up near Coxsackie like Lenny Spinoli, though I could swear her accent was straight out of North Jersey.

"Ricky played in a couple of movies, but it was more of a hobby for him. For me, it was a career move. After I left the Jammers, I worked for Mt. Pleasant Entertainment. They produced a couple of low budget films and gave me some bit parts. That's when I got the bug and decided acting was my preferred calling."

I tucked that piece of information into the back of my gray matter. Actors were also good liars. Part of their training—they had to lie well to be convincing.

Sally Martin sent an unwitting look my way that reminded me again of Cinda Mae, and I nodded in response, encouraging her to continue, even though so far her narrative was more disappointing than the five pounds I'd gained on my last diet. I'm an optimist so I hoped eventually something might come of my questions.

"I'll check out the *Pines* movie on Netflix," I told her. "Did you get the part?"

She shook her head. "No, even though I do a great Schenectady accent." She shrugged as if to say the casting director wouldn't know a Schenectady accent if he or she fell over it. "I lied and told them I grew up in Albany and maybe they found out I didn't, so that's why I didn't get the part."

"Possibly," I said, "though people lie about everything in this town. Nobody seems to hold it against them." I knew if she'd grown up in Albany, she'd pronounce her hometown as *Awbany*, a slipup that might have given her away.

She nodded. "Yeah. I lied about my age, too, but then everybody out here lies about their age. They think you're crazy if you *don't* lie about it. Anyway, Ricky didn't get a part either, but we found each other." She gave me a wide-eyed look. "And that's a lot more important, wouldn't you say?"

Given her current set of circumstances, I *wouldn't* say, but I wasn't about to let that slip. "How long have you and Ricky been married?"

"One year tomorrow." She shifted her eyes to the left while at the same time shifting in the straight-backed chair I keep by my desk. It's my secret weapon for limiting the amount of unpaid time people spend bending my ear.

Her body language prompted me to ask a follow-up. "Has Ricky been married before?"

She hesitated again, causing me to wonder if she was counting up the number of his ex-wives. "Twice," she said, glancing left again. "He says three's his lucky number. I told him it better be. Of course, now I'm thinkin' maybe three was his unlucky number."

"Depends on what's happened to him, I guess."

However, the more she talked, the more encouraged I felt that Ricky Martin might be alive and well and somewhere in Mexico, the Baja peninsula most likely.

A picture popped into my mind of the other Ricky Martin, the famous one, lounging by the pool in Hotel Cabo San Lucas, sunglasses hiding his come-hither eyes. I caught myself about to sigh audibly, even though Ricky Martin was gay, something I knew before he came out of the closet publicly. I couldn't have cared less. He was one gorgeous hunk of manhood. I'd share a closet with him any day of the week.

CHAPTER 7

Bunny returned with a contract in hand and laid it on my desk. I thanked him in a way that gave him permission to stay as I slid the document across to Mrs. Martin.

"This is our standard contract," I told her, taking the last reluctant step to seal our relationship. "If you find the conditions acceptable when you finish reading it, just complete the contact information, initial each page, and place your John Hancock on the bottom of page five. I'll do the same and Bunny will make a copy for you." I pointed to a sentence on the first page. "Initial retainer is two thousand dollars."

Sally Martin took the retainer clause in stride, and Bunny and I waited as she sifted through the remaining three pages of the contract, reading every jot and tittle, including the fine print. As I thought, she was as literal as Cinda Mae. Finally, she reached the end and glanced up at me, ignoring Bunny, which I knew he wouldn't appreciate.

"Your rates are a little higher than Cinda Mae estimated," she said, "but that's okay."

"Cost of living's been going up a lot out here. Not like the rest of the country."

"I know. Doesn't matter. It's worth a lot to me to know what happened to my husband and to find out whether or not he's still alive because maybe he is and I'm wrong about him being murdered by the same perp who murdered Lenny."

A peculiar way to phrase her concern, I thought, wondering how she was so sure someone murdered Lenny Spinoli. I'd have to look up the *Times* article, see if they characterized Lenny's death as a homicide.

I handed my client a pen, and she followed my instructions, signing the paperwork and handing over twenty big ones in cash—crisp hundreds, like they'd just come out of the printing machine. I reached for the counterfeit detection pen in my top drawer and ran it across the top of every bill. The slight yellowish streak told me the bills were real.

"We'll do our best to answer all your questions," I assured her, handing the contract to Bunny. "If anybody can find your husband and Lenny Spinoli's killer, we can."

"That's what Cinda Mae said."

"For starters, you'll need to answer a few questions for Mr. Contreras. We'll need as much BI as you can provide in order to jump start our investigation, including a photo of your missing husband."

"BI?"

"Sorry. Law enforcement jargon for background information."

"No problem. I have a photo of Ricky in my wallet, but it's not very recent."

"As long as it looks like him, it'll do." I nodded to Bunny. "And, Bun, after you take down the information, hook Mrs. Martin up with our favorite accountant."

"Yes, ma'am." This time Bunny actually saluted.

I tuned back to Sally Martin. "Our accountant will let you know if and when you need a lawyer."

She stood up, shook my hand, and trailed Bunny out of the office. I watched to make sure he handed her our accountant's business card, which he did. I heard him add another set of reassurances before escorting Mrs. Martin into the outer office.

Bunny's a sucker for a woman in distress, which is one of the reasons I wish my sister Franny would find another love interest. I didn't trust Bunny not to hurt her, and she's been hurt too much already. I sat there for a few long minutes, wondering what I could do about the situation that wouldn't be harmful to my sister, finally deciding her decisions were hers and not mine. I needed to avoid meddling in her love life, which is hard to do when you think someone you love is making poor decisions.

Returning my thoughts to business, I picked up the landline to dial my ex. Before placing the call, I reviewed our relationship for about the hundredth time. I knew he was upset with me for not agreeing to a wedding date, and I knew I was running out of excuses to postpone marrying him again, which meant that sooner or later he'd deliver another ultimatum.

If nothing else, I had to give him credit for being persistent and for cleaning up his act. Johnny spends a lot of time these days demonstrating how much he loves me, and assuring me he's given up his former womanizing ways, which was the cause of our breakup. I'm not the most forgiving person in the world, but I have forgiven him because it so happens I love Johnny.

But there's more to it than that. He's a cop. More than a cop, he's a big deal detective in the Hollywood PD, who is accustomed to giving orders and getting his way. Me? I'm a PI who works for herself precisely because she *dislikes* taking orders from anyone and, like Johnny, enjoys getting her way. And "there's the rub," to quote Hamlet, which I don't often do.

I punched in Johnny's office number. He answered the phone with, "Hi, sweetheart, missing me?"

"I am, Johnny, but I'm also missing information."

"This is a business call, then," he said, his voice deflating.

I decided to cheer him up, especially since I wanted straightforward answers to a rather large number of questions that were technically none of my business. "Business and pleasure, sweetie, and before we get down to business, I want to double-check on dinner tonight. We're on, right?"

"Is my name Chief Grillmaster of Hollywood?"

"No, it's Johnny Birdwhistle, best grill chef around." I hoped that acknowledgement was sufficient to put him in a good mood.

"You won't be sorry you called."

I could hear the smile in his voice.

"Okay, here's my first question."

"Shoot."

"What do you know about the dead body that washed up on Dockweiler Beach yesterday?"

After a long pause, Johnny replied with, "Jesus, Mary, and Joseph, what have you got to do with that?"

"I asked first."

After a long pause and an even longer sigh, he said, "John Doe, picked up on Dockweiler at four-thirty Sunday afternoon. Apparent drowning victim, probably swimming alone, caught in a rip tide."

His answer surprised me. How did my client know the dead guy's name and the Hollywood PD did not? Or, more likely, did Johnny know, but he wasn't saying?

"That's it?" I said. "That's all you know?"

"If I knew more, wouldn't I share that knowledge with my former and future bride?"

I had to think for a minute about how to phrase my next question without stepping on Johnny's toes.

"Since this John Doe's death has been designated as accidental," I began, caution being my guide, "I'm assuming that means you, Chief Grillmaster and Head of the Homicide Division for the HYPD, are not in charge of said case and therefore your knowledge of the facts would be somewhat limited?"

"You would be correct in that assumption, which I take it means you know something I don't."

"I know the dead guy's name is Lenny Spinoli, full name Leonardo daVinci Spinoli, and that he didn't die swimming at Dockweiler Beach. If the coroner's ruling is death by drowning, then the dead guy probably drowned when he fell off or was pushed from a fishing boat found adrift a few days ago near Santa Catalina Island, now residing in the custody of the US Coastguard. The boat, I mean, not the island."

"Before I say more," Johnny said, sounding exactly like Joe Pesci in *My Cousin Vinnie*, "do you, Miss Know-it-all, mind telling me how you came by this classified information?"

I channeled Marissa Tomei. "From my new client, Sally Martin, wife of one Ricky Martin, who reportedly was on said fishing boat with Lenny Spinoli, and who, like Spinoli, has disappeared and whose wife has hired me to find him, or his killer, since she thinks the perp who snuffed Lenny Spinoli may have offed her husband in the bargain."

I raised my voice on the last syllable of bargain as if it were a question, and heard Johnny audibly suck in his breath. "What have I told you about that tough talk you like to spout? It's not ladylike and it doesn't suit you."

"You're changing the subject."

After a long pause, he said. "The reason you know more about this case than I do is because the feebs swept in here as soon as the body turned up on Dockweiler Beach, notified us they were taking over the case and we had to keep our distance. That meant no freelancing, no Curious George behavior, nothing. Monkey no see, monkey no hear, monkey no do. And now you show up asking all the wrong questions of exactly the wrong person. How do you do that?"

"Just lucky, I guess. I take it you want to keep your nose out of my investigation?"

"No. I want *you* to keep your nose out of the feebs' investigation. This is a high-profile case for some reason, or they wouldn't be interested in it. For you, that means it's dangerous. I don't care what this Sally Martin person is paying you, it's not worth risking your life."

"Already signed the contract and took the down payment."

"Tear it up and give back the money before some dude in a suit shows up at your door askin' a lot of questions for which you've got all the wrong answers."

"I'm not worried about some smartass FBI agent."

"Who says the suit I'm talkin' about is with the FBI? More likely a hitman for the Mafia or the Los Zetas cartel since I hear they're workin' together these days. I'm telling you, if this Spinoli case is not a drowning but a murder, then it's somethin' you need to keep your pretty nose out of. That means distance yourself, and the farther, the better."

"I know you're just looking out for my best interests," I snapped, "but Sally Martin seems like a nice lady. *And* she's a friend of Cinda Mae's."

A long list of swear words flew across our phone connection, followed by, "That right there should be a clue for you to stay as far away from this missing person's case as possible."

"Please, Johnny," I said. "Cinda Mae would be crushed if she heard what you just said. Besides—"

He hung up on me, which told me it would be my butt and not the steak getting grilled at dinner tonight. I might have to reconsider his invitation.

CHAPTER 8

As our phone conversation demonstrated, Johnny can't help himself when it comes to telling people, me included, what to do and what not to do. I have more than a sneaking suspicion that if I marry him again, he'll feel even freer to boss me around, which I also suspect is the main reason he's so anxious to re-tie the knot.

Johnny can be a control freak. He knows it, but that self-knowledge does nothing to stop him, which is why I liked our current status—committed and separate but equal. The way things stand, if I get miffed at Johnny, I can go to my own home where I live alone again, since my sister Franny bought a condo a couple of blocks away, take a beer out of the fridge, flip on the TV, and forget about Johnny's orders. If I marry him, he'll want me to move into his place, or he'll move into mine, and there's no escape. Not exactly like being in prison, but not like being free either. At least, that's how I see it.

As I sat there ruminating about Johnny, the outside door of my office closed, indicating our latest client had left the premises. The loud thump caught my attention. I needed to change the hinges so the door didn't slam every time a breeze flowed up the stairs and snatched it from someone's hands. Otherwise, one of these days a client will be knocked off balance, tumble down my non-carpeted stairs, break a leg, and sue me for all I have, which isn't much, but it's growing.

I picked up a pen and wrote myself a reminder: *fix door—increase insurance.*

Door problem noted, I returned to the two-pronged problem of the missing Ricky Martin and his possible killer. Aside from the personal information Sally Martin provided to Bunny, we needed to run a background check on both parties prior to making an irreversible decision with this case. Irreversible meaning spending money we might not recoup.

I still wondered how my client knew the dead guy's name when Johnny didn't. I'd check out the *Sunday Times* and see if Spinoli's name turned up in the article. Then it was on to finding out as much information on our client as we could.

If we turned up any unsavory links in her past or the past of her missing spouse, I'd follow Johnny's advice and break the contract, returning Sally's money with a clear conscience.

In spite of Johnny's worries, I wasn't about to risk my life for a few hundred dollars, or Bunny's life either, especially now that he was dating my sister. She'd be heartbroken if he disappeared into the ocean around Santa Catalina Island—or anywhere else, for that matter.

I buzzed him on the intercom.

"May I help you, miss?" Bunny's idea of humor wore on me sometimes, as did my recent conversations with Johnny. Ah men, I thought.

"Bring me the background information Sally provid-ed on her husband then contact TLO," I told him, refer-ring to a popular background-investigative service used by law enforcement and PIs like me, "and request a thorough background check on Ricky and Sally Martin. I'll look into Lenny Spinoli."

"That it, boss?"

"And while we're waiting for the TLO info to arrive, let's carry out a BI search of our own." In my mind, I sorted through the list of sites we needed to check, from sex offenders' lists to prison records, tax appraisals, and student records websites, deciding to assign the boring ones to Bunny, but he beat me at my own game.

"Already started. I'm working the social media end right now. I'll handle the criminal stuff next."

I hesitated for a minute because he'd just grabbed all the interesting stuff. "Okay, but add newspaper records to your list, too. Start with *thepaperboy.com* and *newspaperarchive.com*."

Going through old newspaper archives was the worst, which is precisely what motivated me to buy a subscription to TLO in the first place. If it was good enough for law enforcement, it was good enough for me.

"If you figure out how to eliminate all the references to the famous Ricky Martin," I told Bunny, "let me know. That name is likely to hinder our searches big time."

"Right, but I'm using Richard, not Ricky. Makes it a little easier."

"I know," I said, trying to cover my stupidity, "that works unless he uses Ricky."

"I already checked that possibility with Mrs. Martin. She says only his friends and family call him Ricky. He doesn't use it himself."

Bunny was getting way too good at his job, which told me he was dead serious about getting his own PI license. Ever since he started dating my sister, he'd been working on it and I worried way too much that he'd quit on me and go out on his own. If he did, he'd better not take my sister with him or I'd do what I could to shut him down. Knowing how Bunny liked to cut corners, it wouldn't take much. However, bringing him into Berger Investigations as a full partner was probably my best option. Besides, I wanted to keep my sister happy.

I already knew he was the reason Franny moved out of my house and into her own place, not that it wasn't the best thing for her. I simply wasn't certain it was the best thing for me. Identical twins can become co-dependent pretty quickly, and even though we hadn't lived together since we were eighteen, the last few months of having Franny around felt pretty good.

Bunny came through the door with a copy of the background information form our client had completed, focusing my attention on the present. I could worry about Bunny and Franny's future plans another day.

"Here's the BI she provided," he said, sliding the paper across my desk. "There's not much here, though, which is why I started sifting through social media sites looking for more."

I glanced down at the document and saw a number of blank boxes. "She tell you why she didn't answer half these questions?"

Bunny shrugged. "Yeah. Reminded me they'd been married less than a year, and she said she hadn't bothered to ask about a lot of things like his college graduation date because it didn't interest her. 'Besides,' she said, 'a person's past is their past. I didn't want to tell him a bunch of stuff about mine so I didn't ask about his.'"

"Makes sense I guess if you have something to hide. The question is what do they each have to hide?"

Bunny nodded. "Whatever it is, we're bound to find out sooner or later."

"What happens in the meantime, though?"

"We'll be fine," Bunny assured me. "Johnny's tried to scare you off this case, right?"

"I don't respond to rhetorical questions," I replied, as Bunny headed out of the office.

"Except you just did."

He had the audacity to wink at me as he shut the door. I turned back to the blinking-stars background on my computer, realizing I'd have to postpone my date with *Edwina's Husband* to another day, maybe another week.

CHAPTER 9

I'd barely begun my first internet search when I heard cries of distress coming from the outer office. I wondered if Sally Martin had returned to share her grief after receiving news of the death of her husband, except the hysterical howls had a familiar ring.

I vaulted out of my chair once I recognized the sound of my twin sister's voice. The two of us nearly collided when my office door flew open, missing my vulnerable body by inches.

"Franny! What the heck's the matter?"

"Polly," she sobbed, "somebody's trying to kill me."

"What? Where? When?"

"I need to move back to Pennsylvania," she blubbered. I could barely understand her. "Life's too dangerous for me out here."

I put my arms around her and led her to my two-person settee, which is what I call the small sofa across from my desk. Loveseat seems inappropriate for office furniture, and besides, at the time I acquired it, I was not interested in putting ideas in Bunny's head. "Sit down, sweetie, and tell me what has you so upset."

She stared or maybe glared at me, always disconcerting when you're a twin—like looking at yourself in a skewed mirror—and wailed, "Is everybody in Hollywood out to kill you or something?"

I shook my head. "Not that I know of. What happened?"

"Everybody thinks I'm you, and now this is the second time I've been put in harm's way because of it. I mean, first, I'm kidnapped the day I arrive, then some perp follows me from your house—"

"You were at my house?"

"Uh-huh. I returned your pair of Christian Louboutins—" Which she pronounced as *lowboatins*. "—that I borrowed for my fancy date with Bunny on Friday night…"

She sucked in her breath, realizing she'd forgotten to tell me she'd borrowed them. Clearly, she was trying to sneak the shoes back into my closet while I was at work, not that she needed to. She knows she can borrow anything of mine whenever she wants. Besides, Johnny rarely takes me anywhere fancy enough to show off my latest pair of designer shoes. At least with Franny living nearby, my footwear can make a splash somewhere in Hollywood.

"Loo-boo-tah," I said, correcting her pronunciation in a dead-on impersonation of our English teacher mother. "So you were returning my shoes, then what happened? Somebody tried to break into my house?"

"No. He was parked in a black SUV across the street."

"What did he look like?"

"How do I know? The windows were as black as the rest of the car."

"If someone was trying to kill you, surely you could have caught a glimpse of him. Did he shoot at you or something?"

"No. When I came out of the house and saw him

parked over there, I didn't know whether to go back in the house where I'd be a sitting duck as he shot up your house like Geejay did, or get in the car and drive straight over here. I decided the car was less risky, so I ran out, jumped in the car, and headed to your office."

"He try to T-bone you along the way?"

"You mean run into the side of me?"

I nodded.

"No. He just followed me. I tried to lose him by turning down side streets and stuff, but he stayed with me the whole way, which is how I know he was just waiting for a good opportunity to bump me off with no witnesses around. I managed to deny him the privilege, but when I pulled into your parking lot, he drove by real slow like he was giving me the evil eye, warning me that next time he wouldn't miss."

I could feel my heart rate slowing down from the near-infarction levels when she first told me someone had tried to kill her. Franny had been hanging around with Cinda Mae way too much lately and the effect was obvious. Hyperbole, panic attacks, shopping sprees, the whole nine yards. My sister was becoming Cinda-ized. Pretty soon she'd be calling me "counselor" and questioning my investigative skills. Somehow, I needed to intervene in this bosom buddy friendship, but not at the expense of my sister returning to Pennsylvania. I loved her, and I loved having her living near me, even if it meant seeing more of Bunny than I ever wanted to outside of work.

"So actually," I said, "no one tried to kill you. Someone in a black SUV followed you, thinking you were me, presumably, but they never shot at you, tried to T-bone you, played bump and run, or anything else of an aggressive nature. Do I have that right?"

Franny sank a little deeper into my couch, which was pretty easy to do since the twenty-year-old springs have

the energy of a dead battery. Ten minutes on the dilapi-
dated wreck and the floor comes up to massage your bottom. Maybe with my newfound wealth, I'd spring for a
new one, no pun intended.

"Well, yeah," Franny said, "but in my defense, if you
will recall, the first day I arrived out here some perps you
were investigating kidnapped me and scared the bejesus
out of me until you came and rescued me. Ever since
then, I've been suspicious of anybody who looks at me
sidewise, and anyway, I am right about one thing."

"And that one thing is?"

"Whoever was in that SUV was following me, and
he was threatening me."

"That's two things," I reminded her.

She screwed up her face. "You're starting to sound a
lot like Cinda Mae. Maybe you shouldn't be spending so
much time around her."

"I'll take that under consideration while you try to
help me out here with some information that assists my
efforts to find this creep."

"I told you I couldn't see into the car because the
windows were too dark, so I'm not even sure if it was a
guy or a girl in there."

"Okay, good point. Do you know the make of the
vehicle?"

"You know I don't know anything about cars, Polly.
I know it was an SUV with a little antenna sticking out
the back of the roof."

"That's a start. Anything else that might help us ID
this driver?"

"I got the license plate number."

"For heaven's sake why didn't you tell me that
first?"

"I like saving the best for last."

I let out my breath and gave her a hug. Sometimes Franny is more like me than I care to admit. I reached for the yellow pad and pen on my desk and handed them over to her. "Write the number down so you don't forget it. We'll give the number to Johnny so he can run it down for us. Once he hears this guy frightened you, he'll have him behind bars before the perp can spell stalker. And I don't want to hear any more talk about you moving back to PA. You're safer out here than you are around your ex-husband's crazy family, most of whom still blame you for his death."

"I know that, Polly. Maybe if I stay, I should dye my hair black and add a few pounds, except I'm not sure how Bunny would feel about that."

"If he really loves you, he won't care about the color of your hair."

"You're right. How do you think black will look on me?"

"Terrific," I said, "and it'll go great with that pair of Louboutins, which I'll give you if you don't move back to PA."

CHAPTER 10

I'd barely managed to calm my sister down when Bunny stormed into my private office, forgetting to knock first, which is another one of my rules.

"Franny!" He sounded frantic. "Are you okay? I heard you come in, but I was on the can."

He gave us both an apologetic shrug. I didn't know whether he was apologizing for spending time in the loo or for telling us about it.

Franny jumped up and folded herself into his arms. I worried he'd squeeze the life out of her, but I buttoned my lip.

I'm better at doing that now that my sister's here. She's a good influence on me. Franny and I are like a split personality. She's sweet and soft and sentimental—me, not so much.

"I'm okay, Bunny," I heard her mumble into his chest.

"What happened? I thought you were dying or some-thin'."

Franny shot me a look, and I pinched my lips tighter.

"I thought somebody was trying to kill me because they thought I was Polly, but maybe he was just trying to scare me, or, um, scare her."

Bunny glared at me over the top of Franny's head, giving me the stink eye like whatever happened to Franny was my fault.

I felt the need to defend myself. "Franny was over at my house and when she left, some jackass in a black SUV followed her here. She wants to move back to PA, but I talked her out of it."

"Really?" Bunny held Franny at arms' length and stared into her blue eyes, which are a little bluer than mine because she wears colored contacts. "You want to move back to Pencilneck land?" I could hear the hurt in his voice, clearly meant to lay a guilt trip on me, which succeeded.

The shamefaced look Franny gave him rivaled a thief caught with his hand in the till. "Not really, Bunny. I was running scared, but Polly convinced me to stay. I'm gonna dye my hair and get fat instead."

"What color?" he asked.

"What about black?"

"I think red would suit you better."

"Okay, then red," Franny said, giving in way too fast in my opinion. "That way nobody will mistake me for my sister and try to bump me off again."

"Again?" I said. "Again? There's no *again* here. Yes, you were kidnapped that one time, in which Bunny and I rescued you before you were hurt, but today you were only stalked, and you got the license plate number, so Johnny will catch the guy and ensure we're both safe and secure in the land of—"

Bunny interrupted my rant. "You got the plate number? Good work, sweetheart." He sounded like a hard-boiled PI from a Raymond Chandler novel as he lifted Franny's chin and planted a juicy one on her lips.

"Okay. We're working here," I said. "Let's stick to business." I grabbed the pad with the license number and ripped off the top sheet. Once Bunny broke his strangle-hold on my sister, I slapped the paper in his hand. "Run this down ASAP."

"Thanks, boss. We don't need Johnny tracking this down. We can do it ourselves."

Bunny headed out of the office with Franny tagging along, both of them forgetting to close the door behind them.

"I'll come with you," she said. "I wannna be the first to see the name of this stalker so I can take it downstairs to Rosa and ask her to put a spell on him."

I wondered what Rosa would have to say about that. As far as I knew, she concentrated on predicting the future not hexing people, but maybe Franny knew something I didn't.

"Also," Franny said, "I wanna see his picture in case I cross paths with him again."

"You need to get a carry permit," I heard Bunny say. "I'll take you to the shooting range and teach you how to use that gun I gave you."

I could see her head bobbing. "I know. I've been putting it off. You know, after Ronnie was shot to death and all…" Her voice dropped off.

"Remember what I told you," Bunny said, as I shut the door on their conversation. I had a pretty good idea what was coming next.

With the two of them out of my office, I took a deep breath to recharge my brain cells and got back to work. Then I made my second mistake of the day—placing another call to Johnny. I'd memorized the license number Franny wrote down, and I wanted to hand it off to Johnny so he could look into it, too, thinking he might get the job done faster than Bunny.

As soon as Johnny picked up the phone, I told him what happened to Franny and how much it upset her. He has a soft spot in his heart for Franny, which might make me jealous if it weren't for the fact that their relationship was more like brother and sister.

"See?" he said. Not the reaction I anticipated. "You shouldn't have taken that case. Somebody's after you already."

"Nice try, Johnny, but Sally Martin left my office a little more than two hours ago. Hardly enough time for the perps that offed Lenny Spinoli to find out she'd contracted with me."

"I just got a bad feeling about this case, Polly. I don't like bein' kept in the dark, and the feebs have no plans to keep the HYPD in the loop. When that happens, it's a sign of big-time criminal activity, which I happen to think a PI like yourself shouldn't be involved with. I wish you'd stick to trailin' cheatin' spouses and leave major crime to the professionals."

I was so ticked off at him for dissing my professionalism that I hung up on him before I managed to pass along the license number. I sat for a few minutes, fuming, then put aside my pride and sent him an email with the SUV's plate number. At the end of the email I told him I couldn't make dinner later because I'd be busy upgrading my professional PI standing in order to meet the incredibly high standards of the HYPD's detective division.

Once I'd gotten that out of my system, I punched the intercom and told Bunny to hold all my calls, no matter who phoned. I knew Johnny would be on the horn full of apologies as soon as he read my three-sentence e-pistle, but I wasn't in a forgiving mood.

"What if Johnny Appleseed calls?"

"You have wax in your ears? Hold all my calls means—hold *all* my calls."

"So, you two having a little spat?"

I practiced my deep breathing. "How far have you gotten running down that plate?"

"Workin' on it."

"Let me know when you have something." I said, hitting the disconnect button.

In less than a minute, the landline rang and I heard caller ID announce, "Call from Detective Birdwhistle." Of course, Bunny picked up immediately, clearly delighted to inform Johnny I wasn't taking calls. Men are such pains.

I was in one of the foulest moods I'd experienced in years, and I wasn't sure why. What I *did* know was that my mood had nothing to do with Bunny planting a passionate one on my sister in my presence. I might, I thought, be entering the first phase of *MEN*opause, the irony of which I appreciated. Perhaps my brain was telling me to hit the pause button when it came to the men in my life. Bunny and his sophomoric humor had been annoying the heck out of me lately, as was Johnny's nagging, mostly about marrying him again. I was *not* ready for another run on that treadmill and maybe never would be.

Before I could decide where to focus next in terms of the Ricky Martin case, my cell phone jangled. I knew who was calling before I saw Johnny's name dance across the screen. I turned off the phone, opened my bottom desk drawer, and stashed the phone in the outside pocket of my brown-and-black overpriced designer purse.

Next to the purse, I spotted my autographed copy of *Edwina's Husband*, which I removed and shoved into the bookcase behind my desk. He's probably a jerk, too, I thought, hoping Edwina would find out before it was too late.

CHAPTER 11

Fifteen minutes later, Bunny buzzed me to say he was following Franny home and he'd be back in an hour.

"Okay," I said. "Have you got anything on the plate ID?"

"Not yet, so you might have to answer the phone while I'm gone."

"I think I can handle it."

I wanted to add, "smarty-pants," or worse, but I bit my tongue. My mother raised me to believe bad language was the sign of a lazy mind. And besides, after Johnny's slam, I planned to concentrate on consummate professional behavior, no matter my mood, and focus on work since, so far, my day had been a big bust.

Putting Johnny out of my mind, I picked up my phone and called my client. I had a few questions for her, beginning with the two uppermost in mind: number one, how did she know the identity of the body found on Dockweiler Beach when the lead detective at the HYPD didn't know? And second, how did she know Spinoli was murdered? Again, information not known to the local police. A dozen different explanations ran through my mind, none of them good.

Instead of Sally Martin, I reached her voice mail and left a message asking her to contact me. I omitted saying what I called about, hoping her curiosity would prompt a quick return call.

While I waited, I logged into my account at TLO and requested a background report on Leonardo da Vinci Spinoli, hoping my request wouldn't result in a visit from the feebs asking me to back away from their investigation like they'd asked the HYPD. I had a pretty good idea Lenny Spinoli held the key to finding out what happened to Ricky Martin, whose dead body had yet to wash up onto a California beach. I entered what information I knew about Lenny Spinoli, which amounted to his name and hometown, and clicked the Send button.

After logging out of my TLO account, another idea struck me. I turned back to my browser and Googled websites with maps of ocean currents between Santa Catalina Island and the California coastline. Maybe I'd find a quick answer to the question of whether or not Lenny Spinoli's body could have washed up on Dockweiler Beach or been dumped there instead, which is what I suspected.

Once I located the maps of surface currents, they were more detailed than I'd anticipated, with colored arrows going every which way showing the direction of the water flow. After studying the charts for several minutes, I was a little farther along the road to an answer than when I'd started. Not as far as I wanted to be, but sometimes progress is measured in baby steps. Depending on where Lenny entered the water within a rather narrowly circumscribed area around Santa Catalina, his body could have washed up on Dockweiler Beach. Clearly, the possibility could not be eliminated from the equation.

Even so, I wasn't ready to rule out the idea that someone wanted Spinoli's death to *appear* to be an accidental drowning, which left me stuck investigating both possibilities. If I started right away and hustled, I might be able to turn up important information before the FBI beat me to it. No reason I couldn't turn the tables on them. After all, the feebs weren't perfect, and I was a darn good investigator who'd solved more than one murder in the past year alone. I'd stake my record against our local FBI office anytime.

Looking back on those cases, I knew in my heart I couldn't have accomplished half of what I did this past year without Johnny's help, a fact that made me all the more determined to prove myself. The feebs' order to the Hollywood PD that tied Johnny's hands provided an opportunity to do just that, since Johnny was forced to stay away from this case. I could solve it on my own, minus assistance from him and his friends at the HYPD. Feminist pride was at stake here.

I clicked open a new file, which coincided with the sound of my outside doorbell. Bunny locks the office whenever he leaves so no one can enter without my knowing. The option of keeping the outside door open during working hours was a big risk in this part of Hollywood, and I wasn't a huge risk taker, despite my choice of occupation. I reached in my desk for my gun and tucked it into the back of my pants before hustling out to see who was perched at the top of my stairs.

Peering through the peephole, I spotted a man and woman standing side by side, all business, both wearing impatient looks. I cracked open the door and as soon as I did, they held out their hands, not in greeting but to display a matching set of credentials. I glanced from the photos on their cards to the faces in front of me. Same blank stares.

Across the top of each piece of documentation were the words *Federal Bureau of Investigation*, and across the bottom, *Department of Justice*. Sunshine and starlight bounced off the gold badges accompanying their creds. So far, everything looked legit.

I took stock of the guy first, his dark suit, white shirt, and blue striped tie, hair graying at the temples, though I guessed his age at no more than early forties. The name on his card read: Special Agent Joe Foster, and he looked the part of a feeb—physically fit with a strong jaw and taciturn eyes that gave nothing away. I had a weakness for the strong silent type, but now was neither the time nor the place. To reassure myself, I held his stare as I asked him to repeat his badge number. My request failed to intimidate him, and he rattled off the number so fast I could barely follow along. When I checked my recollection of the number against his documentation, they seemed to match.

As a believer in equal rights, I decided to give the same test to Ms. Navy Jacket/Gray Slacks. Her name was Adrienne Peters, and her appearance signaled a no-nonsense personality that matched her partner's. Dark brown hair pulled back in a bun added what I estimated to be a good ten years to her age. Nevertheless, she was attractive, in a masculine kind of way.

I sent her a challenging look. "And your badge number?"

She also passed the test with flying numbers. I thought maybe she was testing me, checking on my processing speed, which is pretty good when I'm stressed.

I opened the door a crack and peered out. "How can I help you?" I asked, still refusing to invite the pair inside.

Ms. Peters spoke up first. "We're here to see Ms. Pauline Berger. Are you she?"

"I am," I said, still blocking the door, which forced the pair to stand close to each other on my four-by-five landing. Keeping them off balance kept me in control because I wasn't about to invite them inside. Not yet, anyway.

"May we come in?" Ms. Peters asked.

I hesitated long enough to let them know I couldn't be bullied. Without blinking, I replied, "You may, as long as you're willing to leave your hardware outside." I pointed to the shelf above the door that held our mail and packages. It contained a long wooden box deep enough to conceal the weapons from view unless someone made a determined effort to peek inside.

The two feds looked surprised, but Special Agent Joe Foster replied first. "We can do that." He removed his gun from the holder inside his jacket and carefully placed it inside the bin. Special Agent Peters did the same, though she seemed less comfortable with the idea.

"One more place to check," I said, squatting down to inspect their legs for ankle holsters.

"Jeez," Joe Foster said, as I stuck my hand through the crack in the door and patted the bottom of his pants leg, the one with the bulge. I couldn't help but notice his east coast accent. I wondered what brought him to sunny California, then realized I'd just answered my own question.

"That gun, too," I told him, glancing in Adrienne Peters' direction.

She bent over and pulled a Glock 23 out of her ankle holster, adding it to the now sizable collection in my mail holder.

"Thank you," I said, drawing myself up to my full five-foot-six-inch height and stepping back to make way for them. "Come on in and tell me what's on your mind."

This should be good, I thought, stepping aside to the let them pass and keeping my hand on the Glock behind my back.

CHAPTER 12

Two cautious federal agents entered and scanned my outer office as though casing the place for explosives. I could only imagine what I'd find missing by the time they left. I crossed my fingers the missing items wouldn't include my PI license, a possibility that caused me to wrack my brain for any recent infractions. I came up empty thanks to the fact that I run a clean shop, which in the PI trade means I'm good at covering my tracks. I have to be or I couldn't stay in business.

Escorting my two guests into my outer office, I pointed to the sofa in the corner of the room across from Bunny's workstation. They took the hint and sat down. I rolled Bunny's desk chair over and sat opposite. Since Bunny's a tad over six feet, his chair provided me with a welcome height advantage over my callers. I crossed my legs, looked down my nose at the visibly uncomfortable pair across from me, and repeated my question.

"What can I do for you?"

Joe Foster spoke first, getting straight to the point. "We understand you took on a new client today, one…" He glanced down at his iPhone as if he couldn't remember the name of my client.

I almost made the mistake of supplying her name before remembering the adage: *never volunteer information in a police interrogation*, which I assumed this visit to be. I waited for Special Agent Foster to complete his sentence.

"...one, Sally Martin?" He looked up from his phone, sending a questioning glance my way as if I'd missed the punctuation mark at the end of his sentence.

I wasn't about to answer without a few interrogatories of my own. "Why is the FBI interested in my caseload?"

Special Agent Peters, clearly the less patient partner, responded more quickly than her colleague seemed to prefer, at least by the look on his face. "It's not your caseload we're interested in," she said. "It's your newest client."

I peeked down at my new watch in order to check the veracity of what I was about to say. "My client left my office barely three hours ago. I'm curious as to how you knew she was here and how you knew she'd signed on as a client." I raised my eyebrow in disapproval. "I mean, is my office under surveillance, or is she, and if so, do you have a warrant that allows you to invade her or *my* privacy like this?"

Special Agent Foster sat forward, which wasn't easy to do while seated on a down cushion that could envelop a full-grown Labrador retriever. "Ms. Berger." He exhaled a long patronizing sigh. "We are not the enemy. We've come to ask your help."

"My help?" You could have knocked me over with the little bottle of hand sanitizer I keep on my desk. "In what way can I *possibly* be of assistance to the largest and best investigative service in the world?" I was feeling generous now that I knew the feebs were not here to shut down my operation or tell me to stay away from the Ricky Martin case.

Special Agent Peters took over at this point. I appreciated their smooth teamwork, which was almost as good as Bunny's and mine.

"By extracting as much information as you can," she said, "from your client Sally Martin with regard to the mystery of her missing husband, about which we know next to nothing."

"That's Zero with a capital Z," Foster said. "Zip, nada, nothing."

"We think she knows something," Peters said, "but is afraid to say."

I agreed. "A similar thought occurred to me in my conversation with her. Speaking of which, I have another question for you. I understand the identity of the body found on Dockweiler Beach hasn't been confirmed in the paper, but since you're here asking for my help, can you possibly share that information with me?"

The agents glanced at each other, clearly deciding which of them would field the question. With an imperceptible signal, Foster handed off to Peters. The San Diego Chargers could use these two, I thought.

"We're not at liberty to disclose to the public information related to the Dockweiler Beach case," Peters said.

"So…" I paused here to let them worry about my willingness to cooperate, "you want me to share information with you, but you aren't willing to reciprocate. Do I have that right?"

Special Agent Foster shrugged one physically fit shoulder, drawing it practically up to his ear. "We're constrained by privacy policies that don't apply to private investigators."

I suddenly saw the picture loud and clear. "In other

words, you want to hire me to do your dirty work for you."

Special Agent Peters shook her head. "It's not like that," she said. "We can't hire you, we can only request your cooperation, which we believe is in your best interest and the best interests of your client."

"In what way is that the case?"

"For the moment, you'll have to trust us on that."

"Trust you? I've only just met you."

Foster broke in, appealing to what he surmised was my patriotic sensibility. "Then trust the Bureau. Again, we're the good guys."

"Right," Peters added. "We're as interested in finding Ricky Martin as you are, maybe more."

Adage aside, I decided to offer some free information at this point, hoping to receive as well as to give. "My client thinks the body on Dockweiler Beach belongs to a man named Lenny Spinoli. She also believes someone murdered Spinoli and her husband and wants me to hunt down their killer, or preferably, find her husband alive and well and in hiding."

"Then our goals coincide," Peters said, without affirming or denying Spinoli's identity. "Which is the best of all possible worlds and a good reason to cooperate."

Before I could respond in the affirmative, which I intended to do, Bunny bounded through the front door. "Why all the fire sticks in the mailbox?" he asked, before spotting our guests.

I stood up to make the introductions. "Bernardo, this is Special Agent Peters and Special Agent Foster from the FBI. They're here about the Sally Martin case." To the agents, I said, "This is Bernardo Contreras, my associate and lead investigator on the Sally Martin case." I figured a little exaggeration couldn't hurt and would puff up Bunny's ego, which meant I'd get more work out of him.

Bunny beamed at the mention of his new title. He'd chafed recently at being called my secretary, even though he still manned the phones. I'd proposed changing his job title to administrative assistant, but he'd vetoed that one, too. We finally agreed on associate investigator, a designation I could live with as long as he agreed to continue his secretarial duties. Besides, I'd worked as a secretary at one point in my life, and I hated the title, too, so I understood.

"May I see your credentials?" Bunny asked, to my surprise.

Both agents reached in their pockets for the same badges and cards they'd shown me, holding them out for Bunny to see. He reached for them, but they drew their hands back.

"Sorry. They can't leave our possession," Joe Foster said.

"No problem," Bunny replied, leaning down for a closer look before glancing at me. "They look legit," he said, pulling out his iPhone.

I spotted the annoyed look that crossed Special Agent Peters' face, but she maintained her cool. "That's because they are."

Bunny held out the phone. "Just to be sure, let's snap a pic."

To my surprise, the agents held out the creds."

"Keep in mind," Special Agent Foster said, "sharing these photos with anyone other than the two of you is a federal crime, and we won't hesitate to go after you."

Bunny stuck out his lower lip. "That means you aren't here looking to shut us down?"

"Right, Bun," I said, hoping to prevent an altercation. "They want our help."

Bunny hooted. "Oh, ho, that's a good one. You have more fairy tales for us?"

"Bernardo!" I could have smacked him. All we needed was to have the agents change their mind and forbid us from working on the Martin case, even though I was having misgivings already about taking it on.

Instead, Special Agent Foster reached over and shook hands with Bunny. "I understand your concern. This might be a first for the Bureau, signing up a PI firm, but it's legit. Not only do we *not* want to shut you down, we're hoping your help will speed along our investigation."

I wondered how that would happen as long as this remained a one-way operation in terms of sharing, so I decided to ask. "I'm interested to hear how you plan to assist us in assisting you, since a few minutes ago, I believe I heard you say you couldn't share information with us?" I turned my statement into a question so they had to answer and not just acknowledge.

"Oh, it's not that we can't share *some* information," Peters said. "Just not information on the Dockweiler Beach investigation. There are plenty of other ways we can help, and when we have something concrete, we'll get back to you. I hope you'll do the same for us?"

"We will," I promised.

"Then we'll be in touch," Foster replied, as the two agents wriggled their butts off the couch and moved in tandem to the front door.

"I appreciate your confidence in Berger Investigations," I said to their retreating backs.

Special Agent Peters turned and handed me her card as Bunny hurried past her to hold the door.

"Email is the best and fastest way to reach me if you have any questions," she said. "Or, you can text me. That's fine, too."

Bunny closed the door behind them and turned to me. Or rather, turned *on* me. "What the blankety-blank is the matter with you?"

"What do you mean?"

"Letting in two armed strangers when I'm out of the office. How do you even know they are who they say they are? I mean, did you contact the Bureau for verification, or call Johnny?"

I admitted I hadn't. "I checked over their creds and you agreed they looked legit—had all the proper markers: solid gold badge, Federal Bureau of Investigation spelled out across the top—"

Bunny sat down, put his elbows on the desk, and cradled his head in his hands. "Wait'll Johnny hears this one."

I wondered if that was a threat or a warning.

CHAPTER 13

My normal good humor was eroding faster than SoCal's vaunted beaches. Maybe food would put me in a better mood. Since I'd canceled out on dinner with Johnny, I knew exactly where I'd go instead.

"I'm heading over to *La Gringa's* for dinner tonight," I told Bunny. "Text me if anything interesting turns up on the Hooper stakeout tonight."

"Okay, I'm leaving now, too. Need to grab a short nap so I don't fall asleep and let Melody Knight slip out of my grasp."

"I doubt you'll have an opportunity to grasp her. Keep an eye on her, that's all."

Bunny grinned. "Just joshin'. You know I only have eyes for Franny."

"Glad to hear it, or you know—"

"Stop worrying about your sister, boss. I love her as much as you do."

I doubted that but decided to change the subject. "I'm hoping we hear back from one of our sources about the Martin case in the next day or two. The FBI's interest in the case has me worried."

"Too early to worry. If we don't hear anything tomorrow, I'll put through a call." He shut down his computer and prepared to follow me out. "By the way, I might be late getting in tomorrow."

"No problem," I said, "though I hope by the end of the day you'll also have a handle on the black SUV that followed Franny."

"My top priority."

With that promise in mind, I tossed my purse over my shoulder and sailed out of the office, taking the stairs down two steps at a time, not an easy feat, but it helps keep me in shape.

Once I hit the outdoors, the noxious odor of LA smog assaulted my nostrils. I knew the sun was still in the sky, but exactly where was a mystery. Even a modest breeze might have chased the haze away, but the air was stiller than silence, clinging to everything, including me. I stood rooted to the sidewalk for a minute or two, scrutinizing the area for any suspicious black SUVs since I was in no mood to take a bullet today simply due to carelessness.

Traffic was light, speeding up my back-of-the-hand calculations, which showed every fifth vehicle to be an SUV, half of which were black. What was the lure, I wondered? I preferred some color in my life, which is why I opted for a red RAV4. Fortunately, no SUVs, black or otherwise, slowed as they passed by me, or I might have ducked for cover behind the parking lot dumpster two feet away.

Once I determined the coast to be clear, I crossed the street to *La Gringa's*, the best Mexican eatery in this part of Hollywood. I hadn't visited with the restaurant's owner, Cinda Mae Bradbury, since our celebration dinner the previous week following the successful wrap of our Holy Kow case and, more important, living to tell about it.

Cinda's place was my favorite eatery, which was a good thing because I felt obliged to eat there on a regular basis.

My mouth started watering before I opened the front door. As I stepped inside, the glorious aroma of fried onions, chorizo, and seafood overwhelmed my olfactory senses. *Baja fish tacos here I come.* I couldn't wait to chow down. Exchanging greetings with Cinda Mae's new receptionist led to a request for my usual table when *Her Royal Highness* appeared in person.

"Hey, counselor. Bunny texted me you were on your way over. What took ya so long?"

"The smog weighed me down," I told her, refusing to admit to my cautious approach and wondering if she'd been watching me out the window. "I could barely walk."

"It *is* thick out there today," she replied, as literal as ever. "But our air purifying system takes good care of things in here." She shot me a sidewise glance as she grabbed a menu and motioned me to follow her. "With those shoes," she added, glancing down at my traditional work footwear—black military cross-trainers, "a little fog shouldn't have affected you."

So maybe she wasn't as literal-minded as she pretended to be. Or, she's finally tired of the dumb blonde act, despite how well it's worked for her in the past.

Determined to move the conversation away from my apparel, I asked about the menu. "What's the special today?"

"Shrimp and tilapia in a spicy Vera Cruz sauce. I think you'll like it."

"Sounds good, though I'm fine with an order of fish tacos."

"You can have fish tacos anytime, counselor. This is a new dish that Pedro prepared, and he'll be offended if you don't try it."

"Okay, you're on," I told her as we reached my favorite booth in the back corner of the dining room where I could observe everything, including the front door.

She gave me a knowing look. "I knew you wouldn't want to hurt Pedro's feelings."

"Does that mean he'll serve the dish in person?"

"Of course. He knows you have a crush on him."

"I do, but I know I'm no competition for you."

"You got that right, counselor. Do you still want to see the menu?"

"Guess not, but I'm off diet drinks, so what do you suggest instead?"

"How about *Chocolate de Leche*?"

I nodded.

"That's chocolate milk made with Mexican chocolate."

"I know," I said, "and I can use a dose of feel-good today."

"On the outs with Johnny again?"

"Sort of. He doesn't want me taking on your friend Sally Martin's case. Thinks it might be too dangerous, and he worries I'll die before I have time to marry him again, which is a good possibility because I'm not so sure I'm taking that route any time soon. I kind of like the single life, though I might like it better if I found a nice-looking guy like Pedro to hang with."

"Hands off Pedro, counselor," she said, giving me the evil eye. "Look, but no touch. Besides Johnny's a good person. Maybe you oughta marry him before somebody else grabs him, like that Sergeant María García, for instance, whom you tried to palm off on Bunny. Anyway, I saw her making eyes at Johnny the other day."

I wanted to say, "Really?" except I figured she was only trying to get a rise out of me. Instead, I told her, "I think she still has the hots for Bunny, but Franny has him wrapped around her little finger."

Cinda Mae slowly lifted one arched eyebrow. "I wouldn't be so sure of myself if I were you."

I let out a disdainful sigh. "Unless you're prepared to tell me Pedro has a handsome friend looking for a date with an almost middle-aged *gringa*, we need to change the subject. Besides, I have a few questions for you about my newest client."

"Okay, let me put your order in first. I'll be back in a sec."

While I waited for La Gringa's CEO to return, I checked my phone. Another text from Johnny, which I decided to ignore as I wondered again what was wrong with me. Normally, I was more positive than this. Maybe I'd caught some kind of bug, but before I could name a disease other than depression, Cinda Mae slid into the booth across from me.

Okay, shoot," she said, settling her well-proportioned bottom onto the booth's leather seat. "What do you want to know about Sally Martin?"

"As much as you can tell me about her and her husband."

"I'm afraid I don't know much about her husband. I only met him once. He seemed like a nice guy, but in my opinion there's something not quite right going on there."

"Not quite right about him or her or them?"

"Everything, I guess. I never quite put my finger on it. Sally told me Ricky tried to get into acting when he first came out here." She shrugged as if the statement were obvious. "Everybody does at some point. Apparently, he got nowhere fast because I've never heard of anything he's been in, not that I necessarily would. If you ask me, which you did, the acting parts, if he had any, dried up and that's when he decided to go into real estate. Something else everybody does who comes out here. That, or open a restaurant."

She sent me a knowing grin, which I returned, realizing how much I liked this crazy person sitting across the table from me. Something about her grows on you. I guess it's because despite everything, she has a good heart and I like good-hearted people.

"Anyway," she continued, "acting would explain the facelift, something—"

I finished her sentence for her, "Everyone gets out here."

She laughed. "Yeah, you took the words right out of my mouth. I'm betting he's a lot older than he claims."

"Which is?"

"Early fifties according to Sally, but my guess is he shaves off a good ten years. Of course, she's had her share of nips and tucks, too. Maybe they're the same age, who knows, and who cares? Not me. Anyway, she seems to believe everything he tells her, which no one should do with an actor in my opinion."

I had to agree. Cinda Mae was no fool when it came to sizing up people, something else I liked about her.

"After I met him," she continued, "I asked Sally if he'd had some work done, but she denied it. Said he has taut skin. 'It's an Italian thing,' she told me. Did you ever hear that one?"

"Nope. And my first husband was Italian."

"No kidding, counselor. You sure do get around when it comes to men."

CHAPTER 14

My dinner arrived in the hands of Cinda Mae's drop-dead gorgeous husband, Pedro—aka Peter—Panza. I always have trouble taking my eyes off him, but the plate of food he delivered looked and smelled so delicious, I could barely keep from drooling. I was on sensory overload in more ways than one.

He set the dish on the table and slid it in front of me in a way that made my heart skip a beat or two. "Here you go, Polly. This is my grandmother's recipe, and when I made it for Cinda Mae, she insisted we add it to our menu. Let me know how you like it."

"Be glad to," I said, leaning over the dish and breathing in the delectable aroma of seafood and exotic spices. "It smells wonderful. Hang on a minute while I take a taste." I dug my fork into a juicy mouthwatering shrimp, rolled it in the dark scarlet sauce, added a small scoop of rice, and popped it into my mouth. "Mm-mm-mmm," I told him. "Cinda Mae's right. This is a mouthful of heaven."

Pedro's ear-to-ear grin was an eyeful of heaven. I might never go back to my office. Maybe Cinda Mae would let me bunk in the storage room until I could sort out my emotions and the problems I have with the men in my life. On the other hand, she probably wouldn't want me that close to Pedro, and I wouldn't blame her.

I helped myself to another serving of his Vera Cruz scrumptiousness, savoring every bite as he stood over me, apparently mesmerized by my ardent appreciation of his culinary skills, until Cinda Mae coughed and broke the spell.

"Pretty good, huh?"

My cheeks bulged with tangy shrimp and tilapia, so all I could do was nod and mumble something unintelligible.

"Aren't you glad you didn't settle for fish tacos?"

I nodded again, finally swallowing enough to reply. "This may be the best thing I ever ate," I told her. "You are one lucky woman."

She gave Pedro a loving glance then arched an eyebrow my way. "Don't I know it, so don't get any ideas in that man-crazed head of yours."

Her unjustified comment offended me, and my face must have shown it, because Pedro beat a hasty retreat in anticipation of my outraged response: "What do you mean calling me man-crazy, and in front of Pedro, too?"

Cinda Mae laughed, happy to have finally pushed one of my buttons. "Just joshin' ya, counselor, except I see the look in your eyes whenever you're around Pedro, and I can't help wondering what's on your mind—"

I interrupted her. "It's a look of appreciation, nothing more."

"I know, and I'm glad you like his cooking as well as his looks. Now, was there anything else you wanted to ask me about Sally and her husband?"

"Sure. I'd like to know the where, what, and whens, like: *where* they came from, *when* they moved out here, *why* they moved out here. I'd also like to know *how* Ricky's real estate business is doing, and anything else of interest that you might know and be willing to share with me."

"As far as I know, she went into the real estate business with her husband when she quit her hairdresser job. Did you know she also used to skate with the Jammers?"

"She told me. Anything else you can think of?"

"Most of your questions Sally would answer if you asked her. Did you ask her?"

"Of course," I lied. "That doesn't mean I trust her to answer truthfully. You said yourself that you can't believe what actors tell you. Besides, it's part of my job to follow up on any and all information my clients divulge."

"So, did you do that kind of follow-up when I hired you?"

"Of course. How do you think I was able to solve your dilemma for you? Dumb luck?"

"No. I know you're smarter than that. Especially with all the help you get from Johnny-come-lately and the HYPD. You know, if you don't marry him again, he might quit comin' to your aid all the time like he does."

I thought about what she said while I scarfed down more of Pedro's tasty morsels. "That's part of my problem," I admitted. "I'd like to work an important case on my own without having to resort to help from Johnny or Harry Barnes."

"So what's he and his partner doing, holding that over your head or somethin'?"

"Not exactly. It's just an offhand remark of Johnny's that I can't get out of my head. He called into question my professional standing in the investigation business. I should just let it fly by and forget about it, but it's been nagging at me."

"I know how you feel. Been in that place myself more than once. Every woman has at some point in her life, but you can't let it get you down. Just keep pluggin' away and believin' in yourself, that's my motto. What other people think don't matter a hill o' beans if you have faith in yourself. You do have faith in yourself, don't ya, counselor?"

I was stunned by the idea of Cinda Mae proffering good advice, not to mention my new willingness to accept it. This was certainly a role reversal extraordinaire, but she was right. I needed to climb out of my funk, stop blaming Johnny for my bad mood—or Bunny either, for that matter—and get on with my work.

"Thanks for the wake-up call," I said, feeling grateful someone's words of wisdom had finally penetrated my stubborn skull and brought me back to my senses. I felt a little humiliated to have that someone be Cinda Mae Bradbury, but I'd get over it. "Time for me to stop feeling sorry for myself and settle down to business."

Her head bobbed up and down, causing me to notice she'd changed her hair color again. "I couldn't agree more."

"Then let's hear what more you have to say about Sally and Ricky Martin. Maybe you can give me some insight into what happened to him and why, or at least provide a clue that starts me down the right trail."

"Aside from the fact that he's an exercise freak, there's not a lot I can tell you. Ricky's a very private person and so is she, which is kind of odd for wannabe actors, or realtors for that matter."

"How so?"

"Never like having their pictures taken for one. And you know realtors. They're a lot like actors, splashing their pictures everywhere, but not Ricky's company. Martin Real Estate signs are as far as they go, and not one of those signs has a picture of either of them. Only the address and telephone number along with pictures of houses for sale. Don't you find that kind of weird?"

"Ordinarily, yes," I said, "but maybe Ricky worried about his image turning up on a wanted poster somewhere, which led somebody out here to recognize him. There's a lot of shady real estate business going down anymore. I'm inclined to believe Ricky murdered Lenny Spinoli over some deal gone bad, dumped his body overboard, and abandoned his boat for a gig on the Baja Peninsula, soaking up the sun and quaffing margaritas."

"I think you're wrong about that, counselor. First of all, if Ricky's in Baja, he's probably downing mojitos. Second, he's crazy about Sally, more than she is about him I'd say, so he'd never abandon her unless he had a pretty darn good reason."

"Beating a murder rap is a pretty darn good reason."

Cinda Mae ran a thoughtful hand across the tabletop like she was feeling for a missing contact lens. "Ricky's no murderer. He's a lover, which means…" She'd let her voice drop, clueing me as to what she was thinking before the words escaped her Temptress 400 red lips.

I finished the sentence for her. "Which means he's most likely shark bait, otherwise his body would have washed ashore with Spinoli's."

"I'm not a bettin' person as you know," Cinda Mae said, with a heavy-hearted look, "but that's where I'd lay my money. Poor Sally. She don't deserve this."

CHAPTER 15

Day 2:

O n my ride into work the following morning, I sorted through what I knew about Ricky Martin that I hadn't known before I talked with Cinda Mae the previous night. I came up with three items. Number one, Ricky was tenderhearted and loved his wife, so he wouldn't have faked his own death to escape a messy divorce, or failed to contact his wife if he were still alive. Provided, of course, he wasn't lying unconscious in a hospital somewhere, which was a possibility I'd only just considered.

Second, Ricky the realtor had an ego, or at least a heavy dose of vanity, as evidenced by the fact that he exercised a lot, copped to being younger than his age, flirted with an acting career, and spent big bucks on major facial rejuvenation. That is, if Cinda Mae's powers of observation were to be believed, and I pretty well trusted her on that score.

Third, there were inexplicable inconsistencies in his behavior, like guarding his privacy and objecting to having his picture taken, which are not typical behaviors for an egomaniac or an actor, not that there's a huge difference based on what I've seen of Hollywood.

I wondered if any portion of Cinda's information held important clues to either Ricky Martin's whereabouts or to the reason someone might want him dead. Maybe I'd know more once I received the background report from TLO. If nothing else, Cinda Mae's comments weren't the kind of information TLO was likely to provide me, or that I'd get from the feebs either, if and when they decided to share.

I tucked away all those elements in the back of my brain as I climbed the stairs to my office. Investigations are a lot like puzzles. Seemingly meaningless pieces can suddenly take on significance and provide answers you never expected. I hoped for a similar breakthrough in this case, and I also hoped Ricky Martin would not be found floating with the fishes off the craggy coast of California.

My mind was still buzzing when I walked through the door and Bunny greeted me with, "Hey, boss, I texted you last night but you didn't answer."

I succumbed to my first lie of the day, only slightly worried I might be struck dead. "Forgot to charge my phone."

"Thought you might be interested in the results that came in from TLO on Ricky Martin. The folder's on your desk."

"Why didn't you call me?"

"Because I texted you and when you didn't answer, I figured you were either busy or you had your phone turned off because you didn't want to talk to anybody while you ravaged your dinner."

I objected to his choice of words and shot him a dirty look, but sometimes there's no stopping Bunny from running at the mouth.

"Like maybe you were too busy ogling Cinda Mae's primary squeeze."

"Give me a break," I said, offended for a second time. "I'm not that obvious."

"Not what Cinda Mae says."

"Actually," I sniffed, "I was questioning Cinda Mae about Ricky Martin. I'm not into stealing other women's men. That's more your style than mine."

"I don't do men," Bunny said. "What did Cinda Mae have to say?"

"Not anything useful, at least not at this point," I admitted. "Did you track down an owner for the SUV that followed Franny?"

"Sort of."

"What do you mean sort of?"

"Traced the plates to the federal government."

"FBI?"

Bunny shrugged. "Probably. We should have checked the plates on that pair that dropped in for a chat yesterday."

"Dang. I never even thought about it."

"You can't think of everything, Polly. That's why you have me."

"Right," I said, at a loss for words.

"By the way, Marko and I switched shifts. He took the all-night night shift." Bunny rolled his eyes. "The guy's a glutton for punishment, so today's my turn. Think you can get along without me here?"

"I'll try." I told him, happy to have the office to myself for a while.

"These Hollywood stars don't climb out of bed much before noon, so I'll clean up a few things here before I leave and try to get there by ten. That'll be plenty of time."

"Thanks. And don't forget to keep me posted on the comings and goings of Mrs. Clive Hooper." With that, I headed into my office, closed the door, and settled into some serious work.

I'd almost finished drawing one of my usual Venn diagrams containing the information I knew in the Ricky Martin case when a racket arose in the outer office. I grabbed my gun again and ventured out, running smack into Rosa and her boyfriend Marko, my newest contract employee. They looked like they might be expecting a party.

Rosa spoke up first. "Guess we caught you at a busy time with Bunny gone?"

"A little, but I can use a break. My latest case is frying my brain."

Rosa's head bobbed up and down like a bobblehead doll. "You sound stressed, Polly, and you know what I told you about meditation. Have you been doing those relaxation exercises I prescribed for you?

"Haven't had time. We've been busy, Rosa, which is the reason I hired Marko to help with our caseload. Is that why you're here? To follow up on your prescription for me?"

"That's one of the reasons," she said, clearly oblivious to my snarky reply. "Marko told me Bunny said you've been out of sorts lately, and he thinks you might be depressed. So, when Marko said he was coming upstairs to report on his surveillance today, I decided to tag along and check up on you."

"You don't need to worry about me," I assured her. "I'm always a little out of sorts. You know that. It's in my DNA, something my twin sister failed to inherit for some reason, and that's part of the problem. Bunny hangs around Franny so much these days he expects me to act like her. But Franny's the good twin, and I'm the evil twin."

Rosa pursed her lips and looked me up and down as

if she were sizing my clothes for an alteration. "You're not the evil twin, so stop thinking of yourself that way. Bunny was right. You are feeling a little down. Maybe you should come downstairs for a reading to lift your spirits."

"I wouldn't dare opt for a reading right now. I'm not sure I want to know what's in store for my future."

If Rosa heard a word I said, she ignored it. "Why don't you stop in before you go home tonight? I'll do a reading, and we can talk about it."

I gave up. "Okay, Rosa. And thanks for your concern. I appreciate it." But she wouldn't let it go.

"Also, I read an article the other day about how to choose happiness. I'll email it to you."

I nodded and turned to Marko. "You have a report for me?"

He nodded about six times. I now had a matched set of bobbleheads. I wondered if the head thing was excitement or he had a tic. Hard to tell.

"Here's the thing," Marko said. "If Melody Knight's stepping out on her husband, then it's with another woman, not a guy."

"Really? Are you sure?"

His head bobbed again. "I'm seventy percent sure. I followed her everywhere. She spent the whole day shopping with a woman friend, another movie star. I recognized her. You'll find her name in my report." He handed me an envelope, which I assumed contained the findings of the previous day's surveillance. "She's not as famous as Melody, but I think she's a better actress." He glanced over at Rosa. "I know, I'm no expert movie reviewer, but I know a good thing when I see it, like I knew you were a good thing, Rosie. Right from the first day we met."

"Let's stick to the report here, can we?"

"Sure, Polly. Anyway, they were tight. Arm in arm

down the sidewalk, sat together in the back of Melody's limousine—"

My curiosity was aroused. "Anything happen in the back of the limo? Like, did you see them kissing, for example?"

"I couldn't tell. The windows were so dark I couldn't see inside even when the light came on." He hesitated, realizing what he'd just said and added, "I did see the light go on, but that's all I could see. It didn't illuminate the inside of the limo at all."

"Okay, then. What transpired to cause you to reach your conclusion?"

"The two of them went home together. To the girl-friend's house, not Melody's. At least I assume it was the girlfriend's house, and shortly after that, another woman arrived, so I'm guessing they were having a threesome. You know how these movie stars are. Anything goes."

This, I thought, from someone who met his current squeeze in a polyamory group.

"Anyway," Marko continued, "that's all I know. The party broke up around ten o'clock, and the women went home, or at least I know Melody went home because I followed her. Since I worked both my shift and Bunny's, I called him and filled him in on my theory about Melody's affair, or maybe I should say 'affairs' if two other people are involved."

"Your hypothesis," I said, wishing I'd managed to bite my tongue.

"Theory, hypothesis, same difference," Marko grunted.

I opened my mouth to disagree but decided to drop the issue. "Good work, Marko," I said instead. "Let's wait and see what Bunny turns up today, and whether or not he finds more evidence to support your, uh, idea.

"Oh, he will." Clearly, Marko had more confidence than his hypothesis deserved. "I'd bet on it."

"Not a bet I'd take," Rosa said. She'd been sitting quietly in Bunny's desk chair listening intently to her boyfriend spout nonsense. "I think you've been reading too many of those movie magazines I have on the tables in my waiting room."

Her waiting room? "Since when," I asked, "do you have a waiting room?"

"Since this past weekend when Marko and his brothers repaired all the bullet-hole damage from that drive-by shooting that made mincemeat of my salon. As long as the insurance was paying, I decided to make some changes I'd been wanting for a while. You know me, Polly. If somebody gives me lemons, I make limoncello. Anyway, Marko petitioned my office."

"*Par*titioned your office?

"Yeah. Not exactly down the middle, but the waiting room's big enough to hold four patients now."

I could see Rosa was taking tarot card reading to a new level.

"People need privacy," she said. "Just like when you go to the doctor's office. You don't want all the other patients to know your business."

She had a point.

CHAPTER 16

If nothing else, our case of the bi-sexual philandering movie star wife of a famous director should keep life interesting, but the investigation currently occupying my thoughts centered on the missing Ricky Martin.

Once I escorted Rosa and Marko out of the office, I opened the TLO folder, contemplating my next step in the investigation. I hadn't gotten far before a call came in from Johnny.

I decided to be magnanimous and answer. "Hi, what's up?"

"Same question I have for you," he grumbled. "What's got you so grumpy, anyway?"

"Stress," I told him, adding yet another fib to the day's growing list. "Bunny and I took on a case for a big Hollywood director who thinks his movie star wife might be having an affair."

"All he has to do is check out one of the scag rags down at Ralph's Grocery. If his wife's playing around, they'll have an article about it on the front page with her picture and the hot stud she's—"

"My bet is he's checked that out already and come up empty," I said, cutting off one of Johnny's choice euphemisms.

"Who is this big-time *director*, anyway?"

"Can't say. Part of the contract."

"Then I guess I won't be able to help you if you run into problems along the way."

"Bunny's on it," I told him, trying not to sound smug. "He and Marko are sharing round-the-clock surveillance duties."

"Marko Polo? Rosa's boyfriend?"

"Yeah."

"I thought he had a barbecue place to run."

"According to Bunny, the restaurant's been running itself. Guess he's hired some good help."

"Probably all family. That's the way they make it when they come to this country."

"Could be, though Marko was born here. Grew up in a small town in North Carolina known for its cue. Lexington, I think."

"So what does he know about tailing people?"

"Bunny's been giving him pointers. Says Marko's been hanging around Rosa's place these days telling Bunny he's available for outside work if we ever need him. Apparently, he's always wanted to be a spy, or so he says."

"Surveillance and spycraft aren't the same thing."

"Don't tell that to Marko. The more important he thinks the job is, the harder he'll work at it. Besides, he's got a good network of people out here. Once he gets word out on the street, there'll be a hundred pairs of eyes watching—" I almost stumbled and divulged Melody Knight's real name. "—watching Chloe Lane's wanderings," I said, making up a pseudonym on the spot and not a very good one at that.

"Chloe Lane?"

"Code name for the errant wife."

"Chloe Lane? Where do you come up with these names?"

"Pseudonyms came with the job, written into the contract," I said. "I'd have chosen better ones. At least I hope I would."

"Did Bunny have some kind of heart attack when Mr. Director walked through your office door?"

"No, because the guy sent a surrogate. Some woman—"

"Don't tell me her name, I don't wanna know. What I *do* wanna know is whether you canceled that contract involving the dead guy on Dockweiler Beach."

Here we go again. I heaved a deep sigh. "I did not cancel, and I have no plans to cancel. It's good money, and both Bunny and I need to increase our meager retirement accounts. What I *will* promise is that I'll be extra careful, and if things begin looking dangerous, I'll let you know."

"By then, it might be too late."

I ignored his downer. "I talked with Cinda Mae yesterday. She's the one who recommended me to my client and she vouched for them. No known associations with criminal elements. Husband's a realtor and wife's a former roller derby skater turned hairdresser turned real estate agent. The husband went missing on a fishing trip with the guy who turned up dead on Dockweiler. Wife thinks they were both murdered and wants me to find the killer, or better yet find her husband alive and well. I'm hoping for the latter, but the chances are slim."

"Well, since I can't talk you out of takin' the case, I'll let you in on a little secret about Lenny Spinoli."

"What's that?"

"Undercover cop from New York. He's been on the inside with the Mob for a number of years. Came out here hot on the trail of one of the feebs' *Most Wanted*. Looks like the mobster might have got to him first."

Johnny's news stunned me. Maybe I *should* dump this case. Last thing I wanted was to get mixed up in a Mob murder. For once I was at a loss for words.

"Cat got your tongue?"

"You think my client's missing husband might be the mobster Spinoli was after?"

"That would be a logical deduction."

"That explains the FBI visit."

"What visit?"

"Two agents. Came by here yesterday. Said they wanted my help with their case."

"That's a new one. Are you sure they were who they said they were?"

"They had the right creds."

"Anything can be counterfeited. You should have called me. I could have verified them for you."

"Well, you can verify them right now if you want. Male agent's name is Joe Foster. Partner's Adrienne Peters."

"Don't recognize either name, but that don't mean anything. I'll get back to you on it."

"Okay. I'll catch you later."

"By later, do you mean you're agreeing to come to dinner at my place tonight since apparently you were too busy to make it last night?"

"Uh, yeah, sure," I said, upping my agreeableness quotient another notch. "I'll see you around seven."

"I'll have the grill fired up. Don't be late."

"I won't," I replied to the dial tone in my ear.

I hung up the phone feeling a little numb, like somebody injected ice water into my veins. If Sally's husband, aka Ricky Martin, was some big-time mobster hiding out from the police, then Cinda Mae's information made more sense—the plastic surgery to change his looks, the opposition to having his picture taken.

But if somebody wanted to stay under the radar, I thought, why would they go into high profile businesses like acting and real estate? Of the two, real estate was the more understandable—a perfect foil for laundering money. Maybe acting was a way to throw people off the scent. No one in hiding would choose an acting career, or at least no one in their right mind. I was still puzzled, but at least Johnny and I were back on speaking terms.

I hated to admit to myself how much better that made me feel.

CHAPTER 17

I'd barely hung up talking with Johnny when Bunny called, barely containing his excitement. "Polly!"

"Yeah, Bun, what's up?"

"Two minutes into my stakeout at the Hooper's place, and an ambulance arrived. I'm not one hundred percent certain, but I think they left with Melody Knight. I'm following the ambulance right now as best I can without getting a ticket. I'm guessing we're headed for Hollywood General if you want to meet me there."

"Okay. I'll turn on the police scanner, see what I can find out before I meet you."

"Great. Give me a heads up on the scanner if it turns up the cops are involved."

"Will do."

I hustled out to Bunny's desk, debating whether to call Johnny or turn on the scanner. Since I was still in feminist mode, I opted for the latter. First conversation that came up involved an attempted suicide call. That's all I needed to hear. I locked up the office and headed for Hollywood General.

Within minutes, I was making my way along DeLongpre Avenue. Another half block and I hung a right into the hospital parking lot. Near the end of the first row of cars I spotted Bunny waving me to a vacant spot, his arms flailing like some deranged puppet. I swung into the parking place, barely missing his arm as he held out his cell, wagging his index finger in the air as if he were pushing an imaginary button hovering over his phone.

I turned off my motor and hit the unlock button, but before I could reach the handle, Bunny opened my car door.

"Bun. Calm down."

"Can't. Take a look at this." He held out the phone.

I squinted at the headline from Hollywood's most notorious online gossip site, which proclaimed: "Suicide in Hooper House!"

The one-paragraph story, which claimed Melody Knight had deliberately overdosed, went on to say she'd recently been under treatment for depression and that her distraught husband would be making a statement later in the day.

I looked up at Bunny and shrugged. "Guess that answers our questions. No need to go inside. Let's head back to the office." As I reached over to close my car door, Bunny put his hand on my shoulder.

"Boss. She didn't commit suicide. He murdered her."

I snapped on my seat belt. "Let's discuss this in the office. It's safer. If you're right, we need to be careful. Clive might worry we saw something we shouldn't."

"I never thought of that, Polly."

I smiled and cocked my head. "That's why you have me."

⁓⁓⁓

Back at the office, I buttoned my lips while Bunny ranted on about Melody Knight's "suicide that wasn't a suicide." Leaning back in his chair, he placed his feet on his desk in a way that wouldn't mess up his papers and worked hard to convince me of the correctness of his conclusion, hoping I suppose, I'd encourage him to look into it on company time.

"Here's the thing, Polly. I know as sure as I'm sitting here looking at you, that Melody Knight did *not* commit suicide. Think about it. She's having fun out shopping with her girlfriend, and I use girlfriend here in Marko's sense of the word, spends the evening enjoying a threesome at their mutual friend's house, and the next morning she wakes up and kills herself? It doesn't make sense."

He went on for another five or ten minutes. basically saying the same thing using different words, like a clever campaign manager who'd denied her boss's recent flip-flop by claiming his position hadn't changed, only his words.

Once Bunny stopped for a breath I chimed in. "As a matter of fact," I said, finally able to respond, "we have no evidence those three women were anything but friends. Furthermore, we only have Marko's guess as to what went on in the house that evening, which could have been nothing more than a figment of Marko's vivid imagination, especially when it comes to matters of sex. Maybe the women met to discuss Melody's struggles with depression. Maybe they were trying to help her, ever think about that? Or, maybe they were just sitting around gossiping over a glass of wine, which is where I'd put my money."

"I might have thought of those things," Bunny admitted, clearly deflated, "if we hadn't been hired by her husband to tail her because he thought she was stepping out on him. I say we go interview her two girlfriends."

"On what basis?"

"We tell 'em we're workin' for Clive and since they were the last people to see her—"

"No can do. It's a lie, and I don't want to lose my license over something that's none of our business."

"Whaddya mean a lie?" Bunny's voice rose at least two decibels. "Clive Hooper hired us. In my book, that means we're working for him."

"He hired us to follow his wife whom he suspected of cheating. If she's dead, our assignment is over, job finished. It's no longer our affair. If there's something fishy about her death, it's a matter for the HYPD, not us."

"Then if it's okay with you, I'd like to take my suspicions to Johnny."

"That's entirely up to you," I told him, "but Johnny will want more than what we have to offer before he can open the case, and neither you, nor Marko, nor me have time off the clock to gather more evidence."

"Gathering the evidence is Johnny's job. We just have to raise his suspicions. Trust me. I can convince him to at least look into it."

"Whatever," I told him, shrugging off the whole idea and heading back to my office. "I'm giving Sally Martin a call. I'd like to have another chat with her. On her turf this time."

෯෯෯

Fifteen minutes later, my cell phone rang. Caller ID read John Birdwhistle.

I opted for cheery. "Hi, babe. What's up?"

"I just spent the last ten minutes on the phone with Funny Bunny. He wants me to look into the suicide of Clive Hooper's wife. Told me she's your *Chloe Lane*. Anyway, he claims Melody Knight was murdered. You agree?"

I hesitated, trying to gather my thoughts together since I hadn't expected a call so soon.

"Well?" Johnny demanded, impatient as usual. "You think she was murdered?"

"I'm not sure, since we have no evidence, but I guess I'm inclined to agree with Bunny. At least to the point I think her death is worth looking into. Could be Clive Hooper hired us because he wanted to pin something on her so he could divorce her on the cheap then decided not to wait that long. Bunny claims he had motive. Says her bad reviews tanked Hooper's films."

"Okay, I'll talk to Harry Barnes, see what he thinks. We can discuss this more over dinner tonight."

"Oh, no. If that's tonight's topic, I'll take a rain check on dinner."

"Okay, okay. I won't mention it if you don't."

"Don't worry, I won't," I told him before hanging up. The Melody Knight case was closed as far as I was concerned. I had bigger fish to fry, like "Most Wanted" Ricky Martin, for one.

At half past six, shortly after the sun had set and darkness closed in, I decided to call it a day. I was more than frustrated over my lack of progress in securing substantive background information on Ricky or Sally Martin. The TLO report contained nothing of interest, and I'd even gone through the FBI's Most Wanted list for the past thirty years, which also turned up nothing. Zip. Zero. Nada.

I locked up my desk and headed out. Maybe a good night's sleep would clear my brain, but first, I had to get through dinner with Johnny. If he brought up Melody Knight or started ragging on me about taking on the Martin case, I'd walk out the door and maybe never come back.

CHAPTER 18

Johnny was on his best behavior over dinner and abstained from any mention of Melody Knight and her maybe/maybe not suicide. Instead, he offered help with the Ricky Martin case.

"I checked on the feebs for you," he said, munching on a grilled chicken thigh, which he'd cooked to perfection. "Called the main office on Wilshire and asked to speak to Foster or Peters. Turns out they're legit. Agency has ten satellite offices. They're called *resident* offices. Makes 'em sound upscale, I guess. Anyway, Foster and Peters work out of the Lancaster resident office."

To my surprise, a sense of relief washed over me. "See? I knew they were legit."

"I'm not sure if that's good or bad."

"What do you mean?"

"I'm glad they're legit, so I don't have to worry about you being in danger from two perps posing as federal agents. On the other hand, and this is no reflection on you so don't go taking it personally, but I've never heard of the FBI asking a PI operation for assistance in an investigation, which makes me think they want an excuse to keep tabs on you as well as your client."

"Why would they want to watch a two-bit PI like me?"

"Good question. Have you or Funny Bunny been playing it fast and loose on any of your investigations, like undertaking illegal searches, sneaking into places you don't belong, anything like that?"

"Absolutely not," I said, holding back on my outrage.

"You mean absolutely not you, but what about Funny Bunny? You can't keep an eye on him twenty-four hours a day, and since he's not so good at knowing the line between legal and illegal, it's easy for him to cross over."

I thought about what Johnny said, but I wasn't convinced. I keep close tabs on Bunny, and other than the Kow case, we haven't had a high-profile operation that might interest the FBI until this week's client walked through our door.

"No doubt something funny is going on," I admitted, "but the feebs aren't after me, that I'm certain of. I'm guessing Ricky Martin is a high-profile valuable target, and the feds are covering all their bases, that's all. If anything, Ricky might have sent his wife to me in order to throw the feds off their trail. Ricky fakes his death, wife grieves, everybody focuses on the murder of Spinoli, and the Martins go back into hiding somewhere else on the planet, probably Mexico."

"How'd you come up with that idea, which I like, by the way?"

"Because I think she's been feeding me a lot of misinformation, hoping it makes its way over to the HYPD and from there, to the feds."

Johnny stabbed another piece of chicken and stuffed it into his right cheek. "Makes a lot of sense. You got a good head on those pretty shoulders," he said, reaching over and kissing me on my left shoulder. I had to hand it to him. He knew how to get on my good side.

I agreed. "It does make sense. Especially when you take into account how the Martins heard about my firm. They probably hatched the whole scheme over at Cinda Mae's place while feasting on one of Pedro's tasty creations, like the one I had for dinner—er, the other day."

Johnny halted midway through another bite. Fork in the air, he pointed its chicken tipped tines in my direction. "You over there ogling Pedro again?"

"What's with everyone accusing me of ogling Pedro?"

"Because you're so obvious about it, that's why."

"You know something? Pretty women are a dime a dozen out here, but it's not often, even in Hollywood, you run across a guy as good looking as Pedro. Who wouldn't look at him now and then? I've seen you ogling him sometimes, too."

"I don't ogle other men," Johnny said, "but I see your point."

For the next minute or two, I concentrated on my meal, wanting to change the subject away from good-looking men, not that Johnny wasn't a looker. Even in middle age, he's a solid eight out of ten, but looks don't matter to me as much as they used to, at least not when it comes to long-term relationships.

"Let's assume," I said, changing the subject, "that my client and her husband are using me to con the government agents who are on their trail, or on his trail. That means I should treat all information she provides me as bogus, starting with the fact that maybe her missing husband isn't missing and her crocodile tears are fake." I knew 'fake crocodile tears' was redundant, but I'd already had two glasses of wine and didn't care, and besides, Johnny would never notice.

"Mrs. Martin," I said, "was an aspiring actress, after all. The problem for me is this. Number one." I held up my index finger and noticed Johnny hiding a smile, but I wasn't deterred. "My client has deep pockets, and I wouldn't mind parting her from her ill-gotten gains. Number two, pardon the expression, Bunny and I have each invested a full day working on her case already, and…" Here I hesitated, wondering if I had a number three. Eventually, I thought of it. "And three, I'd like to beat the feds at their own game. If my client's husband is some big East Coast Mafia hood, then I'm betting there's a sizable reward for his capture—"

Johnny didn't let me finish. "Oh, no. You're not goin' there—"

"Let me finish. A sizable reward for his capture, *or* for information about his whereabouts, which I might be able to provide if we get lucky on this case."

Johnny shook his head so hard I thought he might be having a seizure. "No, no, no, no…"

"Calm down," I told him. "I promise I won't do anything that puts me in danger, or puts Bunny in danger. We'll work this case from a distance."

"So, is that why you were planning to drive to Glendale to visit your client's office and home? To keep your distance?"

"She's not there so it doesn't matter." I hiccupped and this time he didn't bother to hide his smile. "In fact," I said, intent on distracting him both from my present condition and from pressuring me about my investigation. "When I called her cell phone, she told me she was in San Francisco on business and didn't know when she'd be home."

"And you believed her?"

"I did, but…" Hic. "…now I'm not so sure."

Johnny handed me a glass of water. "Drink this."

"Thanks." I held my breath and gulped it down in one long swallow.

"Good job," Johnny said, as if I'd accomplished some unusual feat. "When you're completely sober, I'll be happy to place a bet your client was calling from her bedroom in the back of the house, hoping you wouldn't arrive before she finished packing."

Not a bet I was willing to take, but it helped sober me up. I wish I could handle booze a little better, but one glass of wine can send me under the table. Good reason not to drink a second one. I should have known better.

"The question that remains," I told Johnny in an attempt to gather my dignity, "is where to go from here. Maybe I'll send Bunny over to Santa Catalina Island, let him check out the marinas, pass around some photos of my client and her husband. Maybe somebody will remember having seen one or both of them in the previous week. And maybe said person might remember seeing Ricky rent or buy himself a boat. If so, we can be pretty sure he headed south."

"Not a bad idea. One way for him to avoid security cameras at the border, and he could fish along the way."

Johnny wanted me to stay overnight, but I was tired and knew I'd sleep better in my own bed. By ten, the effects of the wine had worn off, but Johnny was not about to let me drive. He tried to give me a breathalyzer test, but I declined. Who but Johnny, I thought, keeps a breathalyzer in the house? Instead I promised to wait a little longer before leaving.

Half an hour later, I agreed to the test and failed. By that time, I was too tired to object to anything. Johnny carried me half unconscious into his guest room where I managed to snag a solid eight hours of beauty sleep. At my age, I needed all the beauty sleep I could get.

CHAPTER 19

Day 3:

Bunny beat me into work again the next morning. I wondered if this was becoming a habit until I realized I was two hours late. I could hear the excitement in his voice when I stepped through the door.

"Hey, Polly. Listen to this," he said, waving a copy of the *LA Times*. "Clive Hooper talked to the press last night. They were waiting in his driveway and stopped his limo. Wouldn't let him pass until he gave them a statement."

I reached for the paper, but he snatched it back. "I'll read it to you," he said, as I peered over his shoulder at the front-page article:

"'Gentlemen and ladies. I'm sure you understand the deep grief I'm feeling at the loss of my beautiful wife whom I love dearly. I'm haunted by grief and remorse. Had I been home this morning, I might have prevented this unfortunate event, a sorrow I will live with for the rest of my life. That's all I have to say. Thank you for your expressions of sympathy."

"Sounds innocuous," I said.

"Maybe not." Bunny reached for the folder on his

desk and removed the contents. "After I read Clive's statement, I looked up Marko's report from the night before Melody died. According to Marko, Clive Hooper was home yesterday until midnight when his Porsche convertible, not his chauffeured limo, pulled out of the driveway with him at the wheel."

"Meaning," I said, "he wasn't at home for the ten hours prior to his wife's death. So Hooper didn't lie."

"Right. He *conveniently* wasn't home on the morning of the discovery of his wife's *body*, which, this same article points out, occurred when the Hooper's cleaning service arrived, saw Melody's bedroom door open, and found her on the floor by her bed. Sounds to me like she knew somebody had spiked her orange juice and was trying to get help. She could have been dead when he left at midnight."

"Guess we'll have to wait for the coroner's time of death report."

"Which is why I want Johnny or Harry Barnes getting a copy."

"Even then..."

"I know you're skeptical, Polly, but I'm betting Marko's report contains evidence that may prove Hooper murdered his wife. At this point, we don't know what apparently insignificant item might prove to be significant down the line."

"I read it pretty carefully. He's added in all kinds of insignificant details, like cars passing by complete with license plate numbers, the position of the moon, crazy stuff."

"Probably to keep from going crazy with boredom."

"On the other hand, you might be right. Who knows which of those things could end up being important, so let's make a couple of copies of that report for our files and move the original to safekeeping in case an enterprising burglar decides to visit our file cabinets in the middle of the night. It's happened before. Could happen again."

"I'll make three copies for good measure. Keep one here, take the original to Johnny, and you or I can take a copy home. Think the original is safe with him? I mean, somebody could get to his files, too."

"Even if they do, Johnny can testify in court that our copies match the original."

"Good thinking. You want the third copy to stay with me or with you?"

"I think it's safer with you, Bun," I said, heading into my office.

I'd barely stashed my purse in the drawer when my landline rang.

"Good morning, grillmeister," I said, wanting to reward Johnny for his good behavior over dinner.

"Got one more piece of news for you about the Spinoli case," he said.

"I'm listening."

"Had a chat with the coroner about the Dockweiler body."

"He confirm the identity?"

"Wouldn't say, but wouldn't deny, either, which I took as a positive ID."

"You sure?"

"He's beholden to the feebs, but I'm sure. The big news, which he did spill, is that drowning wasn't the COD."

"Huh. And the cause of death was?"

"Blunt force trauma to the head."

"So my client was right. Somebody murdered Lenny Spinoli and dumped his body overboard."

"Apparently. Coroner ruled out the idea that Spinoli hit his head in the fall off the boat, no matter how rough the water was. Also, said the guy must have been in the water a couple of days given all the bloating."

"So how did the coroner make the trauma determination?"

"Big dent in the skull. Caused internal bleeding. Nobody's brain could have survived a hit like that."

"Coroner have any ideas about a weapon?"

"Nope. Said it was a puzzle."

"I have another question for you."

"Shoot."

"If the HYPD is supposed to stay away from the Spinoli case, how is it the coroner had all this information *and* filled you in on it?"

I heard Johnny suck in his breath. "Let's just say he owes me."

I decided to thank Johnny the best way I knew, which was to compliment him. "Good work," I told him, "even though the information kinda puts us back where we started, or back to what my client told me in the beginning, but at least it suggests she wasn't lying about the body on Dockweiler."

"That don't mean," Johnny said, his skepticism evident, "that she isn't lying about whether or not her husband is missing. Still could be the case he killed Spinoli and is on the lam and she's working to keep the police off his scent."

"You might be right. My gut tells me there's more missing pieces here than just my client's husband, whoever or wherever he is."

"If anybody can get to the bottom of this," Johnny said, clearly trying to butter me up, "I have confidence in you. Just be sure and fill me in on what you find. *And*, tell me *before* you go runnin' to the feebs. Once I hear your evidence, I can help you decide what to tell the FBI and when you tell 'em, so nothing bounces back on you. They like having a scapegoat. Usually, it's the local PD, but in this case, they might have traded the D for an I."

It took me a minute to realize he meant trade the PD for a PI, but by the time I figured it out he was on his way to another emergency call.

"Gotta go," he said. "Some kind of standoff. They need a negotiator, and I'm it."

I wondered what the problem was this time. Probably another domestic violence call or drug deal gone bad—typical mid-morning Hollywood stuff.

CHAPTER 20

Bunny must have been listening in on my conversation with Johnny because he appeared at my door two seconds after I returned the phone to its cradle.

"Johnny still trying to talk you into giving up the Martin case?"

I shook my head. "No, he's now resigned to helping us out. Called to say the coroner identified the Dockweiler body as Lenny Spinoli."

Bunny shrugged. "Nothing we didn't already know."

"And," I said, saving the best for last. "Coroner's listing the death as a homicide."

"Again, nothing we didn't already know, or suspect."

"Right, but the coroner's report verifies Mrs. Martin's claim that someone murdered Spinoli and might have murdered her husband. I'm more certain than ever that we aren't going to find Ricky alive."

"Unless he killed Spinoli."

"True, which brings me to your next task."

Bunny raised an eyebrow like I was about to send him on a suicide mission.

"Nothing dangerous," I said, in an effort to reassure him. "I want you to forget about Melody Knight's suicide because I need you to hop over to Santa Catalina Island. Find the marinas closest to where the Martin's fishing boat was found adrift and talk to people. See if anything unusual happened there in the last week."

"What do you mean by unusual?"

"If I knew what it was, it wouldn't be unusual, would it?"

"Don't get on your high horse, boss. I'm just trying to find out what you have in mind, if anything."

"For starters, I'm wondering if Ricky might have bought or rented a boat and sailed off to Mexico."

"See," Bunny said. "That's why I asked."

"Okay. Try to come up with a few ideas of your own while you're over there. It might not amount to anything but a waste of time, but maybe we'll get lucky. You have a good nose for news. Take copies of our pics of Ricky and Sally Martin and snoop around, see if anybody recognizes either of them or remembers seeing them, and if so, find out when, where, and what were they doing."

"No problem."

"I'll tell Marko to submit an invoice for his time. He'll be disappointed at being out of work, but I'll promise to tap him if the need arises. Might mean I have to go to dinner with Rosa tonight, but that's okay. She's been hounding me to come in for a reading. Thinks it'll raise my spirits since she has this nutty idea that I've been down lately."

"Well, she's right. I noticed it, too, and so has Franny, but you know how Franny is. Didn't want either of us to mention it."

I rolled my eyes. "If all you're doing is worrying about my state of mind, you two don't have enough to do. I'll give Franny a call and see if she wants to join Rosa and me for dinner tonight."

"She'll probably turn you down."

"Why?"

"She signed up for a swing dance class, but don't let her know I told you. I think she wants to try it out before she tells you about it."

Bunny and I used to be swing dance partners, so I suspected he was the one encouraging her to learn, which was okay with me as long as he saved a dance for me now and then.

I thought about Johnny, wondering what it would take to get him on the dance floor for a few lessons. No doubt I'd have to marry him first. Maybe, I thought, dancing isn't that important after all.

"My lips are sealed," I told Bunny, when a noise like a bomb blast sounded outside.

Bunny turned and ran out of the office. An Olympic sprinter couldn't have moved faster. All I heard from him was, "What the—"

I followed him down the stairs and onto the sidewalk just as a cacophony of sirens blared a few blocks away. I could see a cloud of black smoke spiraling into the overcast sky. It wasn't a pretty sight.

The two of us stood glued to the sidewalk, my mind running through a hundred scenarios. "What do you think happened?"

Bunny shook his head. "I'm not sure I wanna know. Let's head over there, see what's goin' on."

"Not a good idea, Bun. We might be in the way. Or worse, it could be a terrorist attack with another blast going off any minute, and we'd be in the middle of it."

"You're right. Better go back inside and listen to the scanner."

"I hope Johnny's not there."

"Trust me, he's not out there. More likely, back at the office warming his detective chair. He still have that swivel number?"

"He's not in his office. He hung up on me real fast to answer an emergency call. Said they needed him for negotiations. I'm worried."

Bunny put his arm around my shoulder and steered me toward the door. "Quit worrying about Johnny. He stopped working the streets a long time ago."

"You're right." I wasn't convinced, but couldn't come up with a persuasive counterargument. My intuition meter was in overdrive.

By the time Bunny had the police scanner operational, our local TV channel was blaring news of a bomb blast that occurred three blocks from my office. I hoped it wasn't related to Johnny's emergency. I decided to try his cell phone, the number I always call when he's out on a case, but the TV announcer, who was already on the scene and sharing his observations, stopped me. "An alleged suicide bomber has detonated a bomb in front of a Russian restaurant near Hollywood Boulevard, apparently to oppose Vladimir Putin's actions in Syria. We're trying to ascertain whether anyone else died, but the police are keeping mum." The announcer stopped and put his hand over the mic as a nearby pedestrian tugged his arm. "Okay, okay, thanks." Turning back to the camera, he announced: "Two policemen were injured, we don't know how seriously. Apparently, they were trying to negotiate with the bomber who bystanders say suddenly went berserk, screamed for everyone to leave the area, then boom, pulled the plunger."

"Oh, no!" I screamed to Bunny and anyone else within hearing distance, which could have included half of Hollywood. "I'm calling Harry Barnes. According to the TV, two Hollywood PD officers were injured. They were trying to negotiate with the bomber and I'm worried one of them might be Johnny. He's one of their top negotiators, you know."

"Yeah, I know. Talked you into marryin' him again, so I guess that makes him an expert on negotiations."

I ignored Bunny's cynicism and called Johnny's cell. When he failed to answer, I phoned Harry Barnes, Johnny's partner, who also didn't answer. "I'm driving down to the station," I told Bunny, my heartbeat on free fall. "You stay here and take calls. Let me know if you hear from Johnny."

"Will do, boss. Call me when you have something."

I ran into my office for my purse and car keys. My phone lit up before I had time to reach my car. Caller ID read Harry Barnes. My heart pounded into my throat. "Harry, what's going on?"

"Johnny's been hurt. They're taking him to Hollywood General. I'll meet you there."

Not again, I thought.

CHAPTER 21

Five minutes after Harry's call, I was hanging a hard left from North Gower onto DeLongpre Avenue. Déjà vu all over again, I thought, as a six-story white building popped into view. I could hear the shriek of a police siren until suddenly it stopped. I guessed Harry had arrived.

Swinging into the hospital parking lot, I spotted two vacant handicap spots, both of which beckoned to me. I pulled into the one closest to the door and cut the engine. Rather than risk a ticket, I reached into the glove compartment for my illegal handicapped permit and hung it on the rearview mirror.

Getting out of the car, I had to hold on to the door for a few seconds to steady myself. Images of Johnny flooded my brain—his crazy smile, how his eyes lit up every time he saw me. For maybe the hundredth time, I vowed to treat him better. From there, I moved on to bartering with God, promising to be a better person, to go back to church, and give more money to the poor instead of buying another pair of expensive shoes.

My prayer list grew longer as Harry and I waited in the visitors' room for word on Johnny's condition. I thought about promising to marry Johnny again but held off until I heard the doctor's report. After an hour, in which Harry and I made small talk, drank coffee, read magazines, and stared into space, a white-coated medical practitioner appeared through the double doors and glanced around the room.

"Detective Birdwhistle's family?"

The two of us raised our hands. She motioned us to stay seated and walked over. Harry stood up but my legs had turned to jelly so I obeyed her instructions. Besides, I could tell this woman was a no-nonsense professional. The best kind, in my opinion.

"He's conscious, no broken bones," the doctor said, "but he's had a nasty blow to the head resulting in a concussion and temporary memory loss. No fracture, fortunately, but we have him sedated."

The memory loss sounded serious to me. "How long will the memory loss last?"

"That's something we can't predict. Anywhere from fifteen minutes to days or even weeks. Depends on the strength of the blow, which parts of the brain are affected—"

"Can we see him?" Harry asked.

"Yes, briefly. He's in his room, but I'd recommend you spend no more than five minutes with him. If he's still asleep, please don't try to wake him."

Harry and I took the elevator up to the third floor and checked in at the nurse's stand. The woman manning the desk wasn't the most pleasant person I'd ever run across, but eventually she directed us to Johnny's room with the same admonition we'd heard from the doctor, "Five minutes, no more."

Johnny's eyes were closed when we entered. I figured he was sleeping, but ignored doctor's orders and leaned over to plant a kiss on his lips. His eyes shot open. "Hey there, beautiful," he said. A sense of relief flooded over me until he added, "Whoever you are, I want you in my life."

Harry put an arm around my waist. "It's Polly, Johnny."

Johnny looked puzzled. "Polly?"

"Polly Berger," I said.

Before I could explain any more, Johnny turned to Harry. "And you are?"

"Harry Barnes, your partner."

"I've never seen either of you before. Are you trying to con me or something? Because if you are, you won't get away with it." He reached over for the nurse's call button. "I'm calling hotel security. They'll escort you out."

"No need," Harry said, "we're leaving."

"I love you, Johnny," I said, blowing him a kiss. "Get better."

"You can come back," he told me, glaring at Harry, "as long as you leave your shyster lawyer friend at home."

Harry and I left, closing the door behind us.

I turned to Harry. "How long do you think he'll be like that?"

"Hard to tell, but Johnny's a tough character, so maybe a day or two. I'm just glad nothin' worse happened to him. He'll be okay over the long haul, though concussions can mess up your brain for a while."

I nodded, trying to adopt Harry's positive attitude. "Since we can only see him for five minutes every hour, and since he thinks you're some kind of legal con artist, why don't you go back to work? My office is close by, I can run over here every hour or two, check on him, and keep you posted."

"Okay," Harry said, giving me a reassuring hug. "Let me know if anything changes."

 තිම්

Bunny was packed and ready to leave for Santa Catalina Island when I returned to the office. He stayed long enough for me to fill him in on Johnny's situation. I parroted the doctor. "Johnny's conscious, no broken bones, but he's had a nasty blow to the head. He got knocked down and hit his head on the curb when he fell, which resulted in a concussion. Also, he has what they termed temporary memory loss, at least I'm hoping it's temporary. They have him in a private room." I added, "probably for his own good."

"Jeez," Bunny said, shaking his head, "losin' your memory sucks. Did he recognize you?"

"No. Didn't recognize my name either and thought Harry was a con artist after his money, as if he had any money. Said if we didn't leave he was calling hotel security to escort us out."

Bunny struggled to hide a grin. "So he thinks he's hanging out in some kind of upscale hotel?"

"I guess." A smile crept onto my face as well, and before we knew it we were both laughing uncontrollably. "It's not funny," I kept hissing, which only made us laugh harder.

When we'd finally calmed down, I related Johnny's parting shot as Harry and I left his room. "Johnny grabbed my hand as I stood up to leave," I told Bunny. "Harry was already at the door when Johnny stopped me and whispered in my ear that I could come back if I left my shyster lawyer friend at home."

"Poor Harry," Bunny sputtered, revving up again, "I'm only laughing because I know Johnny's okay. It's the situation." He paused for breath. "Only Johnny could mistake a hospital room for a fancy hotel. Wait till he tastes the food. That'll bring him around to his senses."

"Oh, good idea, Bun! You might be right about food jogging his memory. I'll stop by the deli and buy him his favorites. Food can trigger memories, you know." I grabbed my purse and headed for the door. "You be careful over in Santa Catalina," I called back. "See if you can make it over there and back by tomorrow night with some new information in hand. I have a feeling the key to finding the missing Ricky Martin lies on that island."

"If so, I'll find it," Bunny said, full of his usual confidence. "Anyway, I won't leave here until you get back from the deli."

"Okay, thanks."

"And don't forget the bacon."

Curiosity stopped me. "What does that mean?"

"That's for you to figure out."

Like I needed another puzzle in my life.

CHAPTER 22

Standing in line at the deli, I remembered the title of a kids' book I'd seen on Bunny's desk. Why Bunny was reading a kid's book about not forgetting the bacon was beyond me, unless he was looking for punch lines for one of his standup routines most of which I'd forgotten by now. They weren't exactly memorable.

Putting aside Bunny's nonsense, I decided to call my sister Franny to fill her in on what happened to Johnny, and tell her I could also use her help in the office with Bunny away for the next day or two. She used to work for me when she first moved to LA, so she was familiar with my office procedures. Besides, she was in between private nursing jobs right now and, no doubt, could use some extra money.

I took out my cell phone and scrolled to her number on my contact list.

She answered, sounding depressed, so I knew she'd heard the news. "Hi, Polly. I was about to call you."

I told her about Johnny's amnesia, which choked her up even more. She said Bunny had called and told her about Johnny's accident.

"He's okay," I reiterated about five times before she calmed down. "It's just that he has this temporary amnesia. I'm at the deli now ordering a roast beef sandwich on rye for him, hoping it will jog his memory."

"Don't forget the coleslaw," Franny said.

"I won't. I know how Johnny likes his sandwiches."

"I'm sorry. I know you do. It's just, sometimes—"

"I know. Let's not go into that right now. Hang on a minute while I order." I'd reached the front of the line and the server was giving me the evil eye. "Roast beef on rye with coleslaw, a side of potato salad, and a dill pickle," I told him.

"What about dessert?" Franny asked.

I leaned over the counter. "And a piece of New York cheesecake, plain."

"He'll love that," Franny said in my ear.

I agreed, and added, "Bunny has to take a short trip over to Santa Catalina."

"I know, he told me."

"So, I could use some help in the office today and tomorrow. Are you available?"

"Sure. I figured you'd need me after Bunny called. I'm dressed and ready to go."

"Great. Then head on over and don't forget your key. I'll probably be at the hospital when you arrive."

"Okay. Tell Johnny I was asking for him."

"I will, but he may not remember who you are any more than he remembers me."

"Oh, that's right. Well, good luck, Polly. I hope the food brings him to his senses. The taste, smell, and texture of food can trigger strong memories in the brain, you know, and—"

I cut Franny off before she launched into one of her nursing school lectures. "I do know. Let's hope it works. And thanks for helping me out. I'll call you from the hospital and tell you how things are going."

Before leaving the deli, I ordered a BLT to take back

to Bunny, mainly for laughs and to let him know I hadn't forgotten the bacon. I left the deli clutching my bag of goodies and hiked the four blocks back to my office. As I entered my building, I noticed a black SUV cruise slowly by, which gave me a start. I turned around in time to catch a glimpse of the plate number. Same number I'd memorized earlier and which Bunny had traced to a government owned vehicle.

So, I thought, the feds have me on their radar, which in my mind meant they didn't trust me. For the life of me, I couldn't understand why, but I planned to get on the horn and find out. I pounded up the stairs jumpy as a box of frogs. Bunny swung open the door before my hand hit the knob, and I almost tripped and fell at his feet.

He greeted me with, "I was expecting an elephant. What's got your socks in a knot?"

"Same bleeping black SUV followed me from the deli. The feds must think I'm in league with the Martins, or maybe the Martians, or whatever criminal conspiracy my client's gangster husband is associated with, and that ticks me off. Also makes me nervous." I reached into my deli bag and practically threw Bunny's sandwich at him. "Here's your bacon."

His face lit up like a fifteen-watt LED. "Gee, thanks, Polly. I was only kidding about the bacon. It's the title of a kid's book I found in the Goodwill last week. I was looking for material to use in my standup."

As I'd suspected, I thought, deciding not to respond since I wanted him to leave for his mission in a pleasant state of mind. "Thought you might get hungry on your big trip to Santa Catalina, which you'd better get started on so you aren't calling back here asking me for an extra day or two on the island."

"Oh, ye of little faith," Bunny said. "I'm a fast worker, which you should know by now."

I let that one go, too, as I followed Bunny out the door with my food for Johnny.

"Let me go outside first," Bunny said. "I'll let you know if I see the feds around."

At the bottom of the stairs, he opened the door a crack and peeked out before waving me down. "Coast is clear."

I hotfooted it over to my trusty RAV4, jumped in, and started the engine before Bunny had time to open his car door. A minute later, I was speeding along North Gower, checking my rearview mirror regularly.

If the black SUV three cars in back was following me, which I suspected they were, I hoped they'd be disappointed when I turned into the hospital parking lot. But it did give me one good idea, especially when I thought about the back entrance to the lot, which was hidden by a row of tipuana trees.

CHAPTER 23

The SUV behind me drove on by when I pulled into the hospital parking lot, but if they'd been following me, I had a plan. I could be out on the street and out of sight before my tail managed to find their way to the tipuana tree exit. Next time I spotted a tail, this is where I'd bring them.

Entering Johnny's hospital room, I might as well have arrived by TARDIS, the transporter from *Doctor Who*. The craziness going on inside Johnny's wounded head seemed to obliterate time and space. His current reality, when it came to his surroundings, ranged from fancy hotel to solitary confinement at Guantanamo Bay, and everything in between.

After consulting with the nurse who stood outside his room, clearly ready to tear out her hair, I tiptoed in and opened the deli bag without saying a word. He'd elevated his bed to a sitting position and barely noticed me as I spread his lunch out next to his plastic water glass on the moveable table next to his bed.

"I brought you some lunch from Abe's," I told him. Abe's was his favorite deli and if any food could bring him to his senses, I knew a sandwich from Abe's would do it.

Johnny tilted his head in my direction. From the corner of his eye, he glanced down at the food then up at me. "You look familiar," he said. "What's your name?"

"Polly."

"You the new waitress?"

I nodded. "Brought you some lunch. Your favorite. Roast beef on rye with coleslaw, a side of potato salad, and a dill pickle." I waved my hand over the food like I was rehearsing a TV commercial, which maybe I was, crazy as this day was going. "And a piece of New York cheesecake," I added. "Plain, no gooey cherry pie filling on top."

He reached for a half sandwich. "How'd you know I hate that cherry goop?"

"A good guess," I said.

He took a big bite of the sandwich and chewed it slowly. I could see him savoring the experience. At least his taste buds hadn't been affected.

"This is the best thing I've had all week," he said, licking his lips. "I need to visit this place more often." About to take his second bite, he looked over at me again. "You say you're the new waitress?"

I nodded.

"You married?"

I shook my head.

"You wanna marry me?"

The sandwich was working, I thought. Bits of his memory were returning, which made me happy, except this wasn't the part I hoped he'd remember.

"Sure," I told him, crossing my fingers behind my back.

"Okay, then. Let's set a date."

Now I was worried. Had his memory returned and he was tricking me into setting a date? I decided to have another chat with the nurse.

"In a minute," I said. "I'll be right back."

"Okay," he mumbled, his mouth stuffed with roast beef and rye bread.

I closed the door behind me and glanced around. The nurse had returned to the central nursing station. She raised her head when I approached, and I could see the exhaustion in her eyes. I knew exactly how she felt.

"I have a quick question," I said. "Has his memory returned?"

"If it has," she said, "then he's head of the CIA and I'm a Russian agent out to assassinate the president."

"That bad, huh?"

"You have no idea."

I begged to differ, but held my peace. "He's enjoying the lunch I brought," I said. "I thought maybe his favorite food might jog his memory. When he asked me to marry him, I was hoping maybe he was over his amnesia." I shrugged apologetically. "He's been asking me for a while now."

"I know," the nurse said. "He's been asking the same thing of every female who enters his room. One-track mind if you ask me. Maybe if you say yes, he'll quit pestering the rest of us. His amnesia can't disappear fast enough for me."

"I appreciate what you're going through," I told her, expressing genuine sympathy. "I wish I could say he's better when he's in his right mind."

At least she smiled. "Aren't you the bearer of good news, though? I never thought I'd feel so sorry for the HYPD."

That gave me a laugh. "Well, I'll head back and check in on Crazyville. See what's happening at the moment."

"If you need help, press the blue button beside the bed."

Oh brother, I thought, as I headed back to Johnny's room, realizing he'd been terrorizing the staff ever since he woke up from his coma. Like the nurse, I could only hope he'd return to sanity before half the nurses quit and maybe a doctor or two for good measure. Nothing would surprise me.

I opened the door to Johnny's room to see him polishing off the last of the cheesecake.

"Glad you're back," he said. "I might need another order of this cheesecake, and remember, no cherry or strawberry stuff on top."

He'd provided me the perfect escape. Much as I wanted to stay and help him, I knew the best thing for both of us was for me to leave. "I'll take care of that order right now. Good to see you again."

"Same here," he said, apparently forgetting for the moment his most recent marriage proposal.

As I reached the door, he called me back. "Aren't you going to clean the mess off this table before you leave?"

"Oh, right. Sorry." I went back, gathered the remains of his lunch, and carried them out to the trash container in the hall.

If Johnny's amnesia *had* disappeared once he tasted his favorite sandwich, then he was having a good time playing me right now. I left, wondering if, and, or when, I'd know the truth.

CHAPTER 24

After the hospital, I ran a few errands and reached my office a few minutes before five, wondering if I'd missed Franny, but when I entered the office she was sitting at Bunny's desk tackling the stack of filing he'd left in his inbox. Bunny hated filing and waited until the papers were falling onto his desk before biting the bullet.

I've suggested to him now and then one easy strategy for handling the filing, especially when you dislike it so, which is to file away each paper once you're done with it. That way the papers don't pile up, but so far he hasn't accepted my advice. Now that he's dating Franny, I suspect he's probably hoping she'll handle it for him on a regular basis.

"Hi, sweetie," I said. "Thanks for being a good sport and helping me out like this."

"No problem, Polly. You know I'm always willing to give you a hand. Just lucky for you that I'm in between jobs right now."

"I know and I promise to pay you better than Medicare does. Any calls while I was out?"

"Nope. Quiet as a Kansas cornfield. Rosa stopped by looking for you. Said you were supposed to have a read-

ing with her. I told her you hadn't said anything to me
about it." Franny gave me a squinty-eyed look. "Are you
finally starting to believe what Rosa sells?"

"No, but she thinks one of her readings will put me
in a better mood. Do you think I've been acting down
lately?"

Franny paused, which I knew meant she was thinking about how to phrase her response. "I wouldn't use the
word 'down,' but you have seemed a little distracted. On
the other hand, you have a lot on your mind. Running a
successful PI business might not be rocket science, but
it's a big responsibility."

"Thanks, Franny. I can always count on you to understand. Do you want to have dinner with me tonight
since Bunny's out of town and Johnny's out of commis-
sion?"

"Actually, I can't tonight. How about tomorrow
night instead?"

She didn't say why, but I knew it was her swing
class night.

"Okay, tomorrow night, then."

"Sure. We haven't had dinner together in a while."

"We ate together last week." I said.

"Right, but after living with you like I did and eating
together almost every night, now a week seems like a
long time."

I nodded. I knew exactly how she felt. "I've got a
couple of calls to make. You can head out anytime you
want."

"Okay. I'll see you tomorrow. What time do you
want me to come in?"

"Nine o'clock okay?"

"Sounds good. Have a good night, Polly."

I loved having my sister around. No one knew me
better, which I suppose is the case for most identical

twins. Our minds work exactly alike, but where we differ is in our emotional states. Franny is an emoter—mostly of positive, feel-good sentiments. I'm more of a realist.

However, if I managed to contact one Special Agent Joe Foster of the Federal Bureau of Investigation, I would emote some opinions he'd wish he'd never heard. I headed into my private sanctuary to place my call. Business card in hand, I punched his number into my landline and waited. Foster's answering machine picked up. I should have politely left my number and asked him to call back when he was free.

Instead, I turned on my no-nonsense voice. "Special Agent Foster. This is Polly Berger of Berger Investigative Services, and I have a bone to pick with you about the vehicle with government plates, which I presume belongs to your agency and which has been following me of late. I am not a happy camper, and if I feel my life is in danger from an unknown black SUV tailing me around town, I might become so frightened I send a bullet into your presumably bulletproof windshield or maybe through the airspace between your driver's side door and the frame. Do you get my drift?"

With that I slammed down the receiver and took a deep breath. I felt better already. My phone rang immediately.

I answered in my most sarcastic voice. "Yes?"

"Hey, Polly," a familiar voice said. "How come you didn't answer with Berger Investigations? You expecting a call from someone besides me?"

"As a matter of fact, yes, Bun. What's on your mind? You haven't run out of money already, have you? You've only been there a couple of hours."

"I got plenty of cash, and it didn't take me long to turn up something."

"Okay, good. What is it?"

"Well, before I left the office earlier, I downloaded a pic of Lenny Spinoli that I got from TLO and brought it with me to show around along with the two photos of the Martins. No hits on either Martin, but at the second marina, one of the workers recognized Lenny Spinoli. Told me Spinoli looked like the guy who'd rented a fishing boat a week or so ago. Rumors were it was a pricey rental, and the guy paid cash."

"Interesting. A week ago puts it in the right time frame."

"Yeah. Probably took a day or two for Spinoli's dead body to float over to Dockweiler Beach."

"If that's what happened," I said. "I'm not giving up on the idea of a body dump yet. Were you able to get any information on where Spinoli planned to take the boat?"

"No. 'Privacy concerns' the company said."

"Any chance it's now docked at the Marina?"

"No. From what I could gather, nobody's seen Spinoli since he rented the boat. Took it out and disappeared."

"Took it out alone? Not with another guy on board?"

"If Ricky Martin was with him, nobody I've talked to so far saw the guy."

I sat twirling my number two pencil, thinking about this new information. "We need to find out if this boat is the same one the Coast Guard found floating in the water, and then we need to find out if any of Lenny Spinoli's or Ricky Martin's things were on board."

"I don't know if I'll get anywhere with that, Polly. Coast Guard's not likely to share info with me, but I'll see what I can learn. Maybe I can find a seaman recruit hard up for cash. How's Johnny doing, by the way? Did the food bring back his memory?"

"He's about the same. He liked what I brought, but he thought I was the new waitress. He asked me to marry him then ordered another slice of cheesecake."

I could hear Bunny stifling a giggle. "Sounds like he's playing you."

"At this point, I wish it were the case, but the nurse said he asks every female who enters the room if she'd like to marry him."

"Guy's got a one-track mind," Bunny said. "I'd better get back to work, Polly. I'll let you know if I turn up anything else."

"Thanks, Bun, and good work so far."

"This might mean a raise, you know."

"We'll talk about it when you get back," I said, hoping to spur him to new heights.

Despite my occasional gripes about Bunny, he was a good investigator. If you wanted information, Bunny was your go-to guy. He had a way with people that seemed to lead them to share their deepest secrets with him. They tell him things they'd never tell another soul. I wasn't one of those people, which is one reason we work so well together.

After my conversation with Bunny, I locked up my office and headed across the street for dinner at Cinda Mae's, anticipating how good I'd feel after a serving of Pedro's special of the day. What I hadn't expected was Cinda Mae's news flash of the day. Funny how two unrelated cases can come together in the craziest of ways.

CHAPTER 25

Day 4:

A hubbub greeted me when I reached my office the next morning. Franny was sitting at Bunny's desk with Rosa next to her, both listening to Marko's latest rant. After hearing the first fervent sentences spewing from Marko's chapped lips, I wondered if he'd slept at all in the last twenty-four hours.

As expected, Franny was the first to notice my presence. "Oh, hey, Polly. Wait until you hear this."

Marko turned to me, a big grin spreading across his lined face. "Wait 'til you hear, Polly."

"I'm waiting."

"Well, I found out what Melody Knight was up to in her nighttime visits with her friends—"

I interrupted him. "I told you we were no longer working that case—"

"I'm not charging you for my time, Polly. I'm working this on my own. Think about it as unfinished business. I thought you'd be pleased with my initiative." He paused, waiting to be congratulated, I assumed.

"You're starting to sound like Bunny. He can't seem to drop the case, either."

"Wise minds think alike. Anyway, I needed to clear up something. I was wrong about her and her friends having an affair."

I pursed my lips. "I told you it was a dumb idea."

He rolled his eyes. "It wasn't a bad hypothesis based on the evidence, but yes, I came to the wrong conclusion. It happens."

"Let me guess. She was having a therapy session."

He shook his head. "Guess again."

"Suspense over," I said. "Move on."

"Sorry, Polly. I was just having some fun with you. It's a coloring group."

"A *what*?" I twirled my little finger in front of my ear, uncertain I heard straight. "What do you mean a coloring group?"

"Just what it sounds like. A group of women get together, and they color in these adult coloring books. With crayons."

I heard the words, but incredulity blocked my comprehension. "I thought I'd heard of everything by now. Is this some reversion to childhood or something?"

Rosa glanced over at me, shaking her head in what I could loosely describe as sad fashion. "It's all about relieving stress, Polly. I'm surprised you haven't heard of it."

"I kind of like the idea," Franny said. "And I can see where it might work. You get your mind off your troubles while you color the sky a light aquamarine and the grass a pretty shade of—"

"Sounds like a group you and Cinda Mae should start," I said, not meaning to come off as snarky as I sounded, but this adult coloring book idea was hard to swallow. What came next, Barbie doll parties? "Maybe Cinda Mae will give up part of that storage room in the back of her restaurant."

Franny gave me a dirty look and I apologized for the sass, not that she wasn't used to it by now.

"Cinda Mae wouldn't have to give up a storage room," Rosa said. "I'd be glad to share part of my suite downstairs if the three of you wanted to get together in the evening to color. I'd definitely join you. I agree with Franny. It sounds like an activity that soothes the soul. In fact, maybe I should work it into my practice. I always liked to color as a kid. I had one of those big crayon boxes with about a hundred colors. My favorite coloring books were the ones…"

I turned to Marko in the middle of Rosa's trip down Memory Lane. "I'll talk to you later about how you learned about the coloring group because I have a bad feeling about your methods, but right now I have some news of my own, which I'm sure will interest you most of all. As it happens, I had dinner at Cinda Mae's place last night and, if you remember—" I paused for effect. "—she's the one who personally referred Sally Martin to me." Everyone in the room nodded expectantly, so I dragged out the suspense a little longer. "As you all know, Hollywood is a small world and gossip travels far and fast."

"Cut to the quick," Franny said, sounding more like me than she probably realized.

I gave her a look straight from our mother's repertoire. "Not to get off topic, but from what Cinda Mae told me, I gather you and she had a gab fest recently in which you shared an item or two from our office, like who we were working for?"

"I didn't mean to," Franny said, "but you know how it is with Cinda Mae. She can pull information out of you before you even realize you said something. Anyway, she promised not to tell anyone, even Pedro."

"No problem. In this instance, I'm glad you talked to her because she happened to know something that supports Bunny and Marko's theory—"

Marko interrupted. "About Ricky Martin's disappearance?"

I shook my head. "No. About the Clive Hooper case.

"I can't wait to hear it," he said.

"Here goes. Cinda Mae remembered Sally Martin telling her about selling a house in the Hollywood Hills a couple of months ago to a woman whose *boyfriend* paid cash for the place." I had everyone's rapt attention with that bit of information. I should go on stage, I thought.

"Out with it, Polly," Rosa said. "The boyfriend's name?"

I glanced from one to the other, relishing the sense of anticipation on their faces. "Clive Hooper," I said, trying not to gloat.

"You have the woman's name and address?" Marko asked.

"I have a name. You'll have to do the rest."

"One more guy who thinks he can get away with anything," Marko said. "Sounds like you might want to keep me on the payroll, Polly, because I'm thinking he hired us for one of two reasons: either he hoped we'd find something that let him off the hook so that when his wife found out what he was up to she wouldn't be able to sue his pants off, not that he's all that good about keeping his pants on. Probably hoped we'd find she was fooling around, too. Or, he hired us to provide him with an alibi for when he killed her.

"Interesting ideas," I said, "considering the events of yesterday."

"I guess we know why she was so stressed she had to join a coloring group," Franny said, always the empathic one. "I'm betting she knew about his extra-curricular activities and confronted him when she got home that night and that's when he decided to murder her."

Rosa nodded. "What a creep, but I'm not surprised. Did you see his latest movie? Biggest self-serving pile of crap I've seen on the big screen in a dog's age."

"Okay, okay," I said, cutting off another unwanted line of discussion. "I'll pass this information on to Harry Barnes," I told Marko, "and you can stay on the job. Tail our client. Maybe he'll double our payment just to get us off his back."

"Wouldn't that be blackmail?" Franny asked, sending me one of her patented "shame on you" looks.

"Extortion, actually," I said. "So let's table that idea." Turning to Marko, I said, "Hold off on tailing Clive for the moment. I'll find something else for you to do that keeps you on the payroll."

At this point, all I wanted to do was get rid of Rosa and Marko and regain control of my day.

"Thanks, Polly," Marko said. "I'll stay on the job and if I come up with a good idea about how to use what I learn, I'll let you know."

With that ambiguous promise, he and Rosa returned downstairs to Rosa's newly renovated psycho-astrological chambers.

As soon as they left, Franny asked whether I'd stopped at the hospital to see Johnny before I came in to work.

"Yup, I did."

"How is he?"

"The same. Driving the nurses and doctors crazy."

"That can happen in post-traumatic amnesia," Franny said, switching to nurse mode. "Patients are often confused, can't make sense of things, which can manifest in strange behavior. It's called a post-traumatic confusional state, and it's usually temporary. He'll come out of it. We just need to be patient." She reached over for a file folder on Bunny's desk and handed it to me. "Bunny said to give this to you when you came in."

"Sometimes," I said, thinking about Johnny's situation, "life sneaks up and bites you in the rear, which is how I feel about now."

"Best thing to do in that case," Franny said, "is sit on it 'til it blows over."

I couldn't have agreed more, I thought, trotting into my office with Bunny's folder, hoping whatever was inside would unlock another mystery or two.

CHAPTER 26

Fifteen minutes later, I called Franny into my office. "Hey, can you come in here for a minute? I need a sounding board."

Franny hustled in. "Is this a sit-down conversation or a stand-up one?"

I motioned her to the chair across from my desk.

"So many things about this Lenny Spinoli case smell fishy. I'm starting to think Johnny's right, and we should let the feebs handle it and keep our noses out of it."

"Really? You want to give up five thousand dollars that easily?"

"I want us to stay alive," I said.

"What's got you so upset?"

"The contents of Bunny's folder—the TLO report on Ricky Martin."

"And?"

"There's nothing different from the first time I read through it. There's nothing. Literally. Ricky Martin didn't exist until he showed up in LA four years ago, which Bunny circled with a big question mark."

Franny shrugged. "Don't know what to say. He just handed it to me on his way out, like an afterthought. Said he wanted you to read it again."

I decided to think out loud, hoping something might pop out that made sense of this case. "Johnny filled me in on a few facts the feebs conveniently forgot to tell me, namely, that Lenny Spinoli is, or rather *was* a New York undercover cop who's been inside the mob for a long time. He traveled out here to apprehend some gangster who's on the feebs' Most Wanted list—"

"By the name of Ricky Martin?"

"My thinking exactly. You'd make a good detective, Franny."

"Thanks, Polly, but I think I'll stick to nursing. It's safer."

"Agreed. Anyway, let's think this through together. If Ricky Martin is the big-time mobster Lenny was after, that would explain why TLO couldn't locate his past. Somehow, though, Lenny Spinoli managed to track him down."

"Maybe he got a tip from one of Ricky's gangster pals. Especially if there was a price on Ricky's head. Anything for money with those Mob types."

I stifled a grin, since Franny knew absolutely nothing about Mob types except for what she learned from the *Godfather* movies on Netflix. "Good guess," I told her, "not that the method by which Lenny found Ricky matters. I'm guessing he tried to talk Ricky into giving himself up and Ricky declined."

"But why ask him to go fishing?"

"To get him alone. According to Sally, Spinoli told Ricky he was out here looking to buy property. My guess is Lenny was playing the part of a big spender. Probably told Ricky the boat was his, not a rental."

"So, Ricky went because he liked to fish," Franny said, "but when he learned Lenny knew his identity, he whacked him."

"Exactly. And dumped his body into the great blue

sea, assuming no one would find it, or if they did, the body would be so decomposed no one could identify it. Since Ricky couldn't stay with the boat, I'm guessing he called one of his cronies to pick him up and deliver him to a Baja resort where, as I mentioned to Cinda Mae, he's quaffing margaritas and soaking up the sun while his wife worries herself sick about whether he's dead or alive."

"If he's sunning himself in Baja," Franny said, "then he's quaffing mojitos."

I made the three-finger gesture for "Whatever," which my sister ignored.

"On the other hand, Polly, maybe Sally Martin knows exactly where her husband is and hired you and Bunny, not to find Lenny Spinoli's murderer, but to find the guy who ratted out Ricky. So while Ricky's in hiding, she's out running errands for him."

"I hadn't thought of that," I admitted, "but it's certainly a possibility to consider. On the other hand, her story could be true, and we'll find her husband swimming with the fishes off the coast of Santa Catalina, which brings me to my next request. I'd like to buzz over to the hospital to see Johnny. If nothing's changed, I'll take a little trip up to Glendale and check out Sally Martin's place whether she's there or not. Mind taking care of the office for me today?"

"No problem. Bunny said he thought he'd be able to wrap things up this afternoon in Santa Catalina, so he might get back here before you do."

"Let's hope he arrives bearing news that answers some, if not all, of our questions about this case. It can't wrap up fast enough to suit me." I reached over and gave my sister a grateful hug. "You know I appreciate your help, Franny, and stop worrying about me. I'm firmly grounded even if I don't always act like it."

"I know you are, Polly, but you're my favorite person in the whole world, Bunny included, so I'll probably always worry about you."

"Same here," I said, feeling a bit overwhelmed by how much I loved this person who looks so much like me but was so different. "Keep your fingers crossed that I find Sally Martin at home. I'm giving her no heads up so she won't have time to come up with an unverifiable alibi."

"Maybe you need to hire Marko to keep tabs on her now that he's no longer tailing Melody Knight."

"I thought about it, but I'd like to spend some one-on-one time with her first. See if I can squeeze out more information and get a feel for whether her story is a lie or on the up and up. Most of all, I want to see how she reacts when I tell her Lenny Spinoli was an undercover cop."

"Doubt she'll cop to it," Franny said, winking at me.

Bunny's humor was rubbing off on her, I thought, but kept my peace. "Maybe not, but her reaction to the news might indicate whether or not she already knows. That would tell us a lot."

I took out my cell phone and punched in Sally Martin's home address and the address of the Martins' real estate office, both in Glendale, adding the info to my contact list.

Curious as always, Franny asked, "Is their place a house or an apartment?"

"I drove by on Google maps. Nice three-bedroom place. Zillow pegs the value at over a million."

"Not too shabby," Franny said, adding, "and Zillow's estimates are usually low. Real estate is a great business for laundering money if the Martins are into something shady."

"One more thing to look into," I said, adding a note to my growing "to-do" list.

"In any case," Franny continued, "something's going well for the Martins. If not acting, then the real estate business."

"I know. Makes me realize I'm in the wrong business. Maybe I should start thinking about an alternate career. I could live for a year on the proceeds from one house sale alone."

"That's a great idea, Polly. We could start a business together. I could handle the people and you could take care of the books."

"Except it's way too dull for me," I told her, chafing a bit at my sister's insight when it comes to my people skills. She knows me too well.

"Are we done discussing the case?"

"For now," I said.

"Okay. Well, if you stop by the hospital on your way to Glendale, tell Johnny hello for me. If he's back in his right mind, I'll go over later to visit him. Actually, I'll stop there even if he isn't in his right mind. Good luck in Glendale. I hope you catch up with your client."

"I hope so, too. I don't want her waiting for me with some prefabricated tale when I ask her what she knows about her husband's business connections. I have a feeling those financials she gave us might be totally bogus."

"Yeah. She probably knows they're phony and brought them along to convince you their real estate agency is legit. That way you won't be snooping into what she doesn't want you to know."

"Which is something we should be snooping into. You're getting good at this, Franny. Maybe I can make enough money this year to hire you on a permanent basis. Would you like that?"

"Well…"

I could tell she was thinking it over.

"Here's the thing, Polly. I would like to work with you, but I think Bunny wouldn't like it. He might feel we were ganging up on him or something. You know how he is. Besides, working together is not good for a relationship, which you should know when it comes to your problems with Johnny."

She had a point, and I *did* know it. All the more reason, I thought, to reduce my reliance on Johnny and the HYPD when it came to solving my cases.

CHAPTER 27

On my way to Glendale, I made a quick visit to the hospital only to find Johnny in his room sleeping soundly. I tiptoed in and planted a kiss on his forehead, which failed to wake him. Figuring they'd sedated him again, I stopped by the nurse's station to check in with the desk nurse, who wouldn't answer my questions. Not my business, though it would be if Johnny and I were married. Something for future consideration, I thought, even though the idea failed to bring me much pleasure.

"No change in his condition, I'm afraid," the desk nurse told me, "but we're keeping our fingers crossed."

I'll bet you are ran through my mind. They probably couldn't wait to send Johnny home. "Okay, thanks. I'll check in again later today."

Back in my car, I took Los Feliz Blvd. over to the I-5 north for the seven-mile trip to Martin Real Estate in Glendale. With a population pushing a quarter of a million, Glendale was now the third largest city in LA County. The city's biggest claim to fame seemed to be Forest Lawn Cemetery, the final resting place of many of Hollywood's rich and famous. Ironic, I thought, all that fame and money and you still end up six feet under.

Thinking about Forest Lawn depressed me. I'd driven through the place once before, mostly out of curiosity to see who was buried there. Once was enough. The prospect of spending eternity underground lacked a certain appeal for me, not to mention the fact I'm uncomfortable facing my own inevitable mortality, especially with so much unfinished business on my plate. I glanced down at the GPS map, hoping my route avoided the cemetery.

Traffic was light once I reached downtown, having avoided Forest Lawn, and I managed to find a parking spot on South Brand Boulevard a half block from Martin Real Estate and another half block from Nordstrom's, one of my favorite places to shop. Once I finished interviewing my client, if she was in the office, I might have to stop and check out Nordstrom's shoe selection.

I locked up my car and hiked down the sidewalk to a hole-in-the wall storefront that barely had room for the Martin agency's name on the sign. However, given the location, I could only imagine the monthly rental costs, and how much room do you need for a real estate office anyway?

I reached for the door handle, which is when I noticed the *Closed* sign suspended from a plastic hook on the glass front door. I peered inside. There wasn't much to see: a metal desk, two chairs, not including the desk chair, and a small table containing a printer. Pictures of houses lined the limited wall space. Hard to tell whether the place was legit or simply a front. In any case, they were not open for business at the moment.

I took out my cell phone and retrieved the Martin's home address, which, according to my GPS app was less than two-and-a-half miles away. I debated about popping into Nordstrom's first since I was so close but swatted the devil off my shoulder and climbed back in my car instead. Ten minutes later, I was driving by an attractive stucco house on the hillside next to Glenandale Drive.

Suburbia at its finest, I thought. Tidy neat yards lined winding streets littered with low-slung ranch houses, no two the same, each individualized to suit its owner's up-scale lifestyle dream. I might move here, I thought, after I earn my first million.

I slowed the car in front of a white hacienda-style house set on the upside of the hill. I could picture myself in a house like that, but for some reason an image of Johnny never entered the placid domestic scene I'd paint-ed in my mind. I rang the doorbell twice and put my ear to the door listening for the sound of footsteps. All I heard was silence.

I glanced around, catching sight of a camera embed-ded inside the moldings on one corner of the porch roof. I wondered if the lamppost by the sidewalk contained an-other camera, and had announced my arrival. If Sally Martin knew I was here, she was taking her sweet time answering the door. I waited a few more minutes and tried the bell a third time. Still no answer.

I changed strategies and walked a three-sixty around the house, peering in windows before returning to my car where I placed a call to Sally's cell phone. No answer there either, so I left a message on her answering ma-chine: "Hi, Sally, this is Polly Berger. I was in Glendale shopping and stopped by your house for a chat, which is where I am right now. If you hear this message in the next half hour, please give me a call, and we can decide on a meeting place. I have a few more questions for you that will help in our search for your missing husband."

I sat in the car for ten minutes, hoping Sally might be nearby and would return my call. No such luck. Finally, I turned around and headed back to Nordstrom's. I knew I could kill an hour there with ease. If Sally called, I'd still be close. I'd barely put the car in gear when my phone rang. ID read *Unavailable* but I pulled to the side of the road and answered anyway.

"Polly Berger."

"Polly. This is Sally returning your call."

"Hi, Sally. Thanks for calling me back."

"No problem, but I'm still up in Frisco taking care of business, so a meeting's out of the question today."

I really wanted to see her in person, but at least I could ask for answers as long as I had her on the phone. "I have a few more questions for you, do you mind?"

"Nope," she said. "Shoot."

"Well, first, Bunny did a background check on your husband and came up with nothing earlier than four years ago when Ricky apparently arrived in Hollywood. Any idea why that is?"

After a long silence, Sally said, "You're asking me why there's no information on him before that time?"

"Right."

"Well, you could try to look him up under the name Rob Marlow. It's his Hollywood stage name. You know, so he doesn't get his acting persona mixed up with his real estate business. You might find more information on him under that name. But what is it about his background you want to know? Maybe it's something I can answer."

"Whenever we deal with missing persons," I said, "we start by developing a profile of them. By the way, did you ever file an MPR on Ricky with the Hollywood PD?"

"MPR?"

"Missing Persons Report."

Another long pause. "I thought I explained when I hired you that I wanted to keep the cops out of the matter."

"Can you tell me why?"

"Because I don't want to point a finger of suspicion in the direction of my husband. The police might put two and two together, or what they think is two and two, and decide Ricky killed Lenny, since the two of them went fishing together." She paused for breath. "But two and two doesn't always equal four."

I couldn't think of a situation where it didn't, but I played along. "Okay, I can buy that." I moved on to a different topic. "One more thing. Do you have access to a list of people or companies that Ricky dealt with over the past say, two to three months? Clients, including venders with whom he had dealings?"

"I can look through papers at the office when I return and call you with what I find."

"Sounds good," I said. "I'd still like to meet with you when you're back in town. In these kinds of investigations, questions arise on a regular basis."

"Sure, but I don't know how long I'll be up here." Another pause. "Could be a while."

"I see. In that case, let's keep in touch by phone, okay? And when you return, maybe we can—"

"Sure. Hey, I gotta run. Important meeting and I'm already late."

"No problem," I said, but she'd already hung up. I looked at the digital readout on my phone. Our conversation took less than two minutes, just under the time required to triangulate her location if I'd had the right equipment. I wondered if that was a coincidence and decided probably not. In my business, believing in coincidences doesn't pay.

CHAPTER 28

First thing I did on returning to my office was open my TLO account and request a background check on Rob Marlow. After a long minute wait, two pages of information displayed on my screen. I scanned the pages, realizing immediately that my client had lied to me in our most recent phone conversation. Rob Marlow was not Ricky's stage name, but his real name. He'd legally changed his name to Richard Martin when he moved to LA from his hometown in Poughkeepsie, an hour drive from the hometown of Lenny Spinoli. I filed that "coincidence" in the back of my brain.

I was now more certain than ever that Ricky Martin was a mobster on the run, a run that ended temporarily or maybe permanently, when Lenny Spinoli showed up. However, while adding an interesting twist to my case, the TLO report failed to provide any substantial clues as to either the location or current disposition of my client's husband.

With a little more thought, an idea hit me that maybe Ricky was the one who lied and not my client. Perhaps he'd conned her with the name story, and she'd fallen for it. Wouldn't be the first time, I thought, where a man duped a woman, or a husband his wife, a fact I knew firsthand because my first husband was a con artist *par excellence*. Not that Johnny is totally lacking when it comes to disingenuousness. He is a detective, after all, and a good one. Part of that investigative talent lay in conning crooks. I just wasn't in the market for someone turning those talents on me. Been there, done that.

Pushing thoughts of Johnny and my first ex aside, I turned to my computer and searched a popular movie data website for the name Rob Marlow. I found half a dozen actors listed, but no photos, nary a one, though the absence of promo pics wasn't necessarily an abnormality even in the acting business. I decided to Google images that matched the small photo of Ricky that Bunny had clipped to the top of the TLO report. My search turned up more handsome men than I thought lived on this planet. Must be something about the name. However, as handsome as these guys were, I had to admit none compared to Rob Lowe in the looks department. Unfortunately, none of them matched my client's photo either. Giving up, I printed the TLO pages and stuck them in the Martin folder. That's when a call came in from Bunny.

I let Franny answer, but she immediately called me on the intercom.

"Polly, Bunny wants to talk to you."

My hopes rose. Bunny had barely chatted to Franny before asking for me, leading me to conclude he'd found an important piece of information on his Santa Catalina quest.

I reached for my landline. "Hi, Bun, whatcha got for me?"

"A new development, and this might be important."

My heart beat faster, and I took a long breath to calm myself. "You found a flat broke Coast Guard seamen, and he spilled the beans about the fishing boat?"

"Haven't got that far yet, and I wouldn't get my hopes up if I were you. I spent some time in a local bar last night looking for a pair of loose lips and coming up empty. Your best bet to learn about that boat is to swallow your pride and give Harry Barnes a call, see what he can find out for you."

"I'll think about it," I said and tossed out another hopeful guess. "Anybody recognize Ricky Martin's picture?"

"Nope, not yet."

"Somebody recognized Sally Martin's picture?"

"If you'd stop interrupting me with all your questions," Bunny said, "I'll explain. I've been showing these pics to a lot of people and, in addition to finding someone who recognized Lenny Spinoli, I've had another hit."

"Get to it and stop keeping me in suspense," I snapped.

"The other person on Santa Catalina in the last two weeks besides Lenny Spinoli, was Sally Martin and she was there with someone who was not her husband."

"She was on the island with another man?"

"Apparently."

"Are you sure?"

"Here's what happened. I showed the photos around like you asked. One of the women who works at the marina next door to the one where I got the ID on Spinoli, recognized the pic of Sally Martin."

"She have any idea about who the guy was?"

"No. Stop with the questions already. When this lady at the marina saw the picture of Sally Martin, she told me, 'Yeah, I saw her with some guy who'd been hanging around here last week. He was alone then.' She guessed he was Italian. Said he was nice looking."

"They're all nice looking," I told him, thinking of my first husband—

Bunny cut me off, no doubt also thinking of my first husband. "So I'm guessing Sally Martin had a boyfriend on the side."

The information piqued my interest. "This certainly puts a different spin on things."

"I'm not sure what to make of it offhand, boss, but if I had to bet, I'd wager our client's boyfriend was supposed to knock off Ricky, but when he got to the boat, the only person on board was Spinoli, who wound up dead because he was in the wrong place at the wrong time. Or maybe, he knocked off both of them. It's just that Ricky's body hasn't turned up yet."

"On the other hand, maybe our mystery guy wasn't a boyfriend. Maybe he was a hit man hired by Sally and Ricky to knock off Spinoli. Whatever the case, good work. I need to get back in touch with Sally Martin and find out why she was on Santa Catalina and who was the mystery man accompanying her."

Bunny's self-satisfaction reverberated across the airwaves. I was glad I wasn't there to witness it in person. For a fleeting moment I considered taking the wind out of his sails, but he had done a good job and I wanted him to remain motivated, especially now that he knew Franny was in the office.

"Right, and thanks, Polly. I appreciate the compliment."

"I'd wager the FBI hasn't come close to digging up this information yet," I told him, "and I'm not about to clue them in until we learn the new guy's identity. By the way, how are you getting around the island, bike or golf cart?"

"What do you think?"

"Given your spin classes, I'm guessing bike."

"Right, and this beats a spin class any day of the week. I found a great bike if you don't mind the pink leopard skin paint job. It's an attention grabber, I'll say that for it."

"Really? What about plain black?"

"Hey, they gave me this one for half price."

"Well, don't enjoy yourself too much. You are on the clock, you know."

"I do know, which is why I went for the half price bike rental. How about I give the Coast Guard one more try tonight then head for home? I'm missing Franny."

"I'll tell her, but I'd like you to find someone who can attest to Ricky Martin's presence on the island since maybe he never made it out there. We have to consider that option, too. In fact, I'm back to the idea he's sunning himself on the Baja Peninsula. Also, I'll take your advice and call Harry Barnes about the boat. See if he can dig up more information for us. Knowing the feebs, they'll have gone over that boat with a fine-tooth comb. Harry has friends in the agency. He might loosen some lips for us."

"Okay. Good luck tracking down the identity of your client's mobster boyfriend. How do you plan to start?"

"With another phone call to our client," I said. "Where else?"

"That approach could lead to a peck of trouble, Polly. I wouldn't recommend it."

"I'll take your advice under consideration," I told him and hung up.

CHAPTER 29

Of course, I ignored Bunny's advice and immediately phoned my client. I realized I should have waited until Bunny was back so he could triangulate the call and document her whereabouts for us, but then I'd have to defend placing my call, and I wasn't interested in another argument with Bunny.

Sally Martin picked up on the first ring, which I assumed meant she was not in some important meeting after all.

"Hi, Mrs. Martin?"

A skeptical voice on the other end of the line began the conversation with, "You have some information for me or another question?"

"Both," I said. "But first, a question. I'd like to know why you didn't tell me you were on Santa Catalina with a man other than your husband."

"First, I was over there showing property to a client who happens to be my brother, and second, our presence on Santa Catalina has nothing to do with the disappearance of Ricky."

"Your brother? Mind providing me with his name?"

"Why? What does he have to do with the disappearance of my husband or the murder of Lenny Spinoli?"

"Perhaps nothing, but if you wouldn't mind, any piece of information related to Santa Catalina could help us find your husband."

"Okay, but in a minute. I'll call you right back."

She hung up and I waited. In less than a minute, she returned my call. Once again, I wondered whether she was worried about staying on the line long enough for us to track her. If so, I then had to wonder why she didn't want to be found, at least by me. On the other hand, maybe she really was in the midst of a business conference with someone who kept interrupting her. I've been in the same situation myself.

"Tell me why you need my brother's name," she repeated.

"I'll get to that in a minute," I told her. "I've got a pen and paper ready here, so let's get this out of the way before I fill you in on the latest. Your maiden name is?"

"Caruso."

"And your brother's name is?"

"Since you'll probably turn this up anyway, not that it has anything to do with anything, but I have three brothers. The oldest is Salvatore, then there's Giacomo, and the youngest one is Keir."

I almost choked on Keir. Where the heck did that name come from?

Before I could ask, she said, "My father's best friend was an Irishman named Keir O'Malley. He died when my mother was pregnant with my youngest brother so when he was born they named him after my dad's friend."

"A nice gesture," I said. "Do any of your brothers live out here?"

"No. They're all back east."

"Where back east?"

"Somewhere around Poughkeepsie."

"Your husband's home town, and I assume, yours?"

"Uh, Yeah."

"And you never met until you came out here?"

"Well, let's say, we met up again after we both came out here."

I was not happy with the run around my client was giving me. "And Coxsackie's not that far from Pough-keepsie, so Lenny might have been a friend of your husband's from back home."

She sighed. "Um, could be."

"I don't remember your mentioning any of this when we first talked." What I did remember was that we seemed to have come full circle. Not only did Lenny Spinoli come from Upstate New York, but so did Ricky Martin and, so it seems, did Sally Martin, which she'd conveniently forgot to mention. I now seriously doubted her claim that she didn't know Lenny, and wondered what else she'd lied about. My guess was she told so many lies, she couldn't remember what she'd said and what she hadn't, and I wasn't about to jog her memory, at least not in this point in my investigation.

While I debated with myself about what to say, Sally came to her own defense, "I probably didn't think it was important."

"Well, Bunny's over on Santa Catalina Island right now, and in addition to turning up the presence of your brother…whose name is?"

"Keir."

"Thanks. Anyway. So far, Bunny's learned that Lenny Spinoli rented a boat there about a week ago."

"I could have told you that. Actually, I thought I already did."

I paused, sifting through my cognitive deck in search of an instance where my client had told me about Lenny Spinoli renting a boat on Santa Catalina Island, but my memory banks came up empty. I chided myself for not asking her who rented the boat when I had her in my office, a minor investigative failing I laid at my own designer-clad feet.

"For some reason," I said, "we never discussed the rental of the fishing boat, only that the Coast Guard found it floating off the coast of Santa Catalina. At the time, I assumed the boat belonged to your husband since you mentioned how much he loved fishing."

"Again, what does any of this have to do with my brother?"

"Well, Bunny had photos of Lenny Spinoli, your husband and you, which he showed around to various marina employees—"

"Why my picture? I didn't go fishing with them, and I didn't go to Santa Catalina with them, either. I was on Catalina Island before they went fishing. Are you working for me or trying to implicate me in Lenny Spinoli's death? Like, are you snitching for the FBI or something?"

I realized I'd just stepped in a big pile of doo-doo. I needed to figure out how to get out of it without soiling my shoes or losing a paying client.

"Absolutely not," I assured her. "As I said, it's routine in a missing persons investigation, and no one is trying to implicate you or your brother," I told her, hedging the truth. I hurried on before she could raise any more objections. "However, one of the marina workers said the picture of the guy with you looked similar to one of the men who'd been seen hanging around the marina last week. So of course we were wondering if Ricky wasn't the only person on the boat with Spinoli. Could your brother have gone fishing with them, too?"

"You think my brother killed Spinoli?"

"Not at all. I'm only wondering if your brother could be missing along with your husband."

After a long pause, she said, "If my brother was missing, wouldn't I know it? Hey, I gotta run. I'll phone you tomorrow and see if you found out anything about what I hired you to find, which is, the scumbag who killed Lenny and maybe Ricky."

CHAPTER 30

With Sally Martin's shot across the bow regarding what she hired me to do, she rang off, and I breathed a sigh of relief. The call had gone better than I expected, though if her brother flew out here to warn Ricky that Spinoli was onto him and then helped Ricky kill Spinoli, my client was probably on the horn to him right now telling him to get out of Dodge before we or the police caught up with him.

I was beginning to think Bunny was correct about my client—she was up to her pretty earlobes in this mess. I'd been warning Bunny about being so suspicious of everyone who steps through our door, telling him it's no way to run a PI business, but maybe I'm wrong about that. I've been wrong before. I suppose it could happen again.

I rolled my chair back to my computer. My TOC account window was still open so I went ahead and plugged in the names of the Caruso brothers from Poughkeepsie. While I waited for the first report to appear, I opened a second window and Googled the individual brothers' names just for fun, adding Poughkeepsie to the search phrase. I loved the name of that town. Maybe the next time I traveled east, I'd drop in for a visit, after first checking with my client about where to find the best Italian restaurants. Italian food came in a close second to Mexican as my favorite ethnic eats, despite bringing back memories of my first husband.

While I reminisced about edible pleasures, the best kind in my opinion, the squeak of my outside office door signaled a new arrival. I guessed Rosa, but I was wrong. A distinctly male and not unfamiliar voice reached my ears. Not Marko's voice, I thought, but who? The light on my intercom blinked telling me my curiosity was about to be satisfied.

"Polly?"

"Yes, Franny?"

"Special Agent Joe Foster from the FBI is here to see you. Shall I send him in?"

"Please do," I told her, steeling myself for the encounter. Would he expect me to defend the voice message I left him? If so, *fuhgeddaboudit*, now a perfectly legitimate word according to the OED, and which succinctly embodied the fact that I was in no mood to stand up and graciously greet him when he entered. In fact, I remained seated, barely reaching across my desk to shake his outstretched hand. This forced him to bend down in a position that resembled something close to an honorific bow. I felt better already.

"Have a seat," I said, pointing to the straight-backed chair by my desk, hoping he wouldn't make himself too comfortable.

"I got your message." His mouth formed a rueful grin as he rotated the chair and sat astride the seat, something I've only seen males do. I'd once Googled a body language site and learned the behavior signals a casual, relaxed, nonthreatening, yet attentive attitude. A good start, I thought. "And I'm here to apologize," he added.

Well, knock me over with a soggy tortilla. The FBI had surprised me again. I bit back everything I was about to lay on Special Agent Foster, trying to compose an appropriate response that wouldn't sound too much like eating crow. Foster must have registered my uncertainty, because he quickly followed his apology with, "To demonstrate my sincerity, I'd like to treat you to lunch."

If he weren't so doggone good looking, I would have turned him down on the spot. "Um, today?"

He glanced at his watch. I glanced at the digital display on my computer, which read thirty-six minutes past noon.

"If you don't have plans already…"

"I don't," I said, resisting the impulse to explain why my calendar was lacking for lunch dates. "And I accept your apology. I'm hoping an explanation will accompany lunch?"

"It will," he assured me with a broad grin. He had really good teeth.

I wondered where he planned to go and hoped he had in mind a restaurant and not a birdcage in the HYPD since I wasn't interested in that type of grilling.

I decided to ask. "Have somewhere in mind?"

"What about the Mexican place across the street?"

I screwed up my face. "Well, if we have lunch over there, I'll be subjected to the third degree for the next week since the owner's a friend of mine. Better to go a little farther away from my office."

My brain simmered with the myriad questions I'd hear from Cinda Mae if I showed up at her restaurant with a handsome FBI agent in tow.

Foster came to my rescue. "How about Hugo's Hardware?"

"Is that a restaurant or a euphemism for a torture chamber?"

Foster's face lit up, probably at my honesty more than my wit. Maybe he hadn't encountered too many honest PIs before, not in LA, anyway.

"A restaurant, and if you're interested in giving it a try, I'll call ahead for a reservation. Their pork ribs are out of this world, though the curried lamb chops are my current favorite."

"I'm in," I said, realizing the place must be pricey, which is why I hadn't heard of it. I can't afford to eat in restos that require reservations. I wondered who would be footing the bill, the American taxpayer or Special Agent Foster, not that it mattered much to me.

"Where is this place?"

"West Hollywood. Maybe ten, fifteen minutes. We can take my car."

That gave me pause. I should have kept my mouth shut, but that's not my style. "You're not kidnapping me or anything, are you?"

He let out a huge guffaw that sent Franny running to my rescue. She stuck her head in the door, "Is everything okay?"

I motioned her in. "This is my twin sister Franny."

"Yes, we met," Foster said. "I mistook her for you when I came in, but she set me straight fast."

"Well, there's a reason for that, which we won't go into now." I turned to my sister. "Franny, Special Agent Foster is taking me to lunch at Hugo's Hardware in West Hollywood. Anything I need to do before we leave?"

She gave me a Cinda Mae look and with a totally straight face asked, "Do you want me to take lunch over to Johnny?"

"That would be great," I told her, wanting to ring her pretty neck for bringing up the name of my ex. I knew her motive—surrogate mate protector acting on his be-half. "You know what to order," I continued, as though her question hadn't annoyed the heck out of me. "And better take two pieces of cheesecake this time, or he'll be sending you back for more."

"No problem," she muttered, glancing between me and Special Agent Foster, who'd stood up when she came in, probably because his legs hurt from straddling my wooden chair. "Any idea when you'll be back?" she asked.

"I'll call you," I told her. "You know how to reach me if anything comes up." With that, I grabbed my purse out of the drawer and followed Franny out of my office.

Special Agent Foster brought up the rear, and trailed me down the stairs.

I knew I'd be in trouble with Franny later, but it wouldn't be the first time and by now I was up for the challenge.

CHAPTER 31

If the speed with which the leggy hostess at Hugo's Hardware seated us was a valid measure, Special Agent Joe Foster had more juice than Johnny when it came to the Hollywood restaurant scene.

On the other hand, maybe Foster was dating the woman. She certainly lit up when we arrived, and judging by his smile and the lack of adornment on his ring finger, I'd already estimated his marital status as single and looking. The *looking* bit was merely an educated guess on my part and not an example of wish fulfillment.

Once we were seated at a corner table by the window and finished listening to the list of daily specials, I buried my nose in the menu. Special Agent Foster did the same, indicating he was as uncomfortable with this lunch idea as I was.

The server asked for our drink preferences and I stated my usual: "Water, no lemon," because I didn't want someone's fingers touching the piece of lemon that went into my drinking water. Franny always disapproved of my request. She thought it was an insult to the server.

"It's not lead, Polly, it's a citrus rind. The citric acid kills most of the bacteria."

Remembering Franny's comment set me thinking

about the lead poisoned drinking water in Flint, Michigan. Who would have believed such an episode a few years ago? President Eisenhower must be turning over in his grave, I thought, as Special Agent Foster, who insisted I call him Joe, reminded me the server was waiting to take my order.

I opted for the pork ribs marinated in *gochujang* sauce while "Joe" stuck with his favorite—grilled smoked lamb chops with goat cheese and chive gnocchi. I almost changed my order when I heard gnocchi and a wave of Pittsburgh homesickness hit me.

Ordering our meals seemed to bring an end to the awkwardness between us, as we discussed the relative merits of our dishes, agreeing we'd each made a good menu choice before getting around to the day's business.

"I'm guessing you want me to get down to brass tacks," Special Agent Foster—er, Joe—said.

I nodded, uncertain what to expect.

"First, I want to apologize again, this time for not sharing vital information with you when we first visited your office, but we ordered a tail on you for your own protection."

I listened and shrugged when he stopped for breath. "I wish I'd known the black SUV was there to protect me," I said. "It felt like the opposite."

"I understand. Now back to the first question about the body on Dockweiler Beach."

What he said next would tell me whether he was on the up and up, since he had no reason to know I was aware of the identity of Lenny Spinoli or that Spinoli had been murdered.

"The body recovered on Dockweiler has been ruled a homicide not a drowning."

So far, so good, I thought. "Thanks for the information."

"However, we're keeping the identity a secret. What I can tell you is that the murder involves a detective out of New York by the name of Lenny Spinoli. He's been working undercover with the Mob for a number of years and apparently he was about to score a big catch, but it seems the perp caught wind of the operation and is on the run again."

"A big-time New York mobster?" I asked, as if I hadn't already heard the news from Johnny.

"Upstate, but our New York City office informed us of Lenny's trip out here. Unfortunately, before we could meet up with him, he disappeared. Last his boss heard, he was meeting with a realtor named Ricky Martin, who seems to have disappeared the same time as Lenny. We were at a dead end on the whereabouts of either until the body turned up on Dockweiler Beach."

"And that's when you came to me for help?"

He shook his head. "Not yet. When the two guys went missing, we interviewed Mrs. Martin—" He nodded in my direction. "—your client, and got nowhere with her. At the time, we figured she might be hiding something, but we had no grounds to hold her, so we set up a tail. That's where you came in. Last we saw of her was when she left your place. Somehow, she escaped our watchers—poof, vanished into thin air."

"Wait. You were tailing me an hour after Sally Martin came to my office, except instead of following me you followed my sister Franny and by the way, scared the bejesus out of her. She almost moved back to Pennsylvania, thanks to you, until I talked her out of it."

A shame-faced look crossed his face. "Yeah. We were monitoring your client's phone calls and knew she'd called you, so we tracked down your address. Didn't know you were a PI at the time."

His explanation sounded plausible to me. I wondered what Bunny or Franny would make of it. I'd run it by them both.

"And," I said, not dropping the accusatory tone, "you thought I had something to do with my client's disappearance?"

The words were barely out of my mouth when the waitress arrived with our food, saving him the embarrassment of an acknowledgement.

"Food looks great, doesn't it?" he said, artfully changing the subject.

The food looked and smelled terrific, so much so I almost forgave the feds for suspecting me of involvement in protecting a potential criminal from prosecution.

"Smells heavenly," I said, sucker that I am for good food. Sometimes I can be too forgiving.

"Truth is, we didn't know what to think," Foster said, picking up where he left off, "which is when we decided to pay a visit to your operation."

"And your conclusion after visiting my office?"

"That you probably had no idea of the trouble your client might be in. We decided our best strategy was to solicit your help."

"An on-the-spot decision?"

"Pretty much," he admitted, stabbing his first piece of grilled lamb chop, which looked heavenly. I was dying for a taste, but not about to lower myself and ask. However, like a good mind reader, he reached his fork across and slid the bite onto my plate. "Have a taste. See what you think."

I couldn't resist. The chop was spicy and as scrumptious as it looked. I told him so and offered him a piece of my pork, but he declined, saying he'd ordered the ribs before and knew how good they were. "Used to be my favorite," he added, "until I tasted the lamb."

"Next time I come here," I said with lofty self-confidence, as if I could afford to splurge at a place like this on a regular basis, "I might order the lamb, though these pork ribs are out of this world delicious."

Savoring my first bite of the ribs, I glanced across the table at him, realizing not for the first time that he was a genuine hunk. I'd felt so much animosity toward him and his employer earlier that I hadn't really noticed. Or rather, I noticed, but gave the matter no serious consideration.

"Go on with your story," I said. "I'm waiting to hear more about the protecting me part."

"Sure." He popped another bite of lamb in his mouth, chewed, and swallowed it before continuing. "When the coroner ruled the death a homicide—" He glanced up to gauge my reaction, "—we figured maybe Mrs. Martin was either an accomplice, or at least participated in her husband's escape. At that point, we felt the couple might be using you to throw us off their trail."

His shrug at the end of the sentence hinted at the level of the feds' uncertainty about this case, which I calibrated as high, like over the moon, like they had nothing, maybe even less than I'd uncovered.

"So," I said, toying with the remaining pork rib on my plate, "you're suggesting my client is a felon."

"The point is, we don't know."

"Even if she is, why does that necessarily put me in danger?"

"I can't give you specifics because I don't have any. There are too many unknowns right now. What we do know is that Lenny Spinoli was on the trail of a very dangerous criminal, an ex-hit man for the Mob. Whenever we're dealing with the Mafia, we have a large set of known unknowns, but it's the unknown knowns more than the known unknowns that spell danger for anyone involved, law officer or not."

Did he really say that?

"Seems to me," I said, choosing to avoid acknowledging the elephant in the room, "that you're making a lot of assumptions in this case. First, that Ricky Martin killed Lenny Spinoli, either because Ricky is the mobster Spinoli was after, or because the yet-to-be-identified mobster hired him to knock off Spinoli, and that my client, who was the first person by the way, to raise the issue that someone murdered Spinoli, even before the coroner's report came out—"

Joe Foster interrupted me, his cheek stuffed with the penultimate lamb morsel from his plate, "Who told you the dead body was Lenny Spinoli?"

My turn for the sheepish look. "I can't say."

"What else do you know?" he asked, pointing his fork at me.

I hoped the gesture wasn't a threat.

CHAPTER 32

How is it," I asked Joe Foster, who'd finished his lamb chop and begun digging into dessert, "that you, a member of the highly respected Federal Bureau of Investigation, perhaps the world's foremost investigative agency, is asking me, a two-bit PI, for information?"

I nearly tossed my cookies over the *two-bit* term I used to describe myself, but it comes with the territory. I'd lost count of the number of times I'd been required to eat humble pie for the sake of an investigation.

"Easy," he said. "Thanks to an intransigent, penny-pinching Congress, the agency lacks sufficient resources for shutting down organized crime these days. Too many other priorities. In our West Coast operations, for example, the Mob ranks number six, way down the line in terms of priorities. Different story on the East Coast, of course. In Florida, for example, it's the Russian Mob, but in New Jersey the Mafia's a high priority because they're making a comeback."

"No doubt thanks to their governor," I mumbled, a comment Joe Foster prudently ignored, and I pretended not to notice by asking another question. "Is RICO responsible for the slowdown in Mob activities out here?"

My question arose from an article I'd read about the success of the RICO Act in shutting down organized crime all across the country. Now, if we could only find something similar for Wall Street, I thought.

"Not really. The reasons are more market-related—lack of demand for the services..." He hesitated, I wasn't sure why. "...the services the Mafia offers. Right now, the Mexican drug cartels control the narcotics business, along with human smuggling and prostitution, corporations have shut down the unions, state governments have legalized gambling, and Wall Street's taken over the loansharking business. And then there's the Mob's younger generation. They have no use for the old code of Omerta. Faced with a few years in the slammer away from their wives and kids, the perps talk and walk. When they talk, we move in. Makes things easier than in the old days."

Foster's explanation told me everything I wanted to know, the main part being that I seemed to be in the driver's seat here.

"How about we cut a deal?" I suggested.

He pushed his chair back six inches and leaned forward, elbows on the table, chin resting on his ringless hands. "What kind of deal?"

"I'll tell you what I know and you help me with my investigation, the results of which I promise to share with you before sharing with my client, assuming I still have a client." I knew this was a cheeky request on my part, but why not shoot for the moon?

He studied me, his head tilted to the side in what I assumed to be a measure of his level of incredulity at my request. "I suppose you know I have methods for finding out what you know without offering anything in return..."

I nodded.

"Like, for example, charging you with obstruction of justice for withholding information in a federal investigation."

"Yes, I realize that, but I doubt the publicity subsequent to such a stunt would be appreciated by your bosses."

"True," he said, giving in a lot faster than I expected. "What do you want help with?"

I had to bite my tongue about the preposition at the end of his sentence. The fact that I carry around in my head the voice of my English teacher mother is a burden my sister and I bear and share. I stuck to the topic at hand. "I'd like to know what the Coast Guard found in the boat they captured off Santa Catalina Island, and…" I paused, thinking quickly about what else I wanted to know. "…and, I'd like to know whether Martin Realty is a money-laundering front operation or on the up and up, and—"

"Let's start with the trading information part of this equation. I will tell you what we know about the boat, but first, l want to hear something from you that I might not know."

"Fair enough," I said. "First, I know Lenny Spinoli rented said fishing boat from a specific marina on Santa Catalina Island, took it out, brought it back, and took it out a second time, information I received in a text from my assistant investigator who is on Catalina Island as we speak."

"That may or may not be important," Foster said.

The fact that he blew me off suggested I'd just given him information he didn't know.

"And," I continued, "I'd like to know whether or not Ricky Martin was aboard that boat either time. If he was, then I may have to conclude he went overboard with Spinoli. My client won't like that news, though I doubt it will come as a surprise. In any case, end of investigation for me. I'm done and the rest is up to you."

"I wish I had the answer you're looking for, but we don't know yet whether he was on the boat, although it seems logical. Like you, I'm waiting for the evidence report since it will tell us whether to stick with Ricky Martin as our main suspect or turn our attention elsewhere. Anything else you can give me, now that this trading information thing seems to be working?"

So far, I thought, it was working better for him than for me, but I plunged forward. "A second piece of information that might be of interest to you is the fact that my client's brother was on Santa Catalina Island prior to the arrival of Lenny Spinoli."

"Something else I didn't know, and I appreciate the tip. We will definitely change our focus, not that we'll drop Martin from our suspect list, but we will add the brother."

I flipped open my right hand as if he should put something in it. "Your turn. What do you know about the Caruso brothers, if anything?"

"We know a lot," he said, like it was a given and who was I to cast doubt on the FBI? "But not as much as we'd like."

I appreciated the added humility.

"Can you share?"

"Sure. None of the Carusos have a record, so there's not much to say about them. I suppose Ricky Martin could have hired one of the brothers to take out Spinoli. No way to tell at this point."

"Alternatively," I said, simply to remind him I was still in the game, "Since Lenny Spinoli's target seems to have been Ricky Martin, maybe Ricky, aided and abetted by his wife, contracted her brother to take out Spinoli."

Joe Foster nodded and turned back to his food, picking up the two-tined fork again. Without pointing it at me this time, he added, "Good work finding the brother. Soon as I get back to the office, I'll send a team over to Catalina and see if we can run him down."

"If he's still there."

"Yeah, a big 'if.'"

He jumped on that idea a little too quickly to suit me. "You have reason to believe the brother would still be on the island?"

"Not at all. Just covering the bases. It's as good a place as any to start looking for him."

"Unless, of course, he's back home in Poughkeepsie, which is where I'd start the search."

He ignored the dig and asked, "Got anything else?"

I did have more, but decided to wait until I'd wrung more information out of him now that he seemed to be in a loquacious mood. Must have been the two glasses of Chianti.

"Yes," I said, "but first, what do you know about Martin Realty? Any evidence they're legit and not a money laundering front?"

"Apparently bona fide—" Which he pronounced to rhyme with Heidi. "—but a little shady when it comes to their real estate holdings, at least one of which is a sex pad."

"Sex pad?" I'd never heard the term, but the meaning was obvious. Sometimes I have trouble keeping up with the current lingo, which is another reason to keep Bunny around.

Foster sniggered. "Given your profession, I'm shocked at your surprise. It's a one-hour motel."

"I figured," I said, trying not to sound insulted, "never heard the term. Is this place in San Francisco by any chance?"

"Nope, right here in LA Why?"

"Because in my last phone conversation with my client, she claimed to be in San Francisco taking care of a business matter."

"She give you anything that might help us locate her?"

"No, and she kept ending the call just short of the two-minute mark like she suspected a trace. Don't know if she thought I might be triangulating her call, or someone else might, like your agency for instance."

"Maybe both." The lift of an eyebrow signaled his next question. "And the call dropping didn't seem suspicious to you?"

"Yeah, it rang a few bells in my brain," I admitted, "and I didn't dismiss it out of hand, but considering the circumstances, if I were in my client's expensive designer shoes, which I'm not, I'd be extra cautious, too."

My comment seemed to amuse Special Agent Foster, as evidenced by the slight smirk on his face as he paid the bill with cash and stood up to leave.

I followed him to the front door, which he held open for me, a tradition I appreciated, in spite of my ultra-feminist views. Nearing the car, I hesitated for a moment, glancing between the car and Special Agent Foster, who strode a half step ahead of me. I'd just noticed the license plate on his vehicle. Not a government issue and not the number Franny had provided for the black car tailing her.

Had I made a huge mistake here, I wondered, as I climbed into the passenger seat of Special Agent Foster's personal SUV with my heart pounding?

CHAPTER 33

Franny was out, still at the hospital with Johnny when I returned safe and sound to my now-empty office. I was still in a conundrum about Special Agent Joe Foster as I reviewed our conversation in the car. I'd been quieter than usual, a million contradictory thoughts racing around in my head. Was Special Agent Foster the genuine article or an imposter? If he was for real, why was he driving his personal car instead of a government issue?

Foster had noticed my uncharacteristic silence. "Cat got your tongue?"

"Just thinking," I'd told him. "Trying to make sense of a few things."

"It's a tough case," he replied, apparently assuming my mind was on the case rather than on him. "No easy answers out there, but I hope I've convinced you to join the good guys and work with us. The more we share, the faster we can bring this investigation to a close, find Ricky Martin, maybe lock him up, and throw away the key."

"As long as you keep me in the loop," I said, striving for a cheery tone, "I'll do the same."

"No problem, then." He looked over at me and grinned. He had a killer smile.

I put that thought out of my mind as I decided on my next move, maybe call Bunny, but I ended up phoning Harry Barnes instead.

Harry answered on the first ring. "How are you doing, Polly?"

"Not great, Harry. Have you seen Johnny today?"

"Yeah. Just got back. Franny brought him some lunch. He thought she was you."

My heart pounded, worried he might have remembered that I told him I'd marry him again. "So, he's regained his memory?"

"Not exactly. He remembers everything from yesterday on, but nothing prior to that."

"He thought he remembered me."

"Well, he remembered the waitress who brought him his lunch yesterday, which I gather was you. When he saw Franny, he thought she was yesterday's waitress." I could tell by the sound of his voice over the phone that Harry was having trouble keeping a straight face. "Franny said when she arrived, Johnny thanked her for the good food and asked if she still wanted to marry him."

I wasn't sure this was funny. "How did she handle it?"

"Said, 'of course.' I think she wanted to make life difficult for you. She did add that he'd have to get better first. Said she wasn't up to taking on a nursing assignment in addition to her waitressing job."

Harry and I both broke up laughing. "That's my sister, but thanks for the heads up."

"No problem. Is that why you called?"

"No. Got something else on my mind."

"Shoot."

"Before Johnny went out and got himself hurt doing something he should have left to younger members of the department," I said, "he looked up some information for me on two local FBI agents. He told me which office they're working from, but I need to know more. Can you help me out?"

"Sure. What do you need to know?"

"Pictures if you can dig them up. Maybe Johnny found some, but if so, he didn't have time to send them over."

"I'll check his desk first, see if he left any pics or any notes on that yellow pad of his. How long do you think it'll be before he starts using his computer on a regular basis?"

"Unless the department forces it down his throat," I said, "never."

"The department has forced it on him. He's still fighting it."

"I think the yellow pad is his last-ditch effort to prove he's not dependent on technology like the rest of the world. I don't know how long it will take him to realize it's a losing battle."

"Won't be his first or last losing battle," Harry said, "including trying to convince you to marry him again."

"I know," I moaned. "I wish he'd learn to enjoy the status quo. I thought maybe this blow on the head would knock some sense into him, but it sounds like he's getting worse."

"We'll see. Who are the agents you want pics of?"

"Names are Joe Foster and Adrienne Peters. According to Johnny, they're assigned to the Lancaster resident office. I know I could head over there and check on them first hand but I don't want to do that just yet."

Harry paused in thought. "Can't say I've heard of them, but I don't know all the feds out here. I'll see what I can find. Why are you interested?"

"They paid me a visit shortly after I took a new client. Said they wanted to enlist my help."

Harry guffawed. "That's a new one."

"That's what everyone tells me. At least you didn't say you never heard of the feebs asking for help from a two-bit PI firm."

"Well, it is a bit unusual."

"Harry!"

"You know what I mean, Polly. I wasn't insulting your agency. I think you do a good job, and even though I'm not a big fan of private investigators, I appreciate the honest ones. You're honest, in addition to being good at what you do."

"Thanks, Harry."

"You feel better now?"

"I think so…"

"Okay, let me get to work on this. I'll let you know what I find out. I've got a good friend in the field office over on Wilshire. And he owes me a favor, so this shouldn't take long."

"Thanks Harry. Just one more thing."

"What's that?"

"Did Johnny kick you out again when you visited today?"

"He tried. Said the presence of shyster lawyers ruined his appetite."

"What did you do?"

"I told him he was paying me big bucks to watch over his assets while he was away on business, but I'd leave if he insisted."

I nearly doubled over laughing. "So funny, Harry."

"I've been working with Johnny a long time. I know

which buttons to push, but I've got a feeling you have more on your mind."

"You're a mind reader, Harry. I do have something else. Before his accident, did Johnny mention to you anything about Melody Knight's suicide?"

I heard a long sigh from Harry that sounded like static on the line. "He did not."

"I thought that might be the case, so let me fill you in. Bunny was in charge of the Clive Hooper case when we were still being paid by Hooper to tail his wife. Of course, now that she went and committed suicide, we're no longer under contract. In fact, I'll be writing up an invoice to send him when I hang up with you."

"Yet you still have unanswered questions?"

"Here's the thing, Harry…"

"Ye-e-e-s?"

"Bunny and Marko carried out the surveillance on Hooper's wife, which didn't amount to much. He only hired us a few days before she died. Nevertheless, everyone in my office believes Clive Hooper killed her, and that he hired us to provide cover if he comes under suspicion. Meaning, we're supposed to show up and provide him with an alibi at some point."

"This is Hollywood, Polly. Anything's possible. Do you have actual evidence to back up your suspicions? Since Clive's not under suspicion, what's the supposed alibi?"

"I don't know yet, but we might know after the coroner rules on time of death and stomach contents."

"Coroner's ruled. Says the death was a suicide. Estimates TOD at sometime between five-thirty and seven in the morning, but it could be an hour or two either way."

"And the cause?"

"Sleeping pill overdose."

"Not an opioid or heroine overdose?"

"Nope. Sleeping pills—most common suicide method for women. Anyway, she's an actress. They're always taking the easy way out."

"Harry Barnes I can't believe you said that. That's the most sexist—"

"You're right. I apologize. Don't take it personally, Polly, it's just that we live in one of the most narcissistic cultures in the world when it comes to the movie business. It's easy to get jaded."

"I'm disappointed in you."

"I'm disappointed in myself. Let's get back on topic. You're telling me that your accusation is based on nothing more than an educated guess? That's not good enough, though I can see where Bunny and Marko's imaginations could run wild given Hooper's horror films and all—"

"We found motive."

"Motive?"

"Clive's got a girlfriend on the side, for one."

"He's a director. They all have something on the side."

I let that go, even though I knew it wasn't true. "This relationship seems to be on the serious side since he bought her an expensive house in the Hollywood Hills. Paid cash, and then there's the elephant in the room."

"Which is?"

"Melody's acting ability, or lack thereof, which was tanking his movies." The long silence at the other end of the phone told me I'd set Harry thinking. "And there's more."

"I'm listening."

"I looked up a few things in my spare time, and according to the scandal sheets dating back to Clive's wedding five years ago, the couple have an ironclad pre-nup

that exceeds any reasonable community property settle-
ment. He stood to lose a lot."

Another long pause on Harry's end before he came
through with, "I'll talk to the coroner and the CSIssies.
Ask them to take a second look."

"Thanks, Harry. And you'll let me know what you
find, right?"

"Depends. No promises. Until you hear back from
me, remind Bunny and Marko to keep their noses clean
and stay out of it."

A tall order, but I agreed. "Will do."

"And next time you visit Johnny, give him my re-
gards."

CHAPTER 34

Five minutes after hanging up with Harry I was still laughing about his hilarious report on Johnny. I owed him one for brightening my day. Now I had to decide if I should head over to the hospital, knowing a visit with Johnny would be a downer if his memory hadn't returned and maybe a downer if it had, or call Bunny for a progress report.

Before I could do either, Bunny phoned me, saving me from a guilt trip over not making the hospital visit my highest priority.

I answered with a cheery, "Hi, Bun, what's up?"

"News," he said.

"Good news or bad?"

"Some of each."

"Okay then, out with it."

"I found somebody who recognized Ricky Martin's picture."

I could hardly contain my excitement. "Great! At the same marina?"

"No, at a bar nearby. The bartender said she remembered him because he was a looker. Thought he might be an actor."

"Did she say when she saw him? This week, last

week, before the fishing trip, after? Was Martin with someone or alone—

"Hold on. Give me a chance to answer. First, she said he was alone, which was one of the reasons she remembered him. Said it was unusual for a guy that good looking to come in without a babe on his arm."

"She used that term, 'a babe'?"

"Well, she's older than the pyramids…"

"What else did she say?"

"That's it. Doesn't remember him with anyone, meeting anyone, or talking with anyone. She says he came in for a drink and a hamburger. Didn't stay long, didn't chat, even though she tried to engage him. Said she can't remember having seen him before that day or since."

"How long ago was he in there?"

"She couldn't remember, but she thought it was at least a week ago, maybe more. When I suggested the date Spinoli rented the boat, she said it could have been that day or a day earlier or later, but definitely around the same time."

My mind raced, trying to match dates and times in my head without achieving much success. "Well, at least we know Ricky *was* on Santa Catalina Island and probably the same time as Lenny Spinoli, so our client wasn't lying about that. Still doesn't tell us whether or not they were on the boat together. It's sure looking more and more like Ricky killed Spinoli."

"My guess, too. You want me to stay here longer or what?"

"See if you can dig up anything more. If not, head on home."

"Sounds good. I'll do what I can, but you'll no doubt see me back in the office tomorrow morning."

I hung up with Bunny and that's when Marko

showed up. Again. Two times in one day. I heard the outside door open and shut and went out to investigate at which time I encountered Rosa's favorite male of the species.

"Hey, Polly." Marko's standard greeting à la his home state of North Carolina.

"What's up, Marko?"

"Well, I was looking over my surveillance notes, you know, from the night before Melody Knight died?"

"And?"

"I realized there was one car, a silver Mercedes, that came by the house three times in the early hours of the morning."

"What of it? Maybe somebody left for work early in the morning, forgot something, and returned home for it."

"Could be." Marko's shrug was worthy of a Broadway opening. Apparently, he disagreed with my reasoning. "But it wasn't," he added, with a smugness I'd encountered previously. I began to wonder how Rosa put up with him twenty-four hours a day.

"And you would know this, how?"

"Because I had a hunch—"

My famed patience was being tested. "I'm becoming suspicious of your hunches. I hope you haven't committed a felony or even a misdemeanor that led to this hunch."

"No way."

"Okay. What's your hunch?"

"I thought the car might belong to Hooper's lady friend."

"I take it you mean the woman whose name I gave you?"

He nodded. "Well, Hooper spent the night with her and she owns a silver Mercedes. That's enough for me."

It was enough to convince me, too, but I wasn't quite ready to concede. "You get the license number?"

"I have her license number—" He paused for effect. "—and address. I followed Hooper over there, saw the lady greet him at the door. Totally his type. Well-built blonde…" I noticed the slight smirk he tried to hide.

"Uh-huh." I wasn't about to ask how he came by the rest of his information, but I suspected he had a friend on the force who illegally looked up the license plate and address for him. Before I could ask my next question, he explained his sourcing process.

"Of course, I jotted down the license number of the car in the driveway, which is registered in the name you gave me."

"And it matches the license number of the silver Mercedes that drove by Hooper's house?"

Marko paced around the office, stopping a few steps in front of me. "That's the problem."

"You don't have a match."

"Not yet."

"Am I correct in assuming you have a plan for obtaining this information and you want the okay from me?"

"You are correct."

"What's the plan?"

"Well, I was thinking about how all those fancy houses in Hooper's neighborhood have equally fancy security systems, including cameras, and…" Another Broadway shrug.

"And you plan to hack into somebody's web cam? No way."

"No. I haven't a clue how to hack into anything. I was thinking about stopping by their houses, telling the owners I work for a private investigative service and would like to request access to their security video for the early morning hours of Melody Knight's so-called suicide."

"What reason would any of these wealthy Hollywood residents grant that permission?"

"Well, I thought maybe we could offer a reward."

I nearly choked on his reward suggestion before sputtering, "What kind of reward do you have in mind?"

"Say, a thousand dollars?"

"Let me get this straight. You want me to provide a one-thousand-dollar reward for video of a silver Mercedes driving through one of the wealthiest sections of Beverly Hills, and you think these neighbors of Clive Hooper to whom a thousand dollars is like a ten-spot for you and me, will be sufficiently motivated to allow you to have a look at the video on their security cameras? Are you in your right mind?"

"I know a thousand dollars is a lot of money, but if it gets results…"

"Did you hear what I just said about motivation?"

"Rich people are no different than you and me, Polly, except for the fact that most of them are big-time cheapskates. They hate to spend a dime. The worst tippers at my barbecue joint are the ones with the most expensive clothes on their backs. My wait staff hates seein' them walk through the door and avoids 'em like the plague. For these people, a thousand dollars means more than it does to us. Trust me on that. They won't be able to pass it up, especially when it's no skin off their teeth to let me look at some video they care nothing about."

I tried to comprehend Marko's argument in order to respond point by point, but halfway through, I gave up. "First of all, I don't have an extra thousand lying around, and second, even if I did, rich people *are* different. They care about status and they'd be offended. So let's take the idea of a reward off the table."

Marko shook his head, but I provided him with a bone. "I like your idea of contacting these people, and I'll provide you with our business cards when you inform them who you're working for. That way it'll be up to your powers of persuasion, which I know you have as Rosa is proof, to talk them into cooperating with you. That's the best I can do. Come back with the information, and I'll pay you double for your time."

Marko perked up at the mention of double pay. "It's a deal, Polly, and I won't let you down. We're gonna nail that SOB for what he did to his poor wife."

"I hope so," I told him, unsure he even heard me as he made a beeline for the door.

What a day, I thought, gathering my belongings to leave. One more trip to the hospital to see Johnny, and then it was home to an empty house and a medium pizza with everything on it.

Well, everything except anchovies.

CHAPTER 35

Day 5:

M y visit with Johnny the previous night turned out to be uneventful, mostly because he seemed unaware of my presence. I sat by his bed holding his hand, talking to him now and then while he slept. Had something else happened to him? I wondered. He'd never slept this soundly in his life, at least to my knowledge. I went out to the nurses' station and asked about his status, even though I knew they wouldn't tell me much.

The woman manning the desk assured me he was doing fine and claimed his deep sleep was not unusual, especially if he hadn't slept much the night before. Sometimes, she said, day can turn into night and vice versa during a long hospital stay. In my mind, four days was not what I considered a long hospital stay, but I decided not to take issue with her.

Returning to Johnny's room, I hung around until seven-thirty or so before heading for home, checking along the way for any black SUVs that might be following me. Convinced I'd lost any tail had there been one, I stopped and picked up a pizza, figuring it was safer than home delivery. Too many crime stories involve phony deliverymen to suit me. In my current paranoid state of mind, I wasn't about to take chances.

The pizza I bought had satisfied my hunger cravings and the TV kept my mind occupied for a couple of hours before turning in for the night. But despite being exhausted, my awake mechanism failed to shut off until an hour or two after midnight, which I'd pay for later in the day. Thoughts of Lenny Spinoli, Ricky and Sally Martin, Clive Hooper and Melody Knight, two iffy federal agents, not to mention Bunny wandering around Santa Catalina Island, and Marko wandering off who knows where, all cycled through my brain like a virtual reality *Tour de France.*

Worse, my obsessive thought processes led me nowhere, except to doubt my analytical abilities, and not for the first time. At some point, I gave up, opting to sleep on it. Things always looked better in the morning, according to Mother, a saying my sister adopted and used on me regularly. For once, I tried it out on myself. The result was a fitful night's sleep punctuated by a series of anxiety dreams, but at least I slept.

I woke ten minutes before my alarm was set to go off, rolled out of bed, showered, and dressed in my traditional office attire—jeans, T-shirt, and a jacket, which I'd added for propriety's sake. Breakfast consisted of peanut butter and marmalade on an English muffin accompanied by two cups of joe, one cup for home, one for work. Coffee cup in hand, I slogged to my car through a fog of damp, turbid air.

A pall of smog separated LA from the morning sun. Fortunately, traffic was lighter than usual and, at two minutes past eight, I wandered into my office, still in a mental state that matched the outdoor gloom. My brain cleared slightly once I'd downed the top half of my second cup of smooth, black Costa Rican java, my current favorite brew.

Since I was the first person to arrive, I checked the answering machine, hoping to hear some good news from Bunny, and no bad news from Marko, but the recorded voice insisted on informing me of the absence of messages, which wasn't unusual. It's not like clients were clamoring for my services.

After thumbing through the morning pile of ads in our mailbox, I trotted into my office, made myself comfortable, and turned on my computer, before all hell broke loose.

The outside door banged open and slammed shut. "Polly!" a voice screeched. "Where are you?" my sister screamed, as if I was hiding under a barrel or something, which I used to do when we were kids playing hide and seek. She fell for it every time.

"In here, where else, and what the devil's the matter?"

Franny barreled into my office and nearly knocked me out of my chair. "It's Bunny!"

My first thought was that he'd turned up dead on Santa Catalina Island. Adrenalin shot through me with the force of a bullet. "What's happened to him?"

"That's just it. I don't know."

I could have choked her for scaring me like that. My heart was beating out of my chest, and I couldn't slow it down. I struggled to form enough words to populate my next sentence. "Then—why—are you so upset?"

"Because I've been trying to reach him since ten o'clock last night. We always FaceTime each other when we're apart so we can say good night, but he never answered last night when I called. I kept calling up until midnight and stopped because I was too tired and I knew there was nothing I could do until the morning. I kept

hoping that maybe he'd forgotten to charge his phone—"
She looked over at me with that "you know how he is"
look. "—but then I started calling him again this morning. Still can't reach him." Tears now streamed down her
cheeks as she grabbed me and hugged me. "What are we
going to do, Polly?"

I felt like crying myself. I had assumed Bunny had
left Santa Catalina for home like he said he would, and
that he and Franny had probably spent the night together,
which is the reason I didn't call and invite her to have
pizza with me. Barely able to breathe, I hugged my sister
as I tried to think of what to do and how to comfort her.
Comfort myself, too, for that matter because I was equally worried something had happened to Bunny. Everything
seemed to be going from bad to worse in the Martin investigation, and the Melody Knight fiasco was not pro-
ceeding much better. I was beginning to wish I'd become
a nurse like Franny. At least then I'd know how to clean
up other people's messes.

I dragged Franny over to the loveseat in my office
and sat her down. "Give me a minute to get my head together," I told her, as I ran through options in my head.

Number one, I could run over to Santa Catalina and
see if I could find out where Bunny was and why he'd
suddenly gone incommunicado. Two, I could send Marko, but that seemed like a dumb idea. Or three, I could
call Harry Barnes. He might be willing to go with me to
investigate, even though the island was outside his jurisdiction.

A fourth option existed, which I rejected out of
hand—placing a call to Joe Foster. The FBI had jurisdiction everywhere, and he did say he might send a team
over to the island, but what if Foster was an imposter and
somehow involved in Bunny's disappearance? I still
didn't know if he was legit. Maybe he'd gone to Santa

Catalina, found Bunny and the two tangled. The thought felt like a punch to the stomach, especially if my blabbering to Foster was responsible for jeopardizing Bunny's safety.

"I hope he's not dead," Franny whimpered, refusing to let go of me.

"He's not dead," I told her in as firm a voice as I could muster, but my brain was stuck in the opposite gear.

And that's when Marko arrived. Again.

CHAPTER 36

The outside door to my office banged open followed by Marko hollering my name at the top of his lungs.

Now here's the thing—my office suite has exactly two rooms, not very big rooms at that. Bunny's desk and two chairs sit in the outer office across from a couch with bad springs. In the alcove behind Bunny's desk we have a four-drawer file cabinet, supply cupboard, and a small closet. Next to the file cabinet is a door to our tiny bathroom, which I don't count as a room, and which contains the usual two mandatory items plus a showerhead in the ceiling and a drain in the middle of the floor. Prior to Franny moving to LA from western PA, Bunny often spent his nights at the office, a habit of his that went by the boards once he started dating my sister.

Kitty corner, or catty corner depending on where you're from, to the bathroom door is the door to my office, the point of all this being that if I'm not lounging on the couch across from Bunny's desk, which I seldom do, then odds are I'm ensconced inside my little office working on my computer, thus negating any need to scream my name in order to ascertain my presence. If my door is

closed, which is usually the case, a simple knock is sufficient to rouse me.

"Oh no," Franny moaned. "Marko. Just what we
need right now."

"I'll get rid of him," I told her, but before I could
move in that direction, Marko poked his head through the
door.

"Polly, you in there?"

"Come in, Marko. What's up?"

Marko bounded in, stopping cold when he spotted
my sister and me on the loveseat. "Are you sick, Franny?"

I struggled to my feet. "Bunny's missing, and we're
both upset about it."

"Oh, no. What happened to him?"

I couldn't resist stating the obvious. "If we knew, he
wouldn't be missing, would he?"

My comment flew over Marko's head, drifting into
the ether somewhere or more likely, in one ear and out
the other bypassing his brain along the way. I wasn't sure
which, since he next asked, "When did he go missing and
where?"

"We're not sure," I told him. "Sometime last night
and probably somewhere on Santa Catalina Island. We're
trying to figure out what to do about it."

"Hey, I can head over there and hunt him down for
you."

"It's a big island, but I'll keep that in mind. First, I
want to talk with Harry Barnes. Why are you barging in
here so early in the morning?"

Marko sauntered around my desk and parked himself
on my chair, feet splayed in our direction. I sat back
down. "Because I got lucky last night and not in the way
you're probably thinking, though—"

My eyebrow shot up before I could control it.

"We're not interested in an account of your love life. We know enough about that already."

He looked surprised. "From Rosa?"

Franny recovered enough to join the conversation. "You won't believe what she tells us," she told Marko, barely hiding a smile.

"Don't matter," he said, with a slight head shake. "It's all true."

I intervened. "Let's get to the point here, shall we?"

"Sure. You're gonna love this, Polly. You might want to hire me full-time when you hear."

"I can barely afford to pay you part-time, but go ahead."

Marko puffed out his chest like a sage grouse in full mating display. "I found the smoking gun that proves Clive Hooper murdered his wife."

At that, Franny bolted upright, and I laid back on the loveseat hoping my business wasn't about to face a lawsuit over some privacy violation, trespass charges, or other illegal transgression by Marko in his zealous attempt to gather evidence against Clive Hooper. His declaration rendered me speechless, a feat that rarely happens. At some point, I recovered enough to address my worries. "Dare I ask how you came by this smoking gun?"

Marko drew his feet back, tucking them under my desk chair. I hoped he hadn't planned on appropriating that chair every time we met. Leaning forward, he looked from me to Franny and back. "Let me begin," he began, glancing between us again, "by saying it didn't take no thousand-dollar reward to loosen lips, only my charming personality."

I exhaled the breath I was holding. "As long as everything was done on the up and up, nothing illegal, I'm okay with it." I wanted to remind him that if he *had* crossed the line, not to tell me about it. I needed to maintain plausible deniability or risk losing my license.

"I'm not a criminal, Polly, despite what some warped political candidate might think based on my ethnicity."

"Let's not go there right now and also, try to speed this up. We need to find Bunny, which at this moment is more important than your smoking gun. So, to paraphrase you, what did you find and where did you find it?"

"I got the license plate number of the silver Mercedes from Hopper's next-door neighbor's security camera. As we suspected it belongs to the girlfriend, but guess who was behind the wheel at five o'clock in the morning?"

The answer was obvious. "Clive Hooper."

"You win the door prize," Marko said, clearly in wise-guy mode.

"And you know this, how?"

"Same video. And this neighbor's place was only the second one I visited. The nice lady of the house gave me access when I explained what it was all about."

I held my breath again. "Okay, but, don't tell me anything else. Here's what we're going to do. I'm giving Harry Barnes a call—"

"There's more, Polly."

"Save it for Harry. I'm afraid if you blab too much to too many people, we'll somehow be prejudicing the case before it comes to trial."

"Okay, but I did good, didn't I?"

He'd done a lot better than I'd expected and apparently without crossing the fine legal line. I was proud of him. "You win the door prize," I told him. "I just don't know at this point what that door prize is, but I'll think of something."

I went back to my office and placed a call to Harry Barnes, who said he was just about to call me.

CHAPTER 37

"Good news, Polly," Harry said, answering my call.

"About Johnny?"

"No. Sorry, I haven't been to the hospital yet this morning. Stopped by to see him a little after eight last night, but he was sleeping so I only stayed for a few minutes."

"I just missed seeing you, then. I left about a half hour earlier. He never woke up while I was there, either, and I'm worried about him. What's the good news?"

"Your two FBI agents are legit. Work out of Lancaster. I'll email their pics so you can be certain, but that should relieve your mind."

"Thanks, Harry. I appreciate your taking time to check them out for me. I'm just hoping I recognize their faces."

Until I saw the photos for myself, I still had doubts. Anybody could look up the names and station of two agents.

"What'd you call about, Polly?"

"Two things. First, I'd like to send Marko down to the station to talk with you if have time."

"I'll be here."

"He did a little detecting on his own and found some

interesting material on the Clive Hooper investigation. I won't spoil the surprise for you."

"Send him over."

I waved my hands at Marko motioning him to leave. He responded with a salute, which I found funny. "He's on his way. I think you'll appreciate the evidence he's uncovered, and as far as I know, his methods were legal."

"Good. And the second thing?"

"Bunny's disappeared from the radar as of ten o'clock last night. Maybe earlier, we don't know. Still haven't been able to contact him this morning."

"On Santa Catalina?"

"As far as we know."

"It's out of my jurisdiction, but I can make a few calls."

I hesitated to request another favor, but this was Bunny we were talking about. "I hate to ask this, Harry, but would you be willing to go over there with me and see what we can find out?"

"I'd like to say yes, Polly, but that might cause problems for both of us. Tell you what I *will* do, and that is give a call to the Avalon Sheriff's Station. They police the island. I'll explain the situation and ask them to help you out. I'm not sure it's a good idea for you to go over there alone or even at all, so be sure you check in with them first and don't start snooping around on your own. Whoever killed Lenny Spinoli may still be on the island."

"I can take care of myself, Harry. Franny'll stay here and watch the office if you need anything, but I'll keep my cell on."

"Okay. I'll call Avalon right now and get back to you."

I thanked Harry and turned back to my sister. "Harry can't go to Santa Catalina with me, but the Avalon Sheriff's Department patrols the island. Harry's giving them a call and asking for help. He said he'd call me back with the name of a contact. Will you be okay manning the office alone?"

Franny wiped her eyes. Her voice sounded so small I could barely hear her. "I'll be all right. Just keep me posted, okay?"

"I will and don't worry. It could be anything. Maybe Bunny stumbled across a clue and is carrying out some kind of surveillance, has his phone turned off so it doesn't ring and give away his presence or his location. There's some logical explanation behind this, I'm sure. We just don't know it yet, but that's why I'm headed over to the Island. If Bunny does call, let me know right away, okay?"

"Okay. What about Marko?"

"Right. He'll probably come back here to report on his meeting with Harry. If you're more comfortable having him around for company, then ask him to stay. Let him know he can bill for the hours."

"Thanks, Polly. I might do that. Although I'd rather have Rosa for company than Marko."

"I understand. Then go ahead and ask her. She'll close up her place in a heartbeat if she thinks you need her. Let her know we'll reimburse her for lost revenue."

"Okay, Polly. You be careful, though. I don't want to have to worry about you *and* Bunny."

"Then don't worry until there's something to worry about. Bunny left a lot of papers to file as usual. You can clean up some of that for him if it helps keep your mind busy."

"Okay, though I think I've got most of that done."

I couldn't think of anything else, so I dragged my purse out of the desk drawer and headed into the bathroom. When I came out, Franny was holding the phone out to me. Harry was on the line.

"Thanks for calling me back, Harry. How'd it go?"

"Good. Nice fellas in the sheriff's department over there. When you arrive at the Avalon Station, ask for Doug Vetter. He's your contact. Oh, and I sent the pics of Foster and Peters. Check your email."

"Thanks, Harry. You're a gem." After hanging up, I took a minute to look up the Avalon Sheriff's Department website. On the front page was a picture of Doug Vetter who'd won some kind of exemplary service award. He looked like a good guy, if you could tell from a picture, and I thought I could. Next I checked my email, opening the message from Harry and studying the pics he'd sent of Foster and Peters. They were legit after all, which turned out to be an even bigger relief than I'd anticipated. One more item I could scratch off my worry list.

I wondered if I should call Foster and tell him about Bunny going missing on Santa Catalina, but decided to wait until after I'd made contact with Doug Vetter. I wanted to avoid finding myself in the middle of a turf battle between agencies, and I sure wasn't up for Foster telling me he'd handle the matter and I should stay out of it, the typical alpha male response I'd expect from him.

Been there done that. Not in the mood to go that route again.

CHAPTER 38

I left the office and headed home to pack an overnight bag for the trip to Santa Catalina, hoping I wouldn't run into trouble finding a hotel room once I got there. I was so worried about Bunny and what I might find on the island, I totally forgot to watch for tails on the drive home.

Arriving at my house, I decided against leaving my car in the driveway. Before pulling in, I checked my rear-view mirror, noting the color and style of the few cars behind me. I did the same for cars coming toward me, though I spotted only two in the distance, which passed by quickly never giving me so much as a sideways glance. Having surveyed my surroundings, I hit the automatic garage door opener and pulled my car inside. The garage door closed behind me, hitting the ground with a thud, one more item I needed to add to my fix-it list.

Unsnapping my seat belt, I jumped out and moved to the window in the side door to check on whether any car within sight had pulled to the curb, turned around in a neighbor's driveway, or slowed as it passed my house. Deciding I should keep a written record and not rely on my faulty memory cells, I took out my phone, opened a notes app, and typed in the color and style of every car passing by my house over the next ten minutes.

Fortunately, I live in a residential neighborhood where traffic is light, so the task wasn't as monumental as it sounds. My ten-minute list contained twenty-two cars with no duplicates, meaning no car passed by twice since I starting watching. Feeling relieved, I returned to my car, removed my purse, tucked the phone back in its pocket, and sauntered through the adjoining door into my kitchen, which still smelled like pizza from the previous night. I was almost hungry again. I walked over to the sink reminding myself to drink more water. After downing eight ounces, I dumped the rest of the water along with some ice cubes, into my fancy Sport Line Hydra-Coach water bottle, Bunny's last year's Christmas gift to me.

I left the water bottle and a bag of pistachio nuts on the kitchen table and went back to my bedroom to pack, stopping for a quick peek out my front window where nothing seemed to have changed, at least when it came to noticeable surveillance in the immediate vicinity of my house. The thought gave me pause. Had someone put a tracker on my car? I needed to check before I left for Santa Catalina. Packing took me about two minutes since I planned on only one overnight stay, if that, which meant toothbrush, toothpaste, pajamas, and a change of clothes for the next day. Any decent hotel would have the remaining items I might need.

Bag packed, I hustled my bod out to the kitchen, left my bag on the counter, and made tracks for the garage and the cabinet where I store my professional technical surveillance counter-measure devices. I'd previously relied on a flashlight and a magnet attached to a long stick that allowed me to sweep the whole underbelly of my car. That system works to snoop out the cheap trackers amateurs use, mostly to spy on cheating spouses or significant others. Unfortunately, I learned the hard way that professional PIs need professional tools, so I bit the bullet and invested.

My trusty tracker finder turned up nothing. The car was as clean as a surgical ward unless someone somewhere—I had the FBI in mind here—had equipment so technologically sophisticated as to render my expensive tool useless.

Was I worried or relieved that I'd found nothing? A bit of both. I headed back into the house where I dug a burn phone out of my desk and called a friend for a ride, asking her to meet me at Wendy's on the corner of Sunset and North La Brea in thirty minutes.

Next, I phoned Franny and asked her to get Marko to drive her over to Ralph's Grocery on Sunset, where she was to go inside and meet me near the ladies room.

"When Marko drives you to the market," I told her, "ask him to drop you as close to the front door as possible. Also, grab my raincoat out of the closet and put it on before you leave the office. If there's a scarf or hat in the closet or if Rosa has one, put it on as well. When you go out to Marko's car, try to avoid letting anyone see you leave the building."

"What's this all about, Polly?"

"I'm taking some extra precautions, making sure no one follows me on my trip to Santa Catalina. To that end, you and I are going to change identities at Ralph's. I'm giving you my car keys because you'll be driving yourself back to the office in my car, but I'd like Marko to stay right behind you all the way."

"I'm not going to get kidnapped again, am I, Polly?"

"Of course not. Even if someone is following me around, it's likely the FBI keeping tabs on me. You have nothing to worry about. They just want to know where I am and what I'm doing. Problem is, I don't want Joe Foster to know I'm going to Santa Catalina, at least I don't want him to know *yet*."

"Okay, I'm trusting you on this, Polly, but you know Bunny will madder than a wet hen if something happens to me."

"That's the least of my worries right now. You want me to find Bunny and bring him back safe and sound, right?"

"Of course."

"Then you have a part to play too, and that part is decoy. Are we good?"

"We are."

"Okay, then. I'll see you inside Ralph's in twenty minutes."

I hung up, tucked the burner in my pocket, and left my cell phone on the kitchen table in case some unknown person might be pinging my phone. If so, they could rest assured I was hiding out at home.

Tasks done, I returned to the bedroom and grabbed my black wig, a pair of tight black jeans and, much as I hated to do it, a pair of black Christian Louboutin heels. I stuffed them into my overnight bag, hoping I wouldn't have to sacrifice my shoes to the cause.

Remembering the clothes Franny wore to the office that morning, I tried to match her outfit from my closet, which wasn't hard to do. We pretty much wear the same colors and our casual styles are similar as well. It's just that Franny dresses up a lot more than I do, and wears more makeup, so I visited the bathroom to work on my face, Franny style—eye shadow, eyeliner, mascara, lipstick, the works. Next, I pulled my hair into the sideways ponytail Franny likes to wear, different from me, who opts for the old-fashioned back of the head style.

Once I'd finished and glanced in the mirror I felt I was looking at Franny and not at me. Job well done, I thought, congratulating myself on the quick makeover. Satisfied no one would be able to tell Franny and me apart, I climbed back in my car and headed over to Ralph's Grocery. Halfway there, I could swear a black SUV was sticking a little too close to my tail. I smiled to myself and even slowed down a bit to make it easier on whichever uptight feeb might be behind the wheel. I hoped the driver was a woman by the name of Adrienne Peters. I figured she'd pay more attention to my outfit than a man might.

I was feeling better about this plan already.

CHAPTER 39

I pulled into the parking lot at Ralph's Grocery and drove to a vacant spot a little farther from the front door than I ordinarily might have chosen. I wanted to ensure my FBI shadow caught a good glimpse of me entering the store. The only glitch in my plan might occur if she, or he, decided to come inside instead of wait in the car until I left the store, but I doubted that would happen. Too easy to lose sight of your prey.

Inside Ralph's, I cruised by the ladies restroom to see if Franny had arrived ahead of me, but she was nowhere in sight. I grabbed a can of hair spray and a bottle of shampoo from a nearby shelf and headed for the checkout counter where I could keep an eye on people entering without raising any suspicions. If Adrienne Peters had been tailing me, I knew she wouldn't risk coming in, but the windows of the SUV were so dark I had no idea whether she was indeed the driver. Whoever it was, they stayed a good distance back, clearly hoping I wouldn't notice them. Wrong.

Franny came through the door just as the clerk put my receipt in the bag. My sister spotted me immediately, but pretended she hadn't. *Nice play, twinny*, I thought, as I asked the cashier where to find the bathrooms then set my bag back on the counter. "Do you mind if I leave my bag here?"

"No problem," she said. "I'll keep an eye on it for you."

I thanked her and made my way straight to the ladies room. Since Franny was nowhere to be found, I assumed she preceded me into the restroom, and my assumption was correct. As soon as I entered, she folded me into a huge hug as if she hadn't seen me in years instead of less than an hour ago.

"Oh, Polly, I'm so worried. I'm just not sure you should be going to Santa Catalina alone. What if whoever grabbed Bunny, grabs you? What will I do?"

"We'll set up a code, don't worry. If I'm in trouble, I'll text you, and you can call Harry Barnes." I handed her a piece of paper. "Here's the number of my burner. If you hear anything, or have questions, call me. Now, let's change our clothes and get out of here. I'll put your hat and raincoat in my bag and as soon as I change, I'll dump my clothes in your bag."

Before I'd finished my sentence, Franny took hold of my shoulders and held me away from her. "Oh, my gosh, Polly, you look just like me. I haven't had that mirror experience for a long time now."

"Me neither, now let me change."

I entered the large stall at the end of the row. By the time I emerged with my new casual starlet style, Franny had removed her hat and raincoat. She held the items out for me and I stuffed them in my bag, handing back my jeans and the shirt I'd worn when I walked in from my car. She switched out my shirt for hers and we were done, both of us proud of our efforts.

Franny surveyed my new look—tight jeans and Louboutins, the latter of which added four inches to my height. "Wow, Polly. You look great, but can you walk in those?"

"I only have two blocks to go. I think I can make it. Now let's move, and don't forget to stop and pick up the bag I left with the cashier. It has a can of hair spray and a bottle of shampoo, which you can keep if you can use it since they're more your style than mine."

"You haven't told me yet what you're planning to do."

"After you leave, I'll wait a few minutes, watching from inside the store to see if anyone besides Marko follows you. If I spot someone, I'll give you enough time to get back to the office, then call you and let you know the who and what. You can tell Marko he's been hired as your new bodyguard. He won't mind that a bit. Once the coast is clear here, I'll head down to Wendy's where a cab is meeting me in about ten minutes. So get going."

Franny gave me another hug and kissed my cheek. "Keep in touch," she said, more a plea than an order.

I waited five minutes or so before leaving the restroom and dawdling along the aisles as I wended my way to the front of the store. I arrived at the front door in time to see Franny back my car out of the parking spot and pull away. Marko's blue Ford Focus left right behind her and less than twenty seconds later, a black SUV joined the line waiting to turn right onto Sunset Boulevard.

Even though I seldom curse even to myself, I whispered a few choice phrases directed at the driver of that black SUV as I waited for it to disappear down Sunset. Once the car was out of sight I hustled along the sidewalk three blocks in the opposite direction to Wendy's. Inside the restaurant, I bought a diet Coke, more to assuage my conscience for using their restroom than to satisfy my thirst. I changed back into my work shirt and shoes and sat at a booth by the window waiting for my ride.

I'd barely seated myself when the female Uber driver I'd contacted pulled up to the front door. The driver's name was La-Shonna Johnson, and she was someone I've known since my Holy Death case five years earlier, so I'd felt comfortable calling her. If she hadn't been available, I suppose I would have walked the mile and a half to the rent-a-car place, but why walk when I can ride?

As soon as she spotted me, La-Shonna reached over and swung open the passenger side door, greeting me with her usual, "Hey, girl, how you been?"

I climbed into the front seat and reached over for a hug, also her usual. "Not that great, actually," I grumbled, handing her the address of the rental car agency a mile and a half away, not a fare worthy of her time. I felt guilty. "I know it's a short hop, but I'll pay you double."

"Don't worry about it," she shrugged. "I jack up my rates for short rides, the shorter the distance, the higher the price, kinda like the airlines do. You know what I mean?"

I'd traveled enough to know she spoke the truth. "I do know."

"But I've got another question for you."

"Which is?"

"Why you gonna rent a car from one of these agencies when I can drive you anywhere you want to go?"

The idea of hiring La-Shonna to drive me down to Long Beach simply hadn't occurred to me. However, now that I thought it, by the time I paid the daily rental car rate and the parking fees at the ferry station, I'd be looking at a couple of hundred dollars for probably no more than a twenty-four hour stay. Confronted with the financial realty of the situation, the decision was a no-brainer. "You're on La-Shonna. That is, if you have time to drive me to the ferry in Long Beach, and then come pick me up some time tomorrow."

"No problem, lady," she said, turning the car around. "Why didn't you think of that in the first place?"

I gave her a limp excuse about finding myself in a time crunch with little opportunity to plan, adding, "I did the first thing that came to mind."

"Yeah. Operating on automatic. I know the feeling."

"I appreciate your suggestion, which I should have thought of on my own. You're a lifesaver," I told her, beginning to relax as we pulled onto the 101 and headed down to Long Beach.

Now, I thought, if only I can be the life-saver Bunny needs.

CHAPTER 40

The 101 east merged into the 710, taking us straight south to Long Beach. Traffic moved along at its usual noontime pace—anything from a slow crawl to borderline suicidal if you're from out of town and unfamiliar with our 'stop or slam the pedal to the metal' traffic flow patterns. The disappearing lanes—right hand lanes that turned into exit lanes before you had time to adjust—used to drive Franny crazy when she first moved out here. But she adapted, eventually. We all do.

La-Shonna handled the traffic like the expert she is, relieving me of backseat driver responsibilities. Instead, I let my thoughts wander, thinking about Johnny and whether he'd ever be well, and what would happen to us either way.

I felt guilty for experiencing a certain sense of freedom since he'd been hospitalized. What kind of person was I? I wondered. Not that I was happy at what happened to him—exactly the opposite. My heart broke every time I thought of him sitting in his chair in that stupid blue hospital gown, looking so unlike the tough Hollywood detective I'd known and loved. I still loved him and that was the problem. I loved him too much to lose him, but not enough to marry him.

I could feel my eyes filling with tears, which I tried to hide from La-Shonna's watchful eyes. I covered with a fake coughing fit.

La-Shonna glanced over. "You okay?"

"Yeah, something in the air." I reached for my water bottle and took a few swallows. La-Shonna handed me a tissue from the pack in the console.

I blew my nose and leaned back, supporting my neck on the headrest. Closing my eyes, I shut out thoughts of Johnny and let my mind drift back to when I first met La-Shonna. She went by the name of Mama Cass, and worked as a security guard for a local LA business. She saved my life. In the five years since that trauma-filled first meeting, she'd managed to finally divorce her husband, a white surfer dude by the name of Bobby Cass, who thought his wife should serve as his private punching bag.

She'd fought him off the first time it happened. Gave him a black eye and said she'd kill him if he ever hit her again. Seems he didn't believe her. Came home one night fizzed up and lunged at her. She reached for her service revolver and warned him off. Instead of taking the hint, he grabbed a baseball bat and went after her. As a result, he ended his surfing days with a shattered left knee from the bullet in his wife's Glock. Last I heard of him, he was making custom boards for a Manhattan Beach surf shop.

After the divorce, La-Shonna returned to her maiden name, Johnson. I learned her legitimate first name when we had dinner a week following the trial of the perp who tried to kill me, and whom she'd taken down. I addressed her as Helen, which was the name her bad-guy colleague Jimmy GeeJay used during his aborted attempt on my life.

According to La-Shonna, he used to refer to her as Hell-on-Wheels, which he shortened to Helen. She told me she put up with the name because he had a temper and she had to work with the guy.

"I tried to keep my distance and my mouth shut," she explained, when the name issue rose. "The less I had to do with that creep the better. I didn't care what he called me as long as he left me alone."

"Well, neither of us has to worry about seeing him again," I told her, "thanks to his fifteen-to-life sentence in Corcoran."

La-Shonna grinned and shook her head. "One nasty hell-hole that is. I'm not sure I'd wish it even on him. He's a cream puff compared to the inmates there."

Since it was my life the creep tried to end, I wasn't all that sympathetic about his incarceration in one of the most dangerous prisons in the world. Last news I'd read about the place, some prisoner killed his roommate and eviscerated the body, which started a riot. The guards never found the victim's innards, leading me and everyone else to believe the roommate probably made a pâté out of them for a midnight snack.

At this point, La-Shonna stirred me from my unpleasant reveries. "You're kinda quiet today."

"Thinking about Bunny," I lied. "I sent him over to Santa Catalina on a case, and now he's missing. I'm headed over there to find him."

"By yourself?" She sounded indignant.

"Well, Harry Barnes gave me the name of a deputy sheriff over there. I'm supposed to contact him when I land and—"

"Sounds like a bad idea to me, you travelin' over there without your own muscle. You're right about not plannin' for this operation, but I'm gonna help you out. We're goin' over there together and do a little investigatin' on our own before you meet up with some pantywaist deputy sheriff probably scared of his own shadow in a dark alley."

Another good idea that escaped me, I thought. "Are you sure you have time? What about your business?"

"I got a backup. My sister. I'll call her when we get to Long Beach. My next pickup's at four o'clock, but I know she can take it. Same for tomorrow. She's free, so my time is your time."

"Thanks, La-Shonna. I can use your help. I'm really worried about Bunny."

"I hope you're packin'."

"Always," I told her, "what about you?"

She nodded at the glove compartment. "Always."

"Make sure it's not loaded before we get to the ferry or we'll be in trouble."

"No problem."

The twenty-nine-mile ride to Long Beach took just under an hour, which if my math is correct, meant we averaged about thirty miles an hour. Not bad considering we were traveling in the middle of the day, one of the busier travel times if you don't count morning and evening rush hours.

Arriving in Long Beach, we were greeted with the smell of rotten eggs, an occasional occurrence when hydrogen sulfide bubbles up and enters the water supply. Officials claim it's not harmful. Maybe so, but I plan to stick to Diet Coke if I'm thirsty before we board the ferry.

The view out my window wasn't the prettiest seaside scape, either. Long Beach is a shipping town not a coastal resort. The second busiest container port in the US and one of the largest shipping ports in the world, according to Wikipedia, and if anybody knew, I supposed the Wiki people did. That fact, combined with the oil and manufacturing industries, tells you most of want you need to know about the place. I haven't spent much time there, mostly because there are better beaches, and I couldn't care less about auto racing.

Bunny on the other hand, heads down every April for the Long Beach Grand Prix. I attended the race once, in 2007, when it was still known as the Champ Car World Series. I came in hopes of catching a glimpse of Paul Newman. His team won that year, the last year they entered the race. Newman's driver was an easy-on-the-eyes Frenchman by the name of Sébastien Bourdais, whom I also wouldn't have minded running into.

As for the two-mile race, it was noisy and boring, but since I'm not a fan, my reaction probably doesn't count for much. Fortunately, I'd brought along a pair of professional binoculars that I use for work, so at least I could see Newman up close if not personal. I wouldn't say Bourdais rivaled his actor boss in the looks department, but he did have an appealing nerdy-guy look about him. Maybe it was the eyeglasses. He reminded me of an airline pilot more than a racecar driver, which for me was a point in his favor.

"Here we are," La-Shonna announced as we landed in downtown Long Beach and wended our way to the Santa Catalina Sea and Air Terminal, guided by the voice of Aretha, my driver's trusty built-in GPS lady. Clearly, I wasn't the only person who names their guidance system. Mine is Theresa, for reasons even I don't know.

"Ever wonder," I asked La-Shonna, "why the GPS voices in cars belong to a woman and not a man? I mean, given the sexism and misogyny in the world today, how did a lady land that job?"

La-Shonna shrugged. "Easy. Men hate asking directions, but nothing grabs their attention faster than a sexy female voice. You know any better reason?"

I had to admit I couldn't think of one.

CHAPTER 41

I found myself almost looking forward to the one-hour cruise over to the island. Every year, I try to schedule a couple of weekend getaways on Santa Catalina. The place reminds me of a mini-Hawaii, but without the five-hour plane ride. I could see La-Shonna wasn't sharing my feelings. When we stepped onto the Starship Express, a high-speed catamaran with the look of a drug lord's yacht, she grabbed my arm.

"Maybe this isn't such a good idea," she said.

I tried not to sound surprised. "You can turn around and go home, pick me up tomorrow if you want. I won't hold it against you. Things could get dicey if Bunny's in hot water."

"It's not that. I can't swim, and I'm deathly afraid of the water."

"Don't worry. You'll be fine. Follow me." Fortunately, I'd paid the fifteen dollars for an upgrade, and I led her up to the Commodore Lounge where the seats were large enough to comfortably accommodate La-Shonna's generous proportions.

Before we climbed the stairs, I told her, "I think you'll like it in the lounge up here, but if you still want to leave, you have time."

She grabbed my hand. "Nope. I can do this."

I led her to what is known in proper sea terminology as the ladder, but it looked like a solid set of stairs to me. I moved in front of her and placed her hand on the railing. "Hang on and take the stairs one at a time."

Since we had priority boarding, we were the first to arrive in the lounge. I knew once we'd each had a drink and some food, she'd calm down and enjoy the ride.

"Do you mind sitting here?" I asked, pointing to the blue two-seater by the window in the third row. I liked a window seat and I suspected La-Shonna would be happier sitting on the aisle.

"Sure, that's fine, but you take the window," she said, as I stuffed my bag in the overhead compartment.

"No problem." I glanced around at the spacious seating. "Wouldn't it be nice if the airlines gave you this much room?"

"They do," La-Shonna said, ever the realist. "It's called First Class and it costs a heck of a lot more than fifteen bucks."

We took our seats and I checked on La-Shonna's well-being. "You okay?"

"Yeah, pretty much. I'm gonna trust you on this. By the way, where are the life preservers? Aren't they usually hanging on the walls?"

"In the compartments over our heads. And did you mean the bulkheads?"

"The what?"

I couldn't resist, know-it-all that I am. "The walls on boats are called bulkheads, halls are passageways, the floor's the deck, and the stairs are called ladders."

"Well, listen to you. You get all that from your English teacher mama?"

"No, from Johnny, on our very first ferry ride. I should have known then not to marry him."

La-Shonna guffawed, which set me laughing, too. I hoped maybe her fears were subsiding. I'd never seen her afraid before, especially after watching her stand up to a gun-wielding perp, which I knew she would do again in a heartbeat. In that respect, she reminded me of my grandfather, a tough cop in Upstate New York who'd wade into a bar fight in a hot minute, smacking the soft part of the combatants' upper arms with his blackjack, sufficient to cause pain but leaving no visible injury. On the other hand, the sight of a tiny spider made him cringe, much to my grandmother's glee when she came to his aid, catching the scary invader and returning it to the great outdoors.

Before we left port, safety instructions blared from the overhead speakers, relieving some of La-Shonna's anxieties, though my worry levels increased when I saw a clean-cut guy in his early thirties enter the lounge and glance around before taking a seat somewhere in back of us. He wore khakis and a golf shirt, typical dress for feeb field agents. Maybe my covert exit strategies hadn't worked after all.

But how could they not, short of inserting a tracker on my person or bugging my phone, which wasn't the case because I'd swept the office that morning? My purse. I looked down at the purse parked in my lap. My favorite purse, the same one I carried to lunch with Joe Foster. I almost cried.

I lowered my voice. "Don't look over at me," I told La-Shonna, "but I just spotted a problem."

I barely heard her mumble, "Uh-huh. I spotted him, too. Looks like a fed to me."

"Yup. I think there's a tracker in my purse. If I can't find this bug, I'll have to ditch this bag once we get to the island. I'll remove the things I need and give them to you, surreptitiously, if we can do it."

"No problem." La-Shonna stretched and yawned, like she was about to take a nap, distracting anyone watching from seeing me dive into my pocketbook to remove my wallet and burner phone. At least my car keys were safe with Franny. The rest of the junk I'd leave in the purse even if I had to abandon it, since most of it consisted of tissues, grocery store coupons, receipts, and various and sundry restaurant keepsakes, like packs of matches I'd never use.

Fortunately, La-Shonna had opted to keep her purse with her instead of stashing it in the overhead bin for which I was glad, especially when I watched from the corner of my eye as she palmed my wallet and slipped it into her bag in one slick move worthy of a pickpocket on the streets of Rome.

"Why don't you take your purse to the little girls' room and hunt for the bug?" La-Shonna asked.

D'oh. Why hadn't I thought of that on my own? I seemed to be suffering one brain cramp after another these days, which I decided to blame on my supreme anxiety over Bunny's whereabouts and condition.

"On my way," I told La-Shonna, sidling past her. "Let me know what happens."

Inside the restroom, I scoured through my purse, sure enough finding a tiny transmitter at the bottom, no doubt compliments of Joe Foster during our lunch date. I pulled out the bug, spit on it for good measure, and stuffed it in my pocket. Instead of returning to my seat after washing my hands, I climbed down to the lower deck and strolled around, trying to spot a second FBI agent, because they always seemed to travel in pairs.

I'm good at remembering faces. However, the Starship Express, which was about half full, had a capacity of three hundred passengers. My memory's not that good. What I did instead was focus on stereotypes—buttoned-up feebs types and what in my warped mind constituted assassin types—just in case a killer instead of the feds was responsible for the tracker in my purse. I found more of the latter type than the former, making me realize clean-cut must be out of fashion.

When I returned to the lounge, La-Shonna informed me our friend hadn't moved out of his seat. No surprise, but it meant to me that I'd messed up when it came to identifying his accomplice on the lower deck. I'd also missed the snack and drink I'd paid for with my fifteen-dollar upgrade, not that it mattered. Anxiety has a way of killing my appetite.

"See anything downstairs?" La-Shonna asked.

"Too many people. I walked over the whole dang boat," I told her. "Picked out a few people to remember, but by and large came up empty. If our friend has a col-league, it's probably a woman." And she sure wouldn't be Adrienne Peters, I thought, since the agency knew I'd spot her in a New York minute.

"Your turn to hit the head," I told La-Shonna. "We'll be busy once we land on the Island."

I watched with some amusement at La-Shonna's un-steady progress to the ladies' room. I hoped she'd recover her equilibrium once we went ashore, but I could tell she was fighting to keep down the snack she'd just devoured.

The only question now, I thought, when La-Shonna returned a few minutes later looking a little less green than when she'd left, was whether to ditch the tracker on the ship or wait until we got ashore, a decision that ab-sorbed my attention for the remainder of our hour-long trip.

CHAPTER 42

My watch read four thirty-three when we disembarked from the ferry. La-Shonna and I held hands as we sashayed down the gangplank. I didn't know whether she was hanging onto me or I was hanging onto her. In any case, we both landed on the dock in a standing position, which I considered a win.

I still had the tracking device in my pocket, figuring if I left it on the ship when I went ashore, the feebs would quickly know I'd found their bug. At least I wasn't in the position of having to sacrifice my purse in order to lose our tail. And, I'd come up with what I thought was a good idea when it came to losing the tracker.

"Where we goin' from here?" La-Shonna asked.

"Just follow me," I said. "This isn't my first rodeo."

I reached into my purse for the map of Avalon I'd downloaded before leaving my office. La-Shonna hung over my shoulder as I pointed out the Botanical Gardens at the top of the map.

"As you can see," I told her, "almost everything, including the sheriff's station, is within walking distance, which is both a blessing and a curse. However, we'll be hiring a taxi and taking it up to the Botanical Gardens, where, if no one followed us, I'll get out long enough to toss the tracker into one of the gardens. Then we'll ask the driver to take us on a tour of every street in town hoping to find some sign of Bunny. You take one side of the street, I'll take the other—and, by sign, I mean we'll be looking for the bike Bunny rented. It's one of a kind, Bunny told me."

"Figures," La-Shonna said. "Bunny's one of a kind."

"True. Anyway, it's painted in a pink leopard-skin print."

La-Shonna stared at me like I was the crazy person who chose the design. "Who'd do that?"

"I don't know, but if we find the bike, they're in for a big reward. I know it's a long shot, but it's a place to start."

"What about stopping at the sheriff's department first?"

"Too risky. They might tell us to get back on the boat and let them handle it. Also, it's one of the first places the feebs will look for me. If we don't find the bike, then we can make a decision about checking in with the sheriff. Are you with me on this?"

"Of course, girlfriend. Otherwise, I wouldn't be here, tryin' to protect your precious butt."

కుసిం

I hired the nearest driver who looked like he'd just come in from a day at the beach, which he probably had. Baggy shorts and a wrinkled T-shirt hardly made for a professional look, but this was island living. On the plus side, he said he was available for the rest of the day and into the evening if necessary, and his hourly rate was reasonable.

"Great," I told him. "We'd like a sightseeing tour of the whole town starting with the Botanical Gardens."

He shrugged. "Most people just walk the streets. Good exercise and the town's not that big, but I'm good with it."

His comment irritated the heck out of me. "If you don't want the job, I can look elsewhere. We need a reliable driver, not a fitness guru."

"You're lookin' at the most reliable driver on the island. Not bragging or anything, but I used to drive for a racing team in Long Beach."

Just what I needed—a braggart beach bum, fitness guru, and former Formula One driver all rolled into one. "Okay, you're on," I said, hoping I wouldn't regret my decision.

La-Shonna climbed into the car, opting for the rear passenger side seat. I sat behind the driver who still had sand in his hair from his morning outing.

"Name's Dax," he said, reaching around and shaking hands with La-Shonna.

"Helen," she told him, which made me smile.

He turned back and extended a hand to me. "Polly," I told him, adding, "And no, I don't want a cracker."

No-last-name Dax started the car. "Wasn't even goin' there," he said, clearly miffed. "So, Wrigley Gardens first?"

"Yup." I felt for the tracker in my pocket, hoping to find a spot to leave it that would make things difficult when the feebs went looking for me. Maybe I'd find a cool-looking tree to hide it in, or a thick patch of prickly shrubs, or better yet, a Southern Pacific rattlesnake nest. I was feeling none too kindly toward my friend Joe Foster, whose ears should be burning. If not now, they would be on fire next time I met up with him.

La-Shonna interrupted my revenge plans with, "Wow, this place is beautiful."

Surely, this wasn't her first trip to Santa Catalina, a small paradise less than two hours from her home. "You've never been here before?"

"Nope. My first visit, but I'm comin' back."

"I take a trip here every year," I told her, not to brag, but to share my enjoyment of the place. "Reminds me of Hawaii without the travel time. I can't believe you haven't found an opening in your schedule."

"It's not that." She looked away from the window and turned her eyes on me. "Your world and mine are different," she said. "For me and my friends, this island is pure honkeyville."

That thought never occurred to me, and I felt sad and a little guilty. I wasn't sure what to say, so settled for a cliché. "I understand."

She turned back to the window. "If I thought about this place at all, I figured I'd feel too out of place to enjoy myself. I mean, look around. What do you see?"

I decided to humor her. "Quaint shops and gorgeous mountains set against an iridescent blue sea."

"What I see is very few people who look like me."

"True, but what I know of you," I said, no doubt failing to adequately comprehend her emotions, "with your big personality, kind heart, and a smile that melts ice cubes, you'd fit in anywhere."

La-Shonna guffawed loud enough for Dax to glance in his rear-view mirror. "Well, listen to you, Ms. Psych Professor, but I appreciate the compliments even if you did forget to mention my talent for taking down bad guys."

"I wasn't psychoanalyzing you, just hoping this visit might change your mind about a beautiful place."

"It might," she said, "depending on what's happened to Bunny."

That should have been my line.

CHAPTER 43

At the top of a steep hill, our driver Dax pulled up to the front gate of the Wrigley Memorial and Botanic Garden and asked how long we planned to stay.

"Not long," I told him.

"Yeah, not much to see but a lot o' cactus you can see anywhere on the island without paying seven bucks. The view's great, though."

I wondered about the average length of time people spent here. "What's the average stay?"

"About an hour, I'd say."

"I doubt we'll be longer than fifteen minutes. Where will you be?"

He pointed out his open window. "Parking lot's right over there. You can give me a call." He handed me his card, which surprised me. I hadn't figured him for business cards. "And I'll swing back here and pick you up."

"Sounds good," I said, motioning La-Shonna out of the car and glancing down at what purported to be a business card. The text read: *Dax Jervis at your service. You want it? I got it*, followed by a cell phone number. No specifics on the services he provided. I decided the less I knew the better.

"So, what now?" La-Shonna asked, as we watched Dax swing into a parking lot not far from the entrance.

"We figure out where to put the tracker then get back in the car for our survey of the town." I glanced around, finally pointing to a large cactus. "How about I drop it in that prickly pear cactus? Seems appropriate."

La-Shonna shook her head. "That ain't gonna work. Think about it. If your tracker bug ain't movin', the owners of that little device are gonna know you found it and dumped it. They'll start lookin' all over for you, and this place is smaller than a tick turd. They'll find us faster than Usain Bolt on roller skates."

I had no idea whether Usain Bolt roller skated, but she was right. Again, I wasn't using the brains I'd been given.

"You're right. How about this? There's a shuttle that runs up here from town. We can drop that bug inside the shuttle. Let it ride all over the town and drive the feebs crazy."

"Good idea," La-Shonna said, offering to ride the shuttle back to town and transfer the tracker to a different vehicle, but I didn't want us to be separated.

"No, but thanks," I told her as we moved over to the bench beside the front gate to wait for the shuttle. "I need you to stay with me. When the shuttle arrives, I'll climb onto the step, lean in and ask the driver when the next shuttle will arrive. While he's answering, I will surreptitiously employ my best PI sleight of hand and dump the bug. The feds can have fun tracking me up and down the hill while you and I work on finding Bunny."

La-Shonna nodded her approval. "Sounds like a plan," she said, as the white and beige shuttle bus came into view. "And thar she blows."

"Time to fish or cut bait," I murmured, wrapping my fingers around the tracker.

೧౨౦

I chatted with the female shuttle driver long enough to hide my tracker behind the front seat, which turned out to be easier than I'd anticipated. I thanked her for the information as I backed down the steps, and she wished me a good day. I felt a sense of relief, but not the huge reprieve I'd feel once we found Bunny.

"Mission accomplished," I told La-Shonna. "Now let's find Dax and start our street-by-street surveillance before darkness rolls in and foils our efforts."

"Foils our efforts? You're starting to sound like Sherlock Holmes."

"I talk that way when I'm distracted." I glanced at my watch, realizing we'd wasted nearly an hour already, and I was no closer to finding out what happened to Bunny. We hustled back to the car where we found Dax chilling to the Lagoons, an indi-rock duo out of Austin, Texas. We could see him drumming on the steering wheel from two cars away. I liked the Lagoons myself, especially their laid-back *California* track. Something Dax and I had in common. Maybe the only thing. He sat up when we climbed into the back seat.

"Welcome back, ladies. That was fast. I guess you're not into staring down cactuses, huh?"

"Not exactly my thing," La-Shonna told him, taking the blame for our short stay.

I pulled out my Avalon map. "Here's the issue, Dax. We want a not too speedy tour of every street in town. Can you do that for us?"

"Sounds like you're lookin' for something, or somebody?"

I inhaled noisily. "I have a friend who always answers a question with another question. You're starting to remind me of her."

He responded quickly and without malice. "I have no problem giving you the tour you want. Let me know if I'm driving too fast, or too slow." He hesitated. "And holler if you see something and want me to stop. We could continue on Avalon Canyon Road, but it's a dirt road from here. I'd recommend we stay on the main drags. If we don't find what you're lookin' for, I can take you back country. Up to you."

I realized at that point who he reminded me of. Not Cinda Mae, despite the question responses, but Bunny—a little too smart for his own good. On the other hand, maybe Dax' curiosity would come in handy, depending on what we found or wanted to find.

"Good plan. Let's start with the paved roads."

"Okey-dokey then. For starters, we'll hang us a left on Bird Park Road, short and quick."

Dax was right. Bird Park Road took about a minute and nothing looked promising. I was betting on finding Bunny's bike closer to the water, which worried me a lot. Dax did a good job of driving, extremely methodical in choosing streets and varying his speed depending on the scenery. He seemed to have an intuitive sense about our search and what the outcome meant to us, which I found comforting.

I uncrossed my fingers, which was a good thing because they were cramping up and if I'd waited much longer, I might have been unable to straighten them. What I needed to do instead was pray, because I had a feeling that whatever mess Bunny was caught up in, we'd need the Lord's help to extricate him.

CHAPTER 44

La-Shonna called it a friggin' miracle when we found a bicycle that fit Bunny's description. I considered it an answer to prayer.

She spotted the bike first, which I attributed to the fact that she's ten years my junior and younger eyes are better eyes. And La-Shonna is what I call an observer. Nothing gets by her watchful eyes. I suspect it's a trait nurtured by where she grew up, an environment in which constant danger surrounded her, something she only talks about when she's had too much to drink.

We were near the end of a side street on the edge of town when La-Shonna hollered, "Stop the car!"

Dax would have had to stop and turn around two houses farther along, anyway, but he slammed on the brakes so hard La-Shonna and I, neither of whom were wearing seat belts, slid forward. La-Shonna's greater mass sent her body smashing into the back of the front passenger seat, whereas, I managed to stop myself with my outstretched arms pushing against our driver's seat back.

Once the car game to a halt, Dax turned around, giving us both dirty looks. "Ladies, ladies. Are you not familiar with California's Mandatory Seat Belt Law, violation of which can result in a minimum fine of one hundred and forty-two US dollars? That is, if you're lucky?"

I made excuses for the two of us.

"You were driving so slowly, we figured we didn't need them, and, besides, we were moving around, craning our necks looking for—"

I stopped there, which was a mistake because I'd provided the opening Dax seemed to want.

"Looking for what exactly, ladies, if you don't mind my asking? Perhaps if I knew what you were seeking maybe I could better help with the search."

"We're looking for someone," I finally admitted, before La-Shonna broke into the conversation.

"We're lookin' for someone who was riding a pink bicycle exactly like the one leaning against the side of that house over there."

I still hadn't spotted it. "Which house, where?"

She pointed to a house on the left-hand side of the street. "That gray house over there. See the bike behind the bushes?"

"I do now."

"Got it," Dax said, as if we'd asked for his opinion, or cared to have it.

I sized up the house, a single-story craftsman bungalow of the sort that populates the landscape all over Southern Cal. What to do now? I wondered. Go up and knock on the door or go back and get the sheriff? The latter was the most sensible option, though I'm not always known for selecting what's sensible, as my shoe choices demonstrate.

La-Shonna made the decision for me. Leaning over and lowering her voice, she said, "Let's wait until dark, then come on back here. It's not that far from the hotel, and we can take a peek in the windows, see if Bunny's here or not. Then decide what to do next."

"I like that idea," I told her, even though I knew waiting would raise my anxiety levels. I'm better at taking action than waiting around for something to happen. "But what hotel are you talking about? We haven't registered in one yet."

"But we need to. The last ferry out o' here is at nine, and we're not gonna rescue Bunny before that, even if this is the right house."

"Ladies, ladies," Dax said, joining our conversation again. "No sense whispering. I can hear every word you're saying since I'm only a foot away. Who is this Bunny you're looking for and what does she look like? If she works for *Playboy*, maybe I can help you find her. I'm kinda into those cottontails."

I let out an audible sigh. A surfer Casanova wasn't what we needed right now, but since we were stuck with him, I thought maybe we could keep him with us in case we needed a getaway car. He was a good driver and he seemed harmless enough.

I pulled out my PI creds and handed them across the seat. "This is serious business, Dax. We're on this island looking for my colleague, a private investigator who we believe has been abducted and is being held against his will."

The expression of disbelief crossing Dax's face resembled a crinkled piece of tissue paper. "And the guy's name is Bunny?"

I ignored his question and the manner in which he delivered it. "For now, take us back to one of the hotels, a reasonably priced one, so we can register for the night, then wait outside for us. It'll be dark soon and we might be able to use your help."

"No problem," he said, swinging the car around. "I do some of my best work after dark."

❦❦❦

Dax drove us to an attractive Spanish style Holiday Inn, saying he thought it was the best deal in town, which was exactly what we wanted. He told us he'd wait in the parking lot until we were ready to take off on our mission.

I sensed excitement in his voice and guessed he was anticipating setting off on an adventure. I hoped against hope for the opposite and wondered again if I should contact the sheriff's office, let him know about the bike, and ask if they'd go to the house and check things out, but when I mentioned the idea to La-Shonna, she nixed it.

"The sheriff will go over there and whoever's inside will say Bunny's not there. When the sheriff asks permission to search the premises, he'll be denied until he comes back with a warrant. By the time the sheriff gets a search warrant, *if* he can even talk a judge into giving him one based on a bicycle parked in the yard, the perps will have moved Bunny to a different location, presuming of course, that Bunny's still alive."

La-Shonna's concluding sentence about made my heart stop. Up until that point I had not entertained the possibility of Bunny's death. Now I was more determined than ever to get inside that house and get Bunny out, legal methods be damned. I glanced at my watch as we entered the hotel. We had a good hour and a half to wait until sufficient darkness had set in to cover our dirty deeds.

At the registration desk, we signed up for one room with twin beds. I warned La-Shonna that I snore, but she said it wouldn't bother her because she snores, too, so she's accustomed to the noise.

"No problem at all," she said. "I'll sleep right through it. You should know the brouhas I've slept through in my life, including gunshots comin' from the house next door, and I'm not talkin' about once or twice in the time I lived there, but a couple times a year, every bleepin' year. Uh, uh, uh. All I say is that I am darn glad to be outta there. Now, almost any place looks good to me, and that ain't a bad thing, you know? Makes you appreciate what you got."

I could use a little more of that grateful attitude, I thought. To that end, I sent another prayer heavenward, one of my usual kind that included bargaining with God. *Please God, let Bunny live and I'll be a better person. I'll stop buying expensive shoes and give my shoe money to the poor, etc., etc.* I hoped my prayers would work because, other than La-Shonna and surfer Dax, I had no one else to turn right now. I re-crossed my fingers for good measure.

CHAPTER 45

La-Shonna and I made a quick trip to the gift shop to buy some essentials, like a toothbrush and toothpaste for La-Shonna because unlike me, she hadn't arrived prepared to spend the night. We took a quick look through the clothes rack where I found a long shirt that would work as a nightgown for her. She wanted to pay for it, but backed down when I told her I could deduct the cost as a business expense.

"Do we have time to grab a bite to eat because I'm half-starved?" she asked, pressing her fingers into her diaphragm.

Half-starved was a remarkably incongruous portrayal given La-Shonna's generous proportions, and I admit to hiding a smile.

"We do," I said, checking my watch. I was pretty hungry myself and besides, we both needed fortifications for our mission in order to keep our sugar levels up and our heads clear.

La-Shonna glanced toward the front door. "Should we invite slack Dax to eat with us?"

"If you don't mind having him tag along, it's okay with me."

"To tell you the truth, something about him seems a

little off to me," she said. "I'd feel better if we kept close tabs on him."

I hadn't picked up on any irregularities in our driver's behavior, so wasn't sure what caught La-Shonna's attention. When I asked, she said she couldn't put her finger on what was bothering her. I told her that he seemed to be the typical laidback surfer dude, driving tourists around the island in order to put food on the table and maybe a roof over his head, though I wouldn't have been surprised to learn he slept on the beach, or maybe in his car when the rains came.

"However, I'll trust your intuition," I told her, heading for the door. "If you get us a table I'll go outside and invite Dax to come in and join us. I doubt he'll turn down a free meal."

"*If* he's out there," La-Shonna said to my departing back.

A gentle breeze cut through the late afternoon heat as I wandered out to the parking lot in search of our driver. I found the car but as La-Shonna predicted, the driver was nowhere to be seen. I checked the back seat in case he'd decided to take a nap, but the back seat was as empty as the front. My worry meter rose. I hustled back to the hotel dining room to share the news of Dax's disappearance with La-Shonna.

Halfway through the lobby, I ran into Dax coming out of the men's room, which was a huge relief. I realized I needed to stop functioning on an emotional level and put my brain in gear instead of buying in to La-Shonna's paranoid fantasies.

"Hey, Dax. I was out looking for you."

"You ready to split?"

"No, we're going to have something eat first and you're welcome to join us. Tab's on me."

"Hey, sure. I was about to grab a bite myself."

℘℘℘

Dinner turned out to be uneventful and the conversation uninspiring, except for discussing our proposed course of action such as it was. In fact, we had little to strategize about since we had no idea what we'd face when we returned to the bicycle house. At some point, Dax asked if I had a picture of Bunny, which in fact, I did have from the days when Bunny and I were an item. I removed the pic from my wallet and handed it across the table.

"Hey," Dax said. "This looks like nightclub comic Bunny Slippers. Is that who we're going after?"

"It is," I said.

"So, he's not doin' standup anymore?"

"Only on weekends. He makes more money working for me than for a bunch of club owners who'd sooner stiff a comic as look at him. Or her," I added, remembering my feminist roots. "Another benefit is that nobody in my office steals his material."

Dax shook his head as he reached for another piece of pizza from the one we three were sharing. "Bunny's a funny guy, though. He'll make it big one of these days, and then he can stand up all the owners who stiffed him." Dax sent me a huge grin. "Hey, why not? He's a *stand up* comic."

"You're no competition for Bunny," I told him, chomping down the last bite of my arugula pizza.

Our basic plan consisted of checking for cameras and alarms then creeping up to the house sight unseen and peeking in windows. Dax volunteered for the surveillance task, which served to raise new questions in my mind about his background, but I figured a history of burglary might serve us well in this case.

Whether or not our peeping Tom tactics resulted in locating Bunny, our next ploy would be for me to knock on the door and ask to use their phone, saying my cell battery died and I had car trouble. What might happen next was a mystery to all of us, but we agreed to play it by ear from that point on.

Darkness had finally set in by the time we left the hotel, and I could tell all three of us were stoked to find and rescue Bunny. My minimal reservations about Dax weren't bothering me, even with the burglar possibility. He'd pretty much convinced me at dinner that he was exactly the person he portrayed himself to be, and La-Shonna admitted as much when we stopped back in the restroom before leaving.

Along the way, I decided to phone Harry Barnes and give him a progress report, even giving in and letting him know the bike house address when he asked for it. Despite that, he let me know he was annoyed I hadn't contacted the Avalon Sheriff's office. Eventually, I talked him down but not without having to listen to a lecture first.

"Just be careful, Polly. Don't take any unnecessary risks. If the people inside the house refuse to allow you to come inside and use one of their phones, then leave and go straight to the sheriff's office, even though I think you should check in with them first to request backup."

I crossed my fingers behind my back and said, "I'll call them if I need them, Harry, don't worry. Remember, I have La-Shonna with me. I trust her Afghanistan military experience over the training of some rinky-dink deputy sheriff in a California tourist town."

A deep sigh came from the other end of the phone. Clearly, Harry was exasperated with me but realized there was nothing he could do to dissuade me from my mission. After I returned to Hollywood, I thought, I'd take him and his wife out to dinner at their favorite restaurant. Smooth over the bumpy spots in our relationship.

La-Shonna raised an eyebrow once I disconnected the call. "Getting some flak from Harry?"

"He thinks we should go to the sheriff and not to the bike house, but that's 'follow the rules' Harry. Even Johnny gets annoyed with him sometimes. Says they'd bring down more bad guys if it weren't for Harry's dedication to the law."

Dax butted in as if we'd included him in the conversation. "This Harry sounds like an upstanding guy. Maybe he's right about going to the sheriff's office."

La-Shonna told him in no uncertain terms to stick to his driving and leave the investigating to us.

CHAPTER 46

Dax parked his car a block from the house where we'd located what we thought was Bunny's bike. "Wait, ladies, until I turn off the overhead light, and remember, I go out first, scouting for cameras and any other technical or non-technical surveillance mechanisms that might be in place. Like a big dog, for instance."

I hadn't thought about dogs, but I was glad Dax had. "You can text me when the coast is clear," I told him, volunteering the number of my alternate burn phone. Fortunately, I'd thought to bring a second burner in case Dax turned out to be less trustworthy than we hoped.

La-Shonna and I sat in the back seat of the car straining our eyes to keep track of Dax's whereabouts. For five minutes or more, maybe ten, since time seemed to have stopped for me, Dax disappeared from view.

"I don't know," La-Shonna said. "I still think there's something not quite right about that boy."

"He's a surfer," I told her, an explanation that accounted, in my mind, for everything from manner of dress to certain psychopathic tendencies.

La-Shonna settled back in the seat. "We'll soon see, I guess."

Soon came faster than either of us expected. We nearly jumped out of our respective skins when the driver's side door opened and Dax slipped back inside. Neither La-Shonna nor I had seen him coming, which only reinforced my suspicion that he might be a cat burglar in his spare time.

"Here's the bad news," Dax said, turning around to look at us. "There's a camera at the right front corner of the house monitoring the sidewalk and front door. Same situation out back. The good news is there's no surveillance for the windows on either side of the house, so that gives us a way in in an emergency. Windows are the old-fashioned kind that lift up. The other good news," he turned to me, "is that you've found your boy."

"Is he okay? Did you see any bruises or broken bones? Do they have him tied up?"

Dax shook his head slowly. "He looks in good shape to me."

My patience was wearing thin. I wanted details. "What's Bunny doing? Or, rather, what are they doing to him?"

"Looks to me like they're feeding him."

"How? Through tubes?"

"No. They're sitting around a table and from the amount of laughing, I'd guess Bunny's regaling them with stories from his stand-up routines."

I was confused. "I don't understand this at all."

"Neither do I," Dax said. "Are you sure he was kidnapped because it looks to me like these people are all friends?"

"People, friends," I parroted. "How many people? Males, females, old, young, what? Tell me, who's in the house with him?" I realized how agitated I was becoming when La-Shonna put a hand on my arm to restrain me, but I was ready to kill somebody about now. I just wasn't sure who that would be. Maybe Bunny.

"Two guys plus Bunny."

I had another question, one that might clear things up, in my mind at least. "What are they eating?"

"Looks like spaghetti to me."

"The two guys Italian?"

Dax shrugged. "Could be. Dark curly hair, good looking."

"Italian," La-Shonna said. "They're all good looking."

Dax stared me down, one eyebrow raised. "Sounds to me like you know these people."

"No, but I can guess who they are." I glanced over at La-Shonna. "Sally Martin's brother and husband."

"Who's Sally Martin?" Dax wanted to know.

"Long story," I told him. "What's important to know is that her husband has a target on his back. I'm going in there and find out from Bunny what this is all about and why he went incommunicado, scaring the crap out of Franny and me."

Dax asked, "Who's Franny?"

"Bunny's latest squeeze and Polly's identical twin sister," La-Shonna said. "Identical in looks, but they're as different as night and day, sugar and vinegar, chalk and cheese—"

I cut off La-Shonna with, "He gets the idea," and told Dax, "Franny's the good twin, I'm the evil twin."

"Wow, the dynamic duo. She a PI, too?"

"No, Dax. She's a nurse because she has empathy, unlike me." I opened the car door, and inched my leg to the ground before Dax stopped me.

"Hang on a minute. We still don't know the whole story here. Maybe all three guys are being held prisoner in the house, and there's a guard somewhere that I didn't see. I mean, Bunny could be telling stories to keep their spirits up. I think we still need to take precautions here."

"You're right," I said, again missing the boat. I may have to hand in my credentials if I couldn't improve on my techniques.

"How about you two find a couple of good hiding places outside the house," I said. "Maybe, Dax, you keep an eye on the window where you spotted Bunny, but stay close to La-Shonna. Before I go in, I'll call La-Shonna on my cell phone and keep the call open so she can hear what's happening. In other words—" I paused for breath. "—Dax, you will be the eyes, and La-Shonna, you will be the ears of this operation. If either of you have the slightest suspicion that things are going wrong, call nine-one-one, which should connect you to the sheriff's office."

With that, I took my first determined step away from the car, threw my expensive bug-free purse over my shoulder, and marched toward Bunny's hideout, thinking to myself along the way that Bunny better have one darn good explanation about this whole mess. If he didn't, and if I didn't kill him because of it, Franny might, which would make me very upset. I hated the idea of my sister serving time.

I charged up the sidewalk to the front door of Bunny's bike house, fully expecting the occupants to see me coming. And even though I wasn't expecting trouble, like a bullet aimed my way, I stood off to the side when I rang the bell. Which I rang twice. Like the postman.

I heard voices and footsteps, but no one answered, so I rang the buzzer a third time, leaning on it for a good twenty seconds, hoping to wake somebody up. I was about to place my finger on the button a fourth time when Bunny opened the door halfway, grabbed me, and pulled me inside.

"What are you doing here, Polly?" he demanded, like I was someplace I didn't belong when he was the person who was someplace he didn't belong.

I yanked my arm away and let out a string of words I usually don't use unless I am really, really angry, and I was about the angriest I'd been since the day Franny's husband broke into my bedroom and tried to kill me, and we all know how that turned out.

"I'm here looking for *you*, Dumbledore," I spit out, "because neither Franny nor I have heard a word from you for the past twenty-four hours, and we were worrying ourselves sick thinking maybe you were kidnapped or dead or both, and you have no idea the hell and high water I've gone through to find you. So, Mr. Funny Bunny, you better have a good excuse for yourself because if you haven't, you need to hang on to your privates before someone, namely me, separates my Glock from my purse and fires off a shot that separates you from your manhood."

I made the mistake of taking a breath at this point, a pause that Bunny used to cover my mouth with his hand since it was the only way he could shut me up, and even then, I continued talking through his fingers, debating whether to take a bite out of one of them. I resisted the temptation only because I can't stand the sight of blood.

"I couldn't contact you," he said, "because you've just stumbled into an FBI sting operation and probably friggin' messed up the whole thing. I'll tell you later how I got caught in the middle of it, but right now we have to get out of sight."

Before Bunny could get me anywhere, we heard the sound of fireworks coming from outside the house. Unfortunately, I knew exactly what kind of fireworks they were, which set off an urgent need in me to go back out and help my friend, except that Bunny had me in a stranglehold. I hoped the noisemaker going off belonged to La-Shonna, but who was she shooting at? Dax? And if so, why?

Was Dax the hitman the feebs were after? If so, I thought, I might be responsible for having just made one of the biggest mistakes of my life.

CHAPTER 47

While I stood rigid as a statue paralyzed with regret over my blunders, Bunny dragged me down to the living room floor, not for the first time in our complex, conjoined lives, and hollered, "Get your head down, Polly."

"I have a friend out there," I hissed. "La-Shonna. She came with me." I felt sick. I knew the authentic Persian rug under me would not be upgraded by a sampling of my stomach contents, which I struggled to keep in place.

"Nothin' you can do for her now," Bunny said, "without risking your own life, and I can't let you do that."

Bunny's response was punctuated by more shots, one of which found its way through the front door, embedding itself in the wall directly behind the location of my body seconds earlier. Thank goodness Bunny had dragged me around the corner into what I first thought was the living room, but turned out to be a study. Fewer windows. That's good, I thought, as I began to focus my efforts on staying alive.

I could feel my heart beating into my ears when another round of shots rang out, accompanied this time by the beautiful sound of sirens, the Doppler effect of which told me police were closing in. Instead of feeling a sense of relief, all I could think about was how I should have listened to Harry Barnes and contacted the sheriff instead of riding out here with Dax and putting La-Shonna in danger. If I ended this night dead, I'd have a lot to answer for on the other side.

⁊⊱⊰

Once the sheriff's posse arrived, I expected everything to quiet down immediately, but the fireworks started up again, limited this time to a few brief bursts followed by what's characterized in pulp novels as an eerie silence.

"I'm going out," I told Bunny. "I've got to check on La-Shonna, make sure she's okay."

"Wait a couple more minutes. Nothing you can do right now except satisfy your curiosity and that's not worth getting killed for, even for you."

I glanced around, expecting to find company, but instead, found we were alone. "Who else is in this house with you, anyway?"

"Sally Martin's brother Keir and her husband Ricky, who isn't floating with the fishes by the way."

"Swimming with the fishes, you mean."

"No. Dead bodies float. They get bloated from all the gases released during decomposition and—"

Fortunately, the front door opened and put an end to Bunny's lecture on the putrefaction of waterlogged corpses. A voice I assumed belonged to a deputy sheriff, called out, "Anybody home?"

Bunny and I struggled to our feet. "In here," Bunny said, heading back to the entry where he shook hands with a deputy sheriff who identified himself as Doug Vetter. I recognized the name.

"You must be Polly Berger," Vetter said, when I made my shamefaced appearance.

"I am she," I said, extending my right hand to shake the one he proffered.

"The one and only," Bunny added.

If we'd been alone in my office, I'd have smacked him for that one.

Outside the house, confusion reigned, despite efforts by the police to reduce the chaos. Atop the patrol cars, lightbars flared, drawing endless circles in the night mist, tactical flashlights in the hands of four somewhat puzzled sheriff's deputies roved the premises, and headlamps beamed like spotlights from the dozen or more cars lined up on the road waiting to pass.

The collective luminescence imparted a carnival atmosphere to the scene in front of me, and I blinked a few times to orient myself. Separating good guys from bad guys seemed to have been the problem until Bunny and I entered the picture. Three people stood handcuffed alongside two sheriff's cars: La-Shonna, who looked as healthy as ever, thank goodness; Dax, who looked a little the worse for wear; and next to Dax, a dark-haired, good-looking man—probably Italian, I thought—who looked sullen, but otherwise seemed to be in one piece. Another male, not so lucky, lay on the ground nearby. In the distance, I detected the sound of ambulance sirens screaming our way, but I knew they were too late.

CHAPTER 48

Before either Bunny or I could ask a question or proffer useful suggestions, Ricky Martin and his brother-in-law, Keir Caruso, joined the party. I was still having difficulty dealing with the names when Bunny introduced us, but at least I now knew who was who, or which was which.

Ricky Martin was the more handsome member of the pair, although no competition for his actor namesake. Keir Caruso was another story. With a first name like Keir, he should have had red hair, but no such luck. He and Ricky could have been blood brothers they looked so much alike—same height, same build, same coloring, but Keir was younger, and athletic in a way I'd always pictured a hit man for the Mob. I had a million questions for each of them, but this was not the time or the place.

Deputy Vetter, who'd preceded us out of the house, turned to me, not Bunny, which upped my opinion of him, but which also told me he'd had a recent chat with Harry Barnes.

"Can you tell me what's going here?" Vetter asked.

"Sort of," I told him, "but I'll know more once you uncuff my friend La-Shonna, who's here working a case with me, a case I'm presuming is now solved."

Of course, Bunny couldn't keep from chiming in. "Ms. Berger is correct, and as soon as we touch base with the FBI, you'll have all your questions answered."

To my knowledge, Deputy Vetter hadn't asked any questions of Bunny, and it was my place as so-called lead investigator to share the dirty details, but before I could get to particulars, our friendly driver Dax Jervis piped up.

"Hey," he hollered, even though we were standing less than eight feet away. "I heard you say you're contacting the FBI. Well, you can do that through me."

"Through you?" I said, joining a chorus of surprised voices asking the identical question.

Dax shrugged his shoulders, which was the most he could do given his cuffed extremities. "I know I don't look the part, but that's because I'm working undercover as a local taxi driver."

La-Shonna, who'd been silent for longer than I could remember in all the years I've known her, broke in at this point. "He's tellin' the truth about not lookin' the part, but check out his creds. He's the real deal. Took out these two perps who arrived here tonight plannin' on bumping off—" She nodded at Ricky. "—Mr. Martin and whoever was hidin' out with him." She glanced again at the crowd surrounding her. "From the looks of things, Special Agent Jervis saved a bunch o' lives here, so I suggest you unhook him from those restraints so he can call his boss and teach everybody here a thing or two, 'cause this boy is somethin' else, let me tell you. And while you're at it, you can uncuff me as well, before I have to take matters into my own hands."

My brain shifted into overdrive. Dax Jervis, FBI? He'd set us up. La-Shonna and I were bait he used to lure the assassin to Sally's brother's house. The assassins must not have known where to find Ricky and were paying Dax to help find their target. Did the feebs know where Ricky was hiding? I wondered. Or, were they relying on me to find Bunny, knowing Bunny would lead to Ricky? I suspected the latter, and nothing that happened since has disabused me of the idea.

After La-Shonna's outburst, Deputy Vetter walked over to Dax and asked to see his identification.

Dax complied with, "Right away, sir," which I'm certain scored points with every member of the sheriff's office within hearing range, though I was still trying to come to terms with Dax's new identity. He was about as far from the usual buttoned-up, buttoned-down feeb as I'd ever seen, not that I'd had any previous experience with undercover FBI types, except on TV. Dax did remind me, I realized, of the Marty Deeks character, an undercover cop on *NCIS LA*, one of my favorite shows and one of my favorite characters, so I guess it's possible.

Dax held out his open wallet for inspection, while at the same time reciting from memory his badge number. All four deputies huddled around, staring at the feeb credentials, which led to a brief discussion regarding their authenticity.

Doug Vetter ended the debate by calling in to an FBI field office in LA, announcing at the end of the call, "He's bona fide," which led to the uncuffing of Dax.

"And my lady friend, too," Dax said, nodding over at La-Shonna, a suggestion I knew stole her heart since she had a thing for surfers anyway, as evidenced by her first marriage. I thought she might hug Dax as soon as her arms were free, but instead she hugged me.

I was quick to hug her back, even though I'm not the huggy type, but I was so happy to see her alive I could have cried. "I was very worried about you," I told her, "but Bunny wouldn't let me go back out of the house to find you when the shooting started."

She turned to Bunny—to ream him out, I expected. "Good decision," she told him instead. "Nothin' she could o' done out here 'cept get herself killt." To me, she said, "Girlfriend, sometimes you got no sense. You know I can take care o' myself. But in this case, it wasn't me doin' the caretakin', but our new best friend. That boy can shoot. As soon as those two goons pulled up and got outta the car, he told me to hit the ground, then yelled, 'Federal agents, put down your guns,' but they weren't havin' none of it. We were hidin' behind a coupla garbage cans, but it was enough to protect us from the gang that couldn't shoot straight. Dax took out the dead guy with one shot. The other dirtbag had more sense, dropped his gun, and got down on his knees like he was about to have an audience with the pope."

Speaking of audiences, La-Shonna held the surrounding audience spellbound, including me. When she stopped for breath, Dax grinned and pretty soon everyone was laughing, which is one of those crazy things that happens to people when they're in mortal danger and, all of a sudden, the danger's over. I wondered what the heck the EMTs were thinking when the ambulance pulled up, but their appearance only served to turn the mood somber again.

The craziest part for me was the song running through my head—the Four Seasons, "Oh, What a Night!"

CHAPTER 49

Day 6:

I woke up early the next morning, happy to be in my own bed, but still wound up from the adventures of the day before. After clearing things up with the Avalon Sheriff's Department and thanking them for their help the previous night, Bunny, La-Shonna, and I left with Dax, who drove Bunny and me to the ferry before depositing La-Shonna at the hotel where we'd registered for the night, and where she decided to stay once I told her I could grab a ride home with Bunny.

I suspected one night might lead to another, particularly if Dax stayed around, and I had reason to suspect he might. To thank La-Shonna for all her help, I promised to pay her hotel bill, including meals, for up to three nights, and she was good with that. As for Dax, I hadn't been quite sure how to react to him. On the one hand, I was happy he'd protected all of us from the two Mob assassins, one of whom was being extradited back to Connecticut while his partner returned home to LA in a plain pine box. Apparently, the latter perp was the person who spotted Ricky and ratted him out to his former mobster pals Back East.

My real bone of contention was not with Dax so much as with his boss, one Joe Foster, yes, that Joe Foster. Why couldn't he have been upfront with me? I'd already agreed to work with him. I simply hadn't realized partnering with the FBI meant resigning yourself to being their patsy, but apparently that's the way the feeb cookies crumble. I should have known better, based on the reactions of both Johnny and Harry Barnes when I mentioned the feebs had asked for my help. They turned out to be right. The FBI would never have sought help from a two-bit PI firm like mine.

On the other hand, the feebs hadn't been the ones to locate Ricky Martin, a feat Bunny accomplished in little more than a day. The only questions remaining in my mind had to do with the whereabouts of Sally Martin and why she hadn't told me or the FBI about her brother's condo on Santa Catalina Island. I suppose she had her reasons, but I couldn't think of one that made sense. I glanced over at my alarm, which had yet to go off, and decided to set aside my passel of doubts and reservations until I reached the office. To that end, I rolled out of bed, dressed, and headed to work, stopping at Starbucks along the way.

Even my downstairs neighbor, Rosa, who works on Saturday mornings, hadn't arrived when I reached my office. In fact, I couldn't remember the last time I arrived so early that I beat Rosa. She had a string of single clients, now referred to as "patients," who scheduled early appointments on Saturdays so she could let them know whether they were in for a good or bad weekend. Knowing Rosa, I suspect she vacillated between telling them they faced a great weekend or just a plain old good weekend. Rosa was not the purveyor of bad news.

Sitting alone in my office enjoying the peace and quiet, I thought to myself I should do this more often.

Even the normal city noises outside my window seemed muted. Yep, I could get used to solitude. Unfortunately, the contentment of my tranquil environment lasted only as long as my morning latte. Marko arrived first with Rosa in tow.

"Polly, you in here?"

Seriously? I'd left the outside door unlocked and my office door was open. Did they think I'd made a dummy of myself and sat it at my desk?

Rosa rushed in first. "We're so glad to see you back, Polly. I worried myself sick about you and Bunny. We both—" She turned and waved Marko in. "—we both thought Franny was about to have a nervous breakdown. We stayed with her until you called last night."

"I know," I said. "I could hear you in the background when I called Franny to tell her we were okay."

"Right." She glanced over at Marko again. "But then Bunny called and, by the time Franny hung up talking with him, she was a basket case. He told her you both would have been killed if it hadn't been for some undercover FBI agent. Since you're here this morning bright-eyed and bushy-tailed, I guess we have the FBI to thank, so I don't want to hear another word from you badmouthing them."

Bright-eyed and bushy-tailed? I hadn't heard that nineteenth century adage since my grandmother used it when I was a kid, and how did I turn out to be the bad guy here, anyway?

"When have you heard me badmouthing the FBI?"

"I don't want to go into it, but—"

"Then let's drop it," Marko said. "We got other fish to fry here. Have you talked with Harry Barnes about the Melody Knight case?"

"Haven't had time. What's the status?"

"Harry says they got enough on Hooper to charge him with first degree murder."

"That's great news," I said. "Congratulations! I expect you provided the clincher with that video you turned up at a neighbor's house, am I correct?"

"You are correct."

"Great work, Marko. Hollywood PD could use your talents."

"To tell you the truth, Polly, I'd rather work for you."

At that very moment, fortunately for me, because I lacked the funds to take on another full-time investigator, the outside door opened and Bunny and Franny came in holding hands. I could tell Franny had been crying already. I steeled myself. Predictably, Franny came over and hugged me as if she hadn't seen me in a dog's age instead of just yesterday.

"I'm so glad you found Bunny, and that you're both back here safe and sound. Bunny told me the whole story, how he looked up the sales record on Sally Martin's brother's condo, found the address, and went over there looking for Ricky." She squeezed his hand as if to say, my hero. "I just wish they'd let him call us to say he was safe, but Bunny said they were too worried about phones being tapped, and besides, he knew if you hadn't heard from him, you'd hop right down there and find him, which you did. What a relief."

I had to agree, and relief was an understatement, as long as nothing more happened to interrupt our current jovial mood.

As luck would have it, the doorbell announced more visitors.

CHAPTER 50

I headed for the door, anticipating Cinda Mae, hoping she had Pedro with her, but no such luck. I opened the door to Special Agent Joe Foster in the company of an older man, another agent, I presumed.

"Morning, Polly. I was hoping you'd be in this morning," Joe said, shifting his eyes to the box above the door. "Am I required to deposit my weapon again because we're really not supposed to do that?"

"Not this time. Come on in and join the party." I held the door and waved them inside, announcing, "Looks like party time today. For those of you who haven't met, this is Special Agent Joe Foster…" I hesitated, waiting for Joe, as I now called him, to introduce his friend.

"Pleased to meet you," he said, "and this is Special Agent Lenny Spinoli."

"Risen from the dead?" Bunny deadpanned.

A rueful smile crossed Spinoli's lips. "In some sense."

I was confused. If this was Lenny Spinoli, then whose body washed up on Dockweiler Beach? I glanced over at Joe Foster for clarification. "Are there two Lenny Spinolis?"

"There may be another Lenny Spinoli someplace in

the world," Joe said, "but probably not another Leonardo daVinci Spinoli."

I decided to ask the question on everybody's mind. "So, whose body washed up on Dockweiler Beach?"

I expected Lenny to answer, but Joe seemed to be in charge of the divulgence. "The corpse was a mobster from the East Coast sent out here to assassinate Lenny and Ricky Martin, and that's all I can say at the moment." He motioned to me. "Can we have a word in private?"

"Of course," I said, leading the way to my office.

Once he'd excused himself to Lenny and the rapt crowd around him, Joe followed me in and settled on the settee.

"Since we're working together," he said, "I can share some details with you, but not with everyone outside. Do all these people work for you?"

"Occasionally. Well, all but one. Rosa the Tarot Card Reader is our downstairs neighbor, but her boyfriend sometimes handles surveillance for us. In fact, he just solved a big murder case for the HYPD, which makes me wish I could hire him full time."

"Really?" Joe eyes lit up. "Anything I'd know about?"

"Oh yeah. The Melody Knight/Clive Hooper case. Hooper hired us to tail his wife, but it was all a setup. Long story I won't go into here. What else do you have to tell me? I'd like to know more about the Dockweiler Beach corpse, for example."

"Let's just say that Lenny defended himself, and when he called me about the result, we decided to make it look like the assassin had been successful with at least one his targets. And it allowed us to set up a sting."

"Did you send Sally Martin our way?"

"No, but we kept tabs on both of you from the time of her first phone call. I looked you up, saw you had a good reputation, and figured maybe you could be of some help to us as well as to Sally. Problem was, we had to get her into a safe house for her own good. Ricky, on the other hand, took off when he arrived at the boat and saw Lenny dispatch the two goons, one of whom went overboard and managed to swim back to dry land. We knew he was on the loose and we had to find him." Joe shrugged. "It's complicated, but that's the gist of things and probably more than I should have disclosed."

"I still have questions," I told him, but he reached into his pocket, pulled out a couple of pieces of paper, and handed them to me.

"Maybe this will satisfy your curiosity. This one," he handed me the top sheet, "is a check from the bureau for fifteen hundred dollars for services rendered. I know it won't cover the time and hassle we caused you, but it was the best I could push through the bureaucracy."

The check looked official so I thanked him, which is when he handed me a second check.

"And this one is from Ricky and Sally Martin for five thousand dollars to express their thanks for helping with their case."

"Wow," I said. "That's way more than I'd have invoiced for, but I appreciate it. At least I wasn't almost killed in this case, so even better."

I saw Joe's eyebrow go up when I mentioned almost killed, but I decided not to press the issue.

"One last question," he said.

"Shoot—er, poor choice of words. What's your question?"

"Are you free for dinner tonight and, if so, would you consider allowing me to take you to dinner?"

"You mean like a date?"

"Exactly."

"It turns out I am free," I told him, "and I'd really like to have dinner with you."

Joe's whole face lit up, which touched my heart. I tried to remember the last time Johnny looked that pleased at the idea of spending an evening with me. Of course, thoughts of Johnny were not what I wanted to occupy my mind right now because they came with a large helping of guilt.

"I'll pick you up at seven," Joe said and added, with the sliest of grins. "I know where you live."

✺✺✺

Saturday was not a day I wanted to spend in the office, so as soon as I could, I shooed my fan base out of the office and left. I wanted to stop by the hospital and spend the afternoon with Johnny prior to heading home for my dinner date with Joe. I hoped to get through the evening without feeling sick to my stomach from all the guilt I felt over enjoying myself while Johnny languished in a hospital room.

To make matter worse, when I arrived on his floor, the nurse in charge greeted me with bad news. The swelling on Johnny's brain had worsened and he'd fallen back into a coma. My knees buckled, and I felt like I was about to faint. I grabbed hold of the counter at the nurse's station to steady myself. Poor Johnny, I thought, as tears dribbled down my cheeks.

"Am I allowed to see him?" I asked.

"Yes," the nurse said. "Stay as long as you like."

I went in and sat by his bed, holding his hand. I must have stayed for three or four hours until the long shadows in the room reminded me of the time. I'd read where people in comas can sometimes hear and understand what their loved ones say to them, and I'd been trying out the idea on Johnny, hoping to pull him out of his unconscious state.

In one final effort of the day, I squeezed his hand gently and leaned close to his ear, repeating what I'd been telling him for the last couple of hours. "Johnny, sweetheart. I love you more than you can ever know and the first thing I want us to do when you wake up is to get married again."

I waited a few more minutes, but nothing about his state changed. I gave his hand a big squeeze, kissed him on the lips, and said goodbye. I wished my efforts could have washed away my sadness, but I felt so bad, even the thought of feeling better only brought on more grief. I left Johnny's hospital room feeling worse than I'd felt in a dog's age.

On the drive home to meet Joe for dinner, question after question nagged at my brain. Foremost among them was whether white lies counted against you in the after-life if, in your heart, your motives are pure. And second, when Johnny came out of his coma would he remember the things I whispered into his unconscious ears? And if so, what then?

EPILOGUE

Albany, NY, Day 8:

A few minutes past noon on what turned out to be a sunny Monday, a call came in to the FBI Field Office on McCarty Street in downtown Albany, New York. The agent in charge answered, smiled, and gave a thumbs-up to the three people assembled in the room.

"Looks like you've been resurrected," he told Lenny Spinoli, a local agent who'd worked undercover inside the Mob for more years than he cared to remember.

"Not sure how I feel about that," Lenny replied.

"How many lives you got left, anyway?"

"None. Now that I'm outed, I'm out. Got an offer to transfer to the West Coast, and I'm thinkin' about takin' it. My brother won't like the idea, but he can visit or move out there himself. The sunshine would do him good. Bakers don't get much sunshine. How about givin' him a call and lettin' him know the Coxsackie Police have a case of mistaken identity?"

While Lenny waited for the results of the resurrection phone call, he thought about another hit Angel Bianchi ordered, a hit that was supposed to happen five years earlier when Lenny worked for Angel, hired to kill Angel's wife and her bodyguard lover, Ricky Martin—the two "cannoli" Lenny refused to polish off. Instead, he'd arranged to place the couple in witness protection on the West Coast, a deal they accepted once they learned the alternative. Thanks to a fluke, an accidental stroke of bad luck for Ricky, Angel eventually learned the pair was still alive.

A thousand questions ran through Lenny's head about the resolution of the case, none of which mattered any more. The feds had finally taken Angel Bianchi off the streets. He'd be gone for good, locked up in a high-security prison for the rest of his life. Finally, Lenny felt free. It was a good feeling. Time to celebrate.

e/ɔe/ɔ

A couple of hours later, Lenny sat in the baggage claim area at Albany International Airport where his FBI colleagues dropped him off following the phone call to his brother.

Mickey burst through the door, greeting Lenny with a bear hug that nearly crushed Lenny's ribs.

"Geez, Len. I about died myself when the cops told me somebody killed you and then said I couldn't tell nobody not even Nita. When I asked 'em why, they said it had to do with their investigation, but I couldn't leave things in their incompetent hands. I put a call in to Pauley and he said he'd take care of it." Mickey held his brother by the shoulders, looking him up and down. "Standin' here seein' you, I know Pauley kept his word, even though he pretended he couldn't believe it when I told him the news."

"I wish you'd stay away from Pauley and his pals," Lenny said, trying to hide his annoyance.

"I know you don't like him, but he's a friend."

"How many times I gotta tell you, there are no friends when it comes to the business."

"I know, I know. Geez, Len, how could the cops make a mistake like that? It broke my heart." He reached out and hugged his brother again, eyes brimming with tears.

Lenny shrugged. "Who knows? Cops make mistakes. They're human." He shoved Mickey forward. "Let's find your car and head home. I'm starving."

Reaching Mickey's car in the short-term lot, Mickey turned to Lenny. "Pauley gave me an earful, by the way."

Lenny reached for the driver's side door. "How about I drive and you tell me about it on the way?"

"Sure thing. Anyway," Mickey continued, talking over the hood of the car as he hustled to the passenger side. "Seems the FBI set up some kind of sting on Angel Bianchi's operation. The list of charges is as long as your arm, including murder and attempted murder. I hope he likes the food up in Clinton because he ain't gettin' outta there for a long time." Mickey paused in his story long enough to fasten his seat belt. "Say, I been wonderin—" He looked askance at his brother. "—if Angel's arrest was somehow related to your disappearance."

"Why would you think that?"

"Well, I remember it was Angel who told Pauley Bodin to give you that weird cannoli message, so I figured maybe it had somethin' to do with you takin' a sudden trip, even though you didn't say nothin' to me about it until you asked me to drive you to the airport. I didn't buy your story about a short vacation, but I didn't want to offend you by sayin' so."

Lenny took his hand off the wheel and slapped his brother's thigh with the back of his hand. "I appreciate that, Mick."

Mickey reached over and squeezed his brother's shoulder. "You know, don't you, if you're ever in trouble over somethin' you can count on me to help out?"

"I know, but it wasn't like that."

"You mean your trip really *was* a vacation?"

"Not exactly. A friend of mine in Pittsburgh needed help. Nothin' worth botherin' you with. How's everything on your end, anyway? Those goons in the SUV ever come back to bother you?"

Mickey took out his cell phone, clicked on a text, and held the phone out to his brother. "No, but I gotta show you this text I got right after you left. Came from Eddie Dagostino, who got it from Pauley. Check out the pic he sent."

Lenny glanced down at a photo of a young man with a bruised face and broken arm. It wasn't a pretty sight, sent shudders down his back. "Who's the guy?"

Mickey shook his head. "This is the skinflint who tried to stiff Eddie's kid, but if things hadn't turned out the way they did, that coulda been me."

"Coulda been," Lenny said, "so let that be a lesson to you. Next time somebody asks you for a favor, see me about it first."

"You think I shouldn't o' done Eddie that favor, right? Or maybe you think you could have handled it better?"

"No. You did a good thing helpin' out Eddie and his kid, but I got a lot o' favors I can call in, and if I can put 'em to good use helping you keep your nose clean for the sake of Nita and the kids, I want you to let me do that."

Mickey sent his brother another questioning glance. "Like who owes you favors?"

"A lot of people, Mick, which I'm keepin' between me and them until payback time. Now quit askin' me so many questions while I'm drivin'. Besides, all I can think about is stopping someplace for a big plate of homemade linguini with a juicy red clam sauce, and then when we get back to your place, a couple of your pistachio cannoli, the Holy ones, because I can't afford love handles at my age."

"You got quite a ways to go before that happens, if ever, the way you keep in shape. Geez, Lenny, I'm so glad to see you I can't stop cryin'."

Lenny felt bad for putting his brother through so much pain. He'd make it up to him, starting with a good meal. "How about we stop at Canali's for that linguini? My treat."

"Sure, Lenny. Maybe once we down our first bottle of wine, you'll tell me what you did in Pittsburgh."

"Maybe," Lenny said, already working up a story to tell his brother. Anything but the truth about the cannoli.

THE END

About the Author

Harol Marshall was born during a record-setting blizzard in Upstate New York. In her first book of heartwarming short stories, *Growing Up With Pigs*, she writes about her childhood with her four younger brothers on their family farm. The daughter of a police chief and named for her attorney uncle, Harol's interest in law enforcement comes naturally, spurred on by her father's dinnertime storytelling, and by her grade school librarian who introduced her to Perry Mason mysteries.

An anthropologist by training, Harol retired after thirty years in academia, trading in research papers for mysteries. She has authored ten books and a number of short stories some of which have appeared in e-zines, including: *Akashic Books' Mondays are Murder series*, *The Cynic Online Magazine*, *Southern Women's Review*, and *East of the Web*.

Harol has two children and two stepchildren. Her daughter is an English teacher and blogger, and her son is a former standup comic and author. Harol and her physicist husband live in North Carolina with their three cats. When she's not at the keyboard, she's dancing, cooking, traveling to see her grandchildren, or watching cop shows on TV.